Ay Chihuahua

A Romantic Comedy by

TIFFANY ANDREA

Paperback ISBN: 978-1-990724-29-9
eBook ISBN: 978-1-990724-28-2

Cover Design by: Burden of Proofreading Publishing featuring Graphics by Msanca, Leonido, and A7880S via DepositPhotos.

Interior Graphics by Design & Beyond via Canva

www.boppublishing.com

TABLE OF CONTENTS

1

DIMA

Cool to Hate

hy don't people understand the meaning of a due date? Like it's a difficult concept to grasp. I might be more sympathetic if we were still telling time and estimating dates based on the sun's position, but we literally carry small calendar devices in our pockets now. There's no excuse.

As a lifelong bookworm, I've spent the last five years pursuing my master's in Library Sciences. I dedicated three of those years to getting my Bachelor of Arts in English, and now I'm one thesis away from completing my degree. Every time I tell people that, they seem surprised. As if my curvy figure and curly hair automatically qualify me for ditz status. It's fun for me to prove them wrong.

It's also a surprise for them to learn I have a temper when inconsiderate morons take a book from the library and don't return it on time.

As a frugal university student, my tight budget doesn't allow me to purchase the number of books I devour in a week. I can either have a roof over my head or buy books, so right now, I choose the roof. My library card is my most cherished possession, other than my dog, Nacho. He's an eight-month-old, six-pound chihuahua convinced he's the Lion King, and makes no apologies for protecting his pride—which consists of him and me. He hates everyone and everything, but that doesn't stop me from smuggling him into the library in his purse carrier. Thankfully, as long as he stays in his bag, he's content and doesn't try to kill anyone.

He does pick up on my moods, though, and he can tell I'm angry. He's on high alert.

My name is on a waiting list for a book called *Catalyst*, which is book three in a romantic suspense series that was one of my favourites from last year. More importantly, I need it for my thesis research, and I'm on a pressing deadline. I've been waiting to read the sequel now for... seventy-three days. It was even booked at other Toronto Library branches, so they were unable to do an interlibrary transfer. I've been stuck waiting. And since someone didn't bring the book back three days ago, like they were supposed to, I've trudged my way to the library in this God-forsaken heat, only to be disappointed and leave with six other books from my carefully curated to-be-read list.

If I had to choose an emoji to describe my mood, it would be the one with steam blowing out of its nostrils. Or the red face. Definitely the red face.

Outside of the library, I'm walking across the forecourt, scanning one book I borrowed, when I crash into a freight train—or something that feels like one. Both of my bags fly through the air—one of which has my angry dog in it—and then I'm lying on the hot ground with my eggplant-coloured jersey skirt covering my face.

Wait... if it's covering my face, that means it's not covering my...

I scramble to right my skirt and before I can accomplish anything else, Nacho escapes his unzipped purse and starts terrorizing the nerdy guy wearing chinos and a Charles Dickens

T-shirt. That's some serious dedication to literary arts I'm not even sure I have.

"Shoo. Scram. Go on. Get back in your… bag thing," the stranger pleads with Nacho to no avail.

Not only my own books, but the Dickens fan's books are splayed out on the stamped concrete. I don't have time to sort them right now because I need to halt my dog's attack. "Nacho Dog." As soon as I open my mouth, that prompts a jolt of pain from our collision. I ignore it and continue begging my chihuahua, while sitting on the ground, trying to find my bearings. "Nacho Dog!"

"I know he's not my dog. I'm trying to get him away from me," the blond man states while doing a sort of uncoordinated River Dance to fend off the ankle biting.

"No, his name is Nacho Dog. Nacho? Like the chips."

"Why would you name him Nacho Dog?" He scrunches his face, which could be because Nacho is clamped to his pant leg.

"Because he's not a chip." Duh. I huff a sigh as I push myself to my feet, battling with residual dizziness. "Nacho. Come here. Come to Momma." I open my arms, hoping my little maniac will run into my warm embrace, but he's too intent on shredding the pants and dignity of the man before me. I walk forward, ignoring the brand new aches and pains I'm feeling, and bend over to scoop him up. Except the second I bend over, grasping Nacho's collar, a fresh wave of dizziness strikes. I can't stop myself from tumbling forward. That's bad enough, but here I am, trying to steady myself with my face right in the book nerd's waist. How's that for an introduction?

Once I right myself, I do a slow scan of the area to see if anyone has been watching this catastrophe unfold. Thankfully, all I find is that Nacho is cranky, I'm embarrassed, and the Dickensian nerd is confused.

He tilts his head—looking at me like my dog does when I've baffled him—and informs me, "Your dog is vicious."

I'm about to tell him to stop being a baby, but I look down and discover a copy of *Catalyst* on the pavement. *He's* the inconsiderate book hog.

"That's my book!"

"Your book? This one?" He picks up the paperback, slapping it against his palm. "That was some twist, huh? When the—"

Like a child, I close my eyes, stick my fingers in my ears, and start singing off key to drown him out. Few things are as unforgivable as ruining the end of a book. That's even worse than missing your return date. When I open my eyes, the chino-clad blond is smirking. The nerve of this guy.

I remove my fingers from my ears, one at a time, making sure he's stopped talking, and it's safe to proceed. "That's not cool, you... you..."

"Handsome intellectual?"

He's not wrong. His dark-blond wavy hair is unstyled on top, with an overgrown fade around the sides. His blue eyes shine behind a pair of black plastic-frame glasses. His facial hair isn't long or unkempt, but makes him appear a little carefree. As carefree as someone in chinos and a Charles Dickens shirt could be. It wouldn't surprise me to find a monogrammed pen in a pocket protector somewhere on his person.

His looks aside, he's infuriating. Especially with that stupid lop-sided grin on his face that zaps me out of my thoughts.

"Keep telling yourself that, buddy. I was trying to think of something nice to say, but I came up empty."

He laughs, which starts Nacho's barking again. I'm surprised he stayed quiet as long as he did.

"That dog is part demon. You should crate him when you sleep. I wouldn't trust him with my eyes closed."

I roll my eyes, again wanting to point out he weighs less than a gallon of milk. "He's an excellent judge of character, so if he doesn't like you, it's for a reason." I glare at the six-foot-tall irritant in hopes he'll move along, allowing us both to carry on with our day. "Maybe because you don't return your library books on time." Then I realize he's heading into the library to return the book I came all the way here for. I'd rather not come back tomorrow, which is supposed to be just as hot, so I might as well follow him in and request the book once he returns it.

Rather than defend his poor date-management skills, the nerd stares at his feet, not responding. Please don't tell me my verbal sparring hurt his feelings. I wouldn't feel right not apologizing, but I'm trying to be angry.

"I'm sorry if you were waiting for this." He waves the paperback in question, then proceeds to pick up all the novels we've left littered on the ground around us this entire time, handing me my bag with my books tucked inside.

I hoist Nacho's purse onto my shoulder and walk toward the library entrance. "Well, let's get on with it so I can get home to read it, Dickens."

"Holden," the deep voice says from behind me. "My name is Holden."

I pause in my tracks. No, I'm not conversing with him anymore. There's no way I'm confessing that my favourite book ever is *The Catcher in the Rye*. It's a coincidence that he has the same name as my favourite literary character. I resume walking to the library entrance, eagerly anticipating the air conditioning. "Mine's Dina."

"You're not taking that demon dog in the library, are you, Dina?"

I turn to look over my shoulder and whisper-shout, "I don't see how that's any of your business, Dickens. He's in a purse."

This guy better be careful before I shorten his new nickname to something not associated with a classic author.

"Pretty sure Julie would be bothered." His know-it-all tone aggravates me more than it should. What kind of ultra-nerd name-drops the librarian's first name?

"Julie and I have an arrangement, thank you very much. Mind your business and just focus on returning your books on time." I huff a loud breath, mimicking the steamy-nose emoji, keeping my back to him as I walk through the automatic doors. "I'll show you how it's done, so you know for next time."

HOLDEN

The Blurb

'm a little brother. Annoying my siblings has been my reason for living since I was in diapers. Yet, I've never enjoyed getting someone worked up as much as Dina. The feisty brunette with the golden skin and piercing brown eyes crashed into me, then unleashed her evil dog to destroy my favourite pants. Neither of those things bothered me, but I don't want her to know that. It's much more fun making her eyebrows draw together and cheeks flush.

When we enter the library, she's leaning down to speak to the tiny hellion in her purse. Who names their dog Nacho? Cujo, HellHound, Chopper, all better options than Nacho. But something tells me Dina Unknown-Last-Name has a quirky way about her. A few minutes in her presence and I can already name several of her qualities. She's intelligent, beautiful, stubborn, and thanks to her earlier wardrobe malfunction, I know she wears panties with Minnie Mouse on them. Though I'm not sure what that says about a person who must be in her early twenties. Now isn't the right time to ask.

We arrive at the reception area, where I'd normally drop my books and be on my way into the stacks, but there's a lineup, so I use it to my advantage. I walk past without stopping.

"Where are you going? You need to drop your book off so they can mark it as returned. So *I* can finally mark it off my to-be-read list!" She stomps along behind me, each step louder than the last.

I turn around, placing a finger to my lips. "Shh. It's a library. Do you need the introductory tour that covers proper etiquette?"

She rolls her eyes, releasing an angry sigh. "You are... Why are you so irritating? You're like a... like a... something irritating."

I stifle a laugh. I'm having more fun testing her temper than I ever have with my siblings. This is nearly as entertaining as my best friend Phil's stand-up comedy routine.

"That was poetic."

"I'm a reader, not a writer," she snaps.

Macho Nacho growls from his perch under Dina's arm. He must really hate me, or he's an evil little creature who hates everyone equally. Jury's out.

"See. Even Nacho knows you're being irritating. Just return the book so I can take it home with me, and we can both go back to pretending this encounter never happened."

That's going to be a problem for me. I don't want to pretend this never happened. This woman with the flowing skirt and the wicked dog barrelled into me and jolted something in my brain.

My focus has been on pursuing my PhD in History for over seven years. My next phase is completing three exams in November. I don't have a lot of time for socializing right now, but I've never met someone, other than my two best friends, who I wanted to find time to converse with.

The past few months, I've been so busy, I've almost exclusively used the university library. Today is the first time

I've visited the public branch for weeks. The only reason I am is to return books my sister borrowed and couldn't return after having a baby four days ago.

I could probably explain that to Dina, and it might turn her down a notch, but what fun would that be? The fire in her eyes over a piece of fiction is amusing.

She's still following me as I ascend the stairs to the second level, so I can choose some new material to keep my sister entertained while she adjusts to life as a new mom.

"What does Nacho like to read? I'm guessing psychological thrillers? True crime?" I ask, navigating the second-floor bookshelves.

"What? No... I mean, we listen to audiobooks sometimes, but... what does that have to do with anything?"

I laugh, then clap a hand over my mouth to muffle the sound. Her twisted scowl isn't helping. "Just curious where we're headed. Better find something the little guy will agree with or he'll try to rip my leg off again." I enter a new aisle and start browsing the titles.

"Or you could just return the other books and Nacho and I will be on our way." Her whisper-shout makes me chuckle again.

If I thought I was genuinely upsetting her, I'd cool it on the "irritating", but she's smirking as much as I am. She's not a poet *or* an actress.

"Why do thrillers always have such literal titles? *The Woman in the Attic*? *The Stranger in the Photo*? *The Secret She Told*?"

"It's just smart marketing. You won't pick up a book unless you have an idea what it's about. The cover draws your eye, the title draws your brain, the blurb draws your heart." She rattles off a response to my rhetorical question without stopping for a breath.

"Hm. I never thought about it that way before."

"You should see some of the romance titles." Her playful smile betrays her. She's no longer even pretending to be enraged.

The books on the shelves are not the most interesting things in this section of the library. Of course, I pick them up and they don't put up a fight when I want to read their contents. Dina, so far, is more of a mystery than anything in print.

"Do you like romance, Dina?" I step toward her, which makes Nacho release a low rumble and bare his teeth through his mesh purse window—which, thankfully, is now zipped closed. "Maybe *My Fake Fiance Mafia Boss* or *The Naughty Pirate?*"

She fails to hide her giggle. That feels like a major win.

"Are those your favourites, Dickens? I pegged you for the smut-loving type."

We're still standing inches away, but Nacho has warmed to my presence. Another win. "How'd you figure that?" I play into her hand, even though most of my reads revolve around ancient gender roles and political hierarchies.

"A few of the books you dropped would put *The Naughty Pirate* to shame."

I'm pretty sure I'm blushing. I hope my stubble hides it. "Those were my sister's choices. She… uh… she just had a baby a few days ago. She was bored."

Another smile warms her face, reaching her eyes for the first time since she bumped into me twenty minutes ago. "Congratulations to her. Boy or girl?"

"Girl. Grace."

"Pretty. So you blame your smutty reading choices on the new mother? Sleazy, Dickens." She steps back twice and smooths out her already smooth skirt. "Listen, I really do need to get going and I'd appreciate not having to come back tomorrow. So, can you just return the books and I can get out of here?"

I was having fun messing with her, but I know most people usually have something more pressing to do than waste their time in a library. "Yeah. One sec." I pick up a copy of *Dead Lady on a Train*, just to make it look like I came up here for a reason and wasn't trying to rattle a curly-haired bookworm.

Dina laughs at my selection. "I wonder what that one's about."

"I'll let you know next time you crash into me."

We walk down the stairs side by side, with Nacho safely on her left and me on her right.

"Do you come here a lot?"

She glances at me from the corner of her eye. "Yeah, I don't live far away. I come a few times a week. At least once."

"I wonder why we never ran into each other before."

The right side of her lips tilt upward, and I'm definitely counting that as progress.

"Usually I watch where I'm going."

I laugh loud enough that other library-goers shoot scowls in my direction. Her literal interpretation of our encounter catches me by surprise. The girl has jokes.

We arrive at the checkout and return desk, where I'd normally slide my returns in the appropriate slot, but today, things are different. I don't think the librarians appreciate being rushed into returns and checkouts, but I've wasted enough of Dina's day, so I'll try to sweet talk Julie into making things happen.

When the young blonde in front of us steps away after checking out her impressive stack of books, I move forward to be greeted by my favourite librarian. The elderly woman has been a regular feature in the lives of me and my two siblings since we were kids.

"Holden, dear. How's your sister?"

I fill her in on the arrival of my niece, explaining that little Grace arrived past her due date, which is why these books are past theirs. She waves a hand at me to brush off my apology. I attempt to give Dina an 'I told you so' grin, but she's standing behind me.

She steps around me, putting on a megawatt smile. "Hi, Julie. I've been on the waiting list for *Catalyst,* so I was hoping you could do a quick turnaround on that one."

"Oh, Dina. I forgot you were waiting for this." Julie holds up the paperback and scans through the pages. "Did Phoebe enjoy this one, Holden?"

"I think so, yeah. The scene with the—"

"No, no, no. Please, no spoilers," Dina begs.

Instead of tormenting her like I want to, I hold up my hands in surrender.

Julie processes the book, scanning the barcode, then Dina's library card, tucking the printout into the front cover. With each step toward handing the book over, I try to build up the nerve to ask for her phone number. Her Instagram handle. Her email address. Something. But before I can, she collects the book from Julie, shouts a rushed goodbye in my direction, and she's gone.

3

DIMA

Special Delivery

Air conditioning is a blissful invention. My must-have list wasn't long when I was condo shopping, but air conditioning and walkability to the library were both non-negotiable. It may only be half a kilometre to the nearest branch, but in this August heat, ten metres is too far. Nacho is panting, and he didn't even exert any effort. Minus assaulting Holden.

Desperate for a shower, I drop my book bag, place Nacho on the bed in front of a high-speed fan, and enter my bathroom, leaving articles of clothing in my wake. The water hits me in a refreshing surge and all I can think about is relaxing on the couch with one of my new books. I've been waiting to read *Catalyst* for so long, I'm going to save it as my reward for getting through my other titles. In my thesis-writing process, books I *want* to read have been few and far between.

By the time I've washed my hair, I've decided which of the other books I'm going to curl up on the couch with for the next few hours. Since it's hot as Hades and I'm not going anywhere until Nacho needs to go out again, I don't bother with pants. I pull on my oversized T-shirt and dig through my bookbag in search of *The Cracked Curtain* I've never read anything by the author, Jenny Kempt, but we'll see if the reviews have been accurate.

Where's my book? I pick up the bag and dump the contents, rummaging through the selection of vibrant hard-covers and paperbacks, but my thriller is nowhere to be found. I pull the receipt-like printout from the inside of another book to see if I missed it in my checkout process. There it is, plain as day, second book from the bottom.

How could I have lost it?

Dickens. The slimy bugger stole my book.

After a few colourful words, I consider how I should go about getting it back.

I'll call Julie. She seemed to have some rapport with him and knew him on a more personal level than most librarians in a downtown library would know a patron.

I dial the number from memory—since I've been calling every day recently to see if *Catalyst* had been returned—and a desk clerk answers. After I beg for thirty seconds, she puts me on hold to retrieve Julie.

"Hello?"

"Julie, hi. It's Dina Blake."

"Oh, Dina, dear. What can I do for you? Are you on the wait list for something else?"

"No, no. Not right now. I have a problem though. Earlier today, after I checked out my books the first time, I crashed into that young man you were speaking to, Holden?"

"Crashed into?"

"Nose in a book. You know how it is, I'm sure. We ran into each other outside. Anyway, in the commotion, it appears he picked up one of my books. I'm wondering if he returned it by accident with his other ones."

"Oh, sure. Let me check. Which title was it?"

I give Julie the pertinent information, starting with the catalogue number listed on the printout.

"No, I'm afraid it wasn't returned, Dina."

Dickens. I'm going to throttle him with a hardcover book if I ever see him again. Not only does he return his books late and blame his literary choices on his pregnant sister, but he can't keep track of which books belong to him or not? Unbelievable.

"Would you be able to give me his contact information so I can get in touch with him?"

Julie hums a few bars of a show tune before she replies. "I can't share his personal information, dear. Surely you understand."

That's a bit of a relief, since I wouldn't be thrilled if she gave my phone number to someone else. It doesn't solve my problem, though. "Yes, I get it. What do I do about it? If he doesn't return it, will I be on the hook for it? I could end up with late fees. What if he never brings it back?"

"Well, since it's taken out under your name, you'd be responsible for any charges that accumulate."

I'm digging my fingernails into my palms, trying to remain calm. I can't afford extra expenses because of someone else's negligence. Not if I want to keep Nacho fed and our lights on.

"Try not to worry, Dina. I can't give you his information, but I'll call him myself and see what he says. He may not even have it. Perhaps you set it down somewhere when you came back inside after your… collision."

I'm certain I didn't touch anything in my bag. That can't be it. Holden has to have it. I tell Julie as much. She agrees to call him to get confirmation, then she'll let me know after speaking to him.

The fifteen minutes between when I hang up with Julie and her calling back have me wearing out a path in my bold-patterned area rug situated at the end of my bed.

The library phone number displays on my phone, so I rush to answer.

"Hello?"

"Dina, hi. Julie, here. So I was able to get in touch with Holden, and he said he could return the book to you this Friday at 1pm on the reading terrace. He confirmed he has it."

Serves me right for trusting a complete stranger to sort out our book chaos. "He can't just return it the next time he's there? I can just take it out again after he brings it back."

"To be honest, dear, you should retrieve it yourself to make sure it's returned before the due date."

She has a point. Budget aside, I do not want to become a library criminal, having fines on my file. I've maintained a perfect record thus far, and I refuse to let that be tainted by anyone else.

"Fine. I guess I don't have much choice. Thank you for sorting it out, Julie."

"My pleasure. I'll see you on Friday."

I hang up the phone with a groan that startles Nacho from his perch on my bed. He starts barking like my condo is being invaded. He's not concerned enough about a threat to get up, so I walk into the bedroom and flop on the bed beside him.

No one else will sympathize or understand if I call to complain about my predicament, so I groan again with my face buried in a pillow. Neither my sister, Angel, nor best friend, Hollis, will understand why I'm so annoyed about a book. So that leaves Nacho. Luckily for me, he lies beside me and lets me complain about Dickens for several minutes until he gets bored and falls asleep.

Friday morning, I glance out my window, and it's pouring rain. The only thing worse for curly hair than humidity is rain. A genetic curse in times like these. I decide my best bet is a thin yoga hoodie and leggings, my rain jacket, and an umbrella. Multiple layers of defence.

I put Nacho in his yellow raincoat with a hood, tuck him in his purse carrier, and we set off. A few of the books I picked up on Tuesday have already run their course, so I've got a second bag of books to return. Nacho only weighs as much as a few hardcovers, so at least I'm balanced as I walk the distance to the library, struggling against the brief gusts of wind, attempting to shield myself, my dog, and my books from the onslaught of rain.

The entire walk makes me resent Holden more with each step. By the time I arrive, my face and pants are drenched from the sideways rain, and I'm furious. Nacho and I wear matching scowls as he peeks his head out of his carrier to take in our surroundings.

"Don't worry, baby boy. Momma will tell him exactly how you feel," I mutter as I trudge up the stairs to the reading terrace.

This day has already gone to the dickens.

4

HOLDEN

No Reason Why

When Dina and I collided in front of the library, it was a complete accident that I picked up one of her books. I discovered the error once I got home and wasn't sure how to rectify the situation other than returning it, but once Julie called, I knew it was my chance to see Dina again.

I assumed she'd be angry about my faux pas, but as I walk up the stairs to the reading terrace to find a soaking wet Dina speaking into her purse, I regret my decision. This was a terrible mistake.

Of all the things I could greet her with—an apology, a simple hello, or a kind word—I blurt, "Is your dog wearing a raincoat?"

The furry imp is poking his head out of his purse with a yellow hood on, accentuating his angry eyebrows. Evidently Dina hasn't learned her lesson to keep the bag fully zipped.

"It's raining out, Dickens. Or did you not notice?" She takes in my appearance, likely realizing that I'm dry.

"No, I noticed. That's why I took a taxi. You walked in this?"

"Yes, I walked in this." She waves her hand to show the storm raging outside. "A taxi isn't an option."

I'm not sure if that's on account of the angry creature under her arm or some other reason, but I don't ask. Something tells me I'd end up with an encyclopedia thrown at my head. "I didn't look at the forecast."

"Really? The way our encounters have gone so far, I assumed you were just *trying* to make my life miserable. Give me my book so I can get back home into dry clothing."

Call me a masochist, but getting this woman riled up is becoming my new favourite hobby. Granted, my only hobbies are studying or hanging out with the same best friends I've had since childhood.

"No manners?" I gesture toward the window and see the rain slanting from the blowing wind off of Lake Ontario. "Besides, you can't walk home in that. Think of poor Cuj— Nacho."

"Do people need to use manners to have something returned from a thief? You stole from *me* and *I* have to say please? I don't think so, Dickens. Give. Me. My. Book. And as for what I can and cannot do, you don't get a say in that." She's getting feistier by the second. Her dark eyes are wild with determination.

"How about this?" I sit down on a vinyl, armless sofa and throw my feet up on the adjacent coffee table littered with magazines. "Why don't you pick a book for me to read? Anything you want, and I promise I'll read it."

For a split second, her face relaxes. That offers me a glimmer of hope until she speaks. "Get your own book. I'm not here to play out some weird librarian fetish or whatever this is. I just want to get the book and leave." She pauses for a second. "Please."

I'm surprised she gave in and used her manners. I almost feel bad for pushing her to that point. Almost. "Bring me a book, and I'll give you yours." I smirk. "Please."

She grumbles, which makes Nacho growl in his low, menacing way that makes you feel like he's about to morph into some fantasy sci-fi creature and take over mankind. I might be reading too much into it, but I wouldn't put it past him.

"Fine." She doesn't spare me a glance before she stomps off.

While I wait, I open my backpack and pull out the book that set this meeting in motion: *The Cracked Curtain*. It makes me think of our discussion from the last time we were here and wonder if there is, in fact, a cracked curtain in the story. I flip through it and get sucked into reading a few pages, where, sure enough, there's a shady old lady who spies on her neighbours through her tattered old curtains. Then I hear a throat clearing.

I raise my eyes from the book to find Dina standing over me with a book that is better described as a brick.

"Here." She hands me a copy of Tolstoy's *War and Peace*, no hint of amusement on her face. "This should keep you busy."

I grab the faded hardcover monstrosity with two hands. "Indeed. Of all the choices, this is what you picked? Why not Proust?"

"Well, *In Search of Lost Time* comes in seven volumes, so it was this or *You Forgot Your Manners, Tales of the Grumpy Octopus*. You obviously haven't read that one."

I laugh, again receiving looks from nearby library patrons. "Most people find me delightful."

She stares at me for a second, then puts out her hand and gestures toward her novel with her eyes. "Book."

I'm a man of my word, so I hand her the cliche thriller. "You sure you don't want *The Naughty Pirate*?"

"Maybe I've already read it." She raises her dark eyebrow and for a second, she takes on a playful demeanour. It's gone just as fast as it arrives. "See ya never, Dickens." Then she's off toward the stairs.

"Dina, wait." I jump up out of my seat and walk in her direction, carrying the massive 1,200 page novel. "Does this mean war or peace?" I hope she understands I'm referring to the dynamic between us and not the piece of Russian literature.

"Mess with my books again and the Battle of Borodino will look like a picnic. Your choice."

Yep. She understands. But I never did find picnics very exciting.

I return home once the rain lets up, so I am able to walk. The entire way, I question Dina's thinly veiled threat, curious what kind of battle plan she'd implement. No doubt she'd use Nacho as her Lieutenant-General. Assuming he passed the psych testing.

I change into dry track pants and a T-shirt, preparing to spend the afternoon reading this massive book that will take the better part of the three-week checkout window to finish. For what purpose? I don't know. Dina and I haven't run into each other before, so chances of seeing her again are slim, but if I do, I want to be able to say I kept my word. Plus, maybe It will spark some inspiration for my dissertation. My plan for my thesis is to research the impact of the industrial revolution on gender roles. There were defined roles in the early 1800s, so this book could help spark some baseline ideas to dive deeper into. It's far more useful than a grumpy octopus.

The book is heavy and awkward to hold in the early pages. I consider myself a fast reader, but this mammoth of a novel is one where, instead of turning a page and getting involved in the story, you realize there are still 1136 pages to go. An hour in, my phone buzzes, which is a perfect excuse for a break.

Sam: *Bro, you busy?*

When either of my best friends message me something like this, it's almost always because they've got a gig they want my input on or they're having woman trouble. Both areas, I do not consider myself an expert, but I'm not the type to leave the guys I've known since kindergarten high and dry.

Holden: *Studying.*

That's a semi-truth at best, but explaining the reality is too involved.

Sam: *Always. You need a break. I've got a gig booked tomorrow. Can you look at my set list?*

Michael, my childhood best friend, is a musician, whose stage name is Two Dollar $am. For that reason, we've called him Sam for as long as I can remember. It's because of him that I learned to use music to escape when my brain feels overloaded. He's always had my back. The least I can do is give him a thumbs up on his song choices.

Holden: *Sure, man. Be there in twenty.*

I change back into more suitable clothing and head west toward Sam and Phil's place, which is just over a kilometre down King Street.

The entire walk, all I can think about, is how my exams start in eleven weeks, and the trajectory of my future depends on them. My focus has been jolted from where it should be, and by wasting the rest of my day, I'm not doing myself any favours. I need to zero in my focus on comparative, transnational, and global history, which is the topic of study I chose for my first exam. Eleven plus weeks might seem like a lot of study time, but the thing with history is, there's no shortage of information to cover.

So much of society's past is set in stone—literally, if we're talking about hieroglyphics—but our understanding is also ever-evolving. It's fascinating and we learn so much about our present and future by analyzing the past. That's what makes it easy for me to develop tunnel vision every time I open a scholarly journal or textbook.

Except, my tunnel has been infiltrated by deep brown eyes and curly hair.

Today, as I weave through foot traffic along King Street, all I can focus on is whether I'm in a state of war or peace with a spunky bookworm and her persnickety dog. For once in the lifetime of our friendship, I hope my best friends can return the favour when it comes to advice on women, because Dina is a riddle I want to figure out.

With history, sometimes the real answers come from piecing together facts and drawing the most logical conclusion. With Dina, I have a feeling she'll be a harder mystery to solve than Cleopatra's tomb.

5

Gotta Get Away

A week after my miserable encounter with Dickens, I'm still irritated. Every time I think of his obnoxious ocean blue eyes, I want to simultaneously dive in and punch him in the throat. No one has ever left me with such polarizing feelings, and to be honest, it's exhausting.

After all the hassle, I finished *The Cracked Curtain*, and it was underwhelming. Disappointing, really. At least *Catalyst* was phenomenal. Now, I have six more books on my reading list I need to read by the end of next week to keep my ambitious thesis-writing schedule on track. Nacho and I are headed to the library in hopes we can pick up most of them.

Working toward my future should be the main reason for my rapid steps, but it's not.

When I enter the glorious climate-controlled building, I drop my borrowed books into the return slot and head to the second floor. Even as I ascend the stairs, my breathing accelerates, and it's not from the minimal exercise. At the top of the stairs is the reading terrace where I last left Holden. I'm not ridiculous enough to think he'd come back on a regular schedule, and I certainly wouldn't think he'd come here to chance running into me. I mean, that's definitely not why I came back, Friday at 1pm. Pssh.

Why would I even want to see him again? To ask him if he's actually spending a good portion of his life reading *War and Peace* because he told me he would? No, he wouldn't waste his time on that.

Stop. He shouldn't even be crossing my mind. My education needs to be my sole focus. Plus, Nacho is the only man I need in my life. I don't need to worry about him getting offended by how much time I spend studying or how little time I have for other things. He doesn't tell me how awful I am at dating.

Nacho and I gather all six books I need to continue the compilation of data for my thesis. But instead of heading home to read in the peace and quiet of my fourth-floor condo, I park myself on one of the armless sofas and crack open a notepad and my book.

To my surprise, a few chapters in, a voice to my left asks, "Do you mind if I sit here?"

I look up to find an average-height, pale-skinned man with bright orange hair pointing at the adjacent sofa. He looks like a scrawny Ed Sheeran. But even if he burst into song right now and serenaded me with the buttery smooth voice of the ginger Yorkshireman, I still wouldn't be thrilled with his company. Nevertheless, I don't own this library.

"Be my guest."

The stranger settles into the seat opposite me, causing Nacho to grumble in his bag.

"What was that?" the man asks, swiveling his head around.

As sly as I can, I reach over to pat Nacho, trying to sooth him. "What was what? I didn't hear anything." I glance at him from the corner of my eye with my face still directed toward my book.

"Never mind. I'm Ed."

Of course he is. "Hi, Ed. I'm reading."

"Hi, Re… Oh, I gotcha." He chuckles and unzips his backpack he set on the table. "Do you live around here?"

I release an exasperated sigh because, clearly, Ed didn't "gotcha" at all. "Yep. I have a tent under the Gardiner. Rent prices. Am I right?"

"That's Canada's second-most expensive city for ya. Do you come here a lot?" Kudos to Ed for not being deterred by my apparent lack of an address. Or lack of interest.

This is not the first time I've been approached by a man who wanted to strike up a conversation. It's not even the first time it has happened at the library. The three years it took to obtain my bachelor's degree were marked with plenty of awkward, one-sided conversations I didn't want to be part of. It's obvious I need to work on my do-not-approach face.

I'm going to make myself a fake book cover with the title *How To Murder People Who Interrupt You and Get Away With It*. It's a working title. Needs revision.

After several seconds of silence, I assume my lack of an answer has discouraged Ed from wanting to speak with me anymore, but when I look up, he's staring at me with his forehead creased, eyebrows raised over his blue eyes. I close my book and tuck it in my bag that's now concealing the only male reading companion I like.

"I do come here often. It's nice to have indoor plumbing sometimes… and silence."

"I bet. Good place to warm up or cool down too." He opens his textbook titled *Physical Anthropology* with two cute monkeys on the cover, but he doesn't start reading. "Hey, uh, if you ever need a place to crash, you could stay with me and my parents."

Ed here needs to read a few true crime books instead of learning about theories of evolution. Though, I suppose that could be fitting, too. Survival of the fittest, and all.

"I appreciate the offer, Ed. Now, if you'll excuse me." I stand, hoisting both of my bags, one on each shoulder, and march toward the stairs. Poor Ed is left in my wake, scratching his head when I glance back.

Social cues are not my strong point because I've always been one to dive into books with little regard for the real world or the actual people in it, but even I could give Ed some pointers. Though, on that note, Nacho could learn a thing or two from Ed about being more approachable. I pat my little reading companion as I reach the stairs and mutter into my bag, "You should've growled louder. Maybe I could've finished my chapter."

I'm so distracted by speaking to my dog, I misjudge the top step and nearly plummet to my death. That might be dramatic, but I would die from embarrassment. In a turn of events—considering the last time we ran into each other, I ended up *on* the ground—this time Holden appears out of nowhere to keep me off of it.

He hooks his arms under mine as he straightens me on the top step and steps back two stairs. "You good?"

Nacho hasn't made a peep, which is out of character for him. That makes two of us, because I can't think of anything to say, either. I nod, taking a second to soak in Holden's incredible blue eyes. My reaction to his versus Ed's has nothing to do with the shade.

"Fancy running into you here." His lips tilt in an irritating grin, but I can't find the sense to be angry with him for existing this time.

I stare into his eyes, trying to come up with something clever to say. "Thank you." Brilliant.

"Are you on your way out?"

I glance down at Nacho, who is glaring at me as if he's awaiting instruction to growl or not. "Yeah, I was trying to do some reading, but some people can't respect the sanctity of the reading terrace."

"Sanctity?"

"Yes. I was sitting there, nose in a book, when Ed Sheeran, *sans* charming accent, interrupted me and wouldn't stop yapping."

Holden chuckles as he looks past me at the reading terrace. "Guard dog didn't help?"

A teenage couple holding hands manoeuvres around Holden and me, making me realize we're blocking the stairs. I start descending, ready to leave this place behind for the day. "Later, Dickens."

Only a few steps down, I realize Holden is in stride with me, marching to the first floor.

"What are you doing?" I'm not taking my eyes off these stairs and risking face-planting again.

"Aren't you going to ask how my reading is going?"

"*War and Peace*? I didn't think you'd actually read it, so no, I'm not going to ask." No matter what my traitorous brain is telling me about engaging in further conversation with a man who is more frustrating than pop-up ads with a tiny x in the corner.

That's why I'm surprised by his reply.

5

HOLDEN

Can't Get My Head Around You

My friends were less than helpful when I visited them last week. Both of them whooped and hollered, telling me I should "Just ask her out." That doesn't feel like the right course of action, though. *War and Peace* has taught me that making an appropriate plan is critical to achieving success. Really, everything I've done since high school has been carefully planned and executed. I set goals and I achieve them. The gorgeous enigma in a floral sundress walking two steps ahead of me shouldn't change that.

"I should be done by next week."

Dina stops walking in the middle of the library's entryway and turns to face me. "You're actually reading it? Nothing better to do?"

That makes me laugh. "I have a lot of things to do that would be a better use of my time, but I said I'd read it, so I am."

"Wow. Integrity. I wouldn't peg you for the type, Dickens."

"Ouch. That's offensive."

She scrunches her face like my niece does when she has to fart. It's adorable on Dina, too, but I doubt it's for the same reason.

"Sorry. Sometimes I speak without considering people's feelings. This is why I stick to books. Speaking of, I have work to get done. I really need to get going."

I get the impression she's an eager reader, but work? "What do you do for work?"

She heaves a sigh and rolls her eyes, making me wonder if Nacho gets his attitude from her. "You're the second man today to keep me from it, so at this point, absolutely nothing. Have a good day, Dickens."

Before I can apologize this time, she spins on her heel and walks through the motion-sensored doors and into the humid summer air. I watch her walk away until she's almost out of sight. Julie is staring at me with a concerning grin on her face when I finally look away from Dina's retreating back. I smile and wave to play off how ridiculous I must look right now.

My plan to show up, hoping to meet Dina, only half worked, because I was late. I had gone down a rabbit hole when studying this morning, and by the time I looked up, it was almost 1:30. The walk from my house was more like an Olympic test event for race walking. I wasn't sure she'd be here anyway, so as I was walking up the stairs and saw her approach the top, my surprise almost prevented me from sprinting up the few steps to keep her from tumbling down. It was a good thing I did my race walk training.

Not going to lie. The brief time she was in my arms felt even better than crashing into her, as one would assume. It felt right; like the kind of cheesy moment Phoebe reiterated at family dinner from her latest romance read, much to the chagrin of her husband.

As quickly as possible, I retrieve the suggested reading material for my sister and rush to check out so I can get back home. Might as well dive back down my rabbit hole.

My week is occupied by studying, attending one event for each Sam and Phil, regular chores and adult tasks, and more studying. Between those things, I spend a lot of time wondering if I moved my study sessions to the public library, would I run into Dina again? The problem is, a public library and academic library are not on the same level in terms of content or study atmosphere. The public library has great resources, but their scientific journal selection is limited at best, and the environment, sitting amongst people reading best-sellers and self-help books, isn't as conducive to studying.

Plus, I'm pretty sure that would put me square in stalker territory. I'm smart enough to know that's not a category I want to be roped into, so my better judgement prevails and I stick to my regular routine.

But I'd be lying if I said I didn't revisit that decision multiple times.

I'm grateful for my sister being a quick reader. That means I have a legitimate excuse to go back to the library to pick up some new X-rated romance novels for her. My library checkout list is starting to look like I should be placed on a sex-offender registry, but I love Phoebe enough to risk it. Okay, I do love my sister, but that's not why I'm going back for a third Friday in a row.

Julie is seated at her spot behind the reception desk, glasses perched on the end of her nose, hair up in a tight bun like a stereotypical librarian. She winks when she sees me, which is uncomfortable... and confusing. She never seemed like the winking type, but maybe she's getting the wrong idea about me and my recent habit of only checking out books with shirtless men on the cover. I need to talk to my sister.

For now, I send Julie a polite wave and high-tail it up the stairs toward the reading terrace. I reach the top, taking in the large windows overlooking the main intersection outside, but that's definitely not the most exciting thing I see.

Dina is seated on one of the uncomfortable modern sofas across from a redhead who is engrossed in an animated conversation. It doesn't look like Dina is too enthused about his intrusion on her reading time.

She doesn't need a rescue, but I'm up for a little fun today.

I stop at the edge of the sofa and wait for her to notice me. "Hey, babe. Were you waiting long?"

She looks at me with wide eyes. "Um. Hi. Just been here talking to Ed... for forty minutes," she deadpans.

I resist the urge to chuckle at her expense, because that will result in both her and Nacho grumbling at me.

"Sorry. I got tied up." I reach my hand out to the talkative ginger. "Hey, man. I'm Dickens."

My introduction makes Dina giggle and the Ed Sheeran lookalike scrunch his face.

"Hi... I'm Ed. Nice to meet you. Are you two"—he waves his finger between me and Dina—"a thing or something?"

I sit on the sofa beside Dina and put my arm around her shoulders. I'm aware it's a move that could get me slapped, and to be honest, I'd be okay with that if she was uncomfortable. But to my surprise, she leans into me like this is where she belongs.

"You betcha. He's my cutesy schmootsie wootsie woo." Dina pinches my cheek like an affectionate grandmother, cautioning me with her eyes.

Ed is shifting in his seat. I'd be willing to bet he's not used to nor comfortable with confrontation. He stands, brushing off his navy slacks with a seam ironed down the front. I'd also bet his mother did that for him.

"Well, I'll leave you two lovebirds alone. Uh... thanks for... the chat?" He poses a statement as a question, which, again,

I'd bet is because he's feeling awkward. The poor chap scurries away in his loafers and argyle sweater. It's summer.

"So, nutter butter, having fun?" I squeeze her shoulder gently.

She shifts on the sofa, sliding out from under my arm. For the first time, I notice Nacho in his bag, glaring at me from behind the mesh. I'm not convinced that's sturdy enough to stop him if he decides to eat my face.

"Nutter butter?" Dina asks, placing a gentle hand on Nacho's bag.

I shrug. "You gave me a rhyming nickname."

"That's a terrible nickname. I'm disappointed you can't come up with something more creative."

I lean back against the sofa and kick my feet up on a turquoise stool. "What's wrong with nutter butter? I think it's cute."

Dina scoffs. "It's *not* cute." She sets her book down, which she hasn't even glanced at since I got here. "You have to come up with something better."

"Better? I don't think it's possible." I'm trying and failing to hide my smirk as I run through potential options. "Okay, I've got one."

Now she's intrigued, made clear by her new smile.

"Minnie." I'm sporting a full grin, wondering how long it will take for her to make the connection.

"What?"

I stare at her for a moment, really noticing her striking features in the natural light from the windows. Pouty lips. Narrow nose. Dark, mysterious eyes. She's beautiful. I knew that from the first day we crashed into each other, but that wasn't what caught my attention. There's much more to her than her appearance.

"Minnie... as in Minnie Mouse?"

Her cheeks flush a bright pink that the sunshine enhances. "I kind of hate you right now." She pauses for a moment, fanning herself with her paperback. "I'll have you know... never mind. Are you here to pick up more books for your 'sister'?" She adds air quotes, making it clear she doesn't believe my book choices aren't for me. Her and Julie both.

"That's one reason." I won't mention that I offered to come pick up new books. My actual goal was this interaction.

"Oh-kay, then. I can respect maintaining a little mystery." She tucks her book in her non-Nacho bag, signalling she's ready to leave. To my surprise, she places her hands in her lap and asks, "So what's our story, Dickens?"

"Our story? I don't follow." The split second I have to run through different possibilities, nothing clicks.

She tilts her head and shrugs one shoulder, then clarifies, "Everyone loves a fake dating trope."

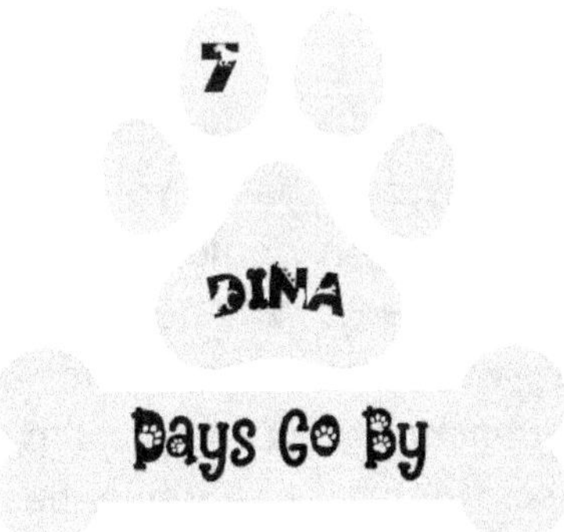

Holden has been nothing but a source of conflicting feelings and annoyance since the moment I met him. But given how irritated I was with poor Ed when he's been nothing but nice, I'm starting to wonder if that's more to do with me than with anyone else. Chances are, I've spent so much time in fictional worlds, real people are too much to handle.

Especially people who have seen my laundry-day underwear I've kept around for far too many years. What can I say? I'm on a tight budget.

But he's the one who interrupted my conversation with Ed—if you can call listening to someone talk about rising property taxes for twelve straight minutes a conversation—by implying we're a couple. He's the one occupying too much of my brain right now, interfering with what I need to be doing. He's not doing anything to uncomplicate our interactions. Or my feelings about them.

So what am I doing when I should be walking away? I'm playing along. Feeding into his game.

"Do you want to know how the story starts or how it ends?" he asks.

Curse my inability to hide my emotions. A smirk tugs at my lips, and I'm powerless to stop it. "No one likes a spoiled ending, Dickens."

He smiles at me wide enough his cheeks lift his thick-framed glasses. If nerds ever had a role model for exhibiting allure and confidence, Holden would be it. He's enchanting in a geeky Clark Kent kind of way. Why do I find myself *wanting* to talk to him? I rarely *want* to talk to people. Though, if he even utters the words *Dungeons and Dragons*, I'm out of here.

Mischief dances in his eyes while he stares at me in silence. Finally, he speaks. "Obviously, we had a chance meeting at the local library, where you immediately fell for my charms."

I shout a one-note "ha!", drawing the attention of our seat neighbours. "*Obviously,* this is fiction."

"I don't read a lot of fiction, but I'd like to read that story... to see how it ends."

For some unknown reason, that statement, coupled with how Holden is looking at me, makes my throat go dry. His intense, but kind eyes are peering at me, as if he has more to say but can't get it out. We're both unable or unwilling to speak.

Today, I know how our story ends. I stand and choke out, "See you around, Dickens," as I scoop up my dog and books, then walk away.

I tell myself I'm leaving because I have work to get done. Because I'm committed to my education. Because there's only one male I need in my life—one who has fluffy ears and a bad temper.

After I check out the six books I'm planning to read over the next week, I spot Julie, who sends me a wink from her small office behind the reception area. That's atypical. A wave or a smile, cool. A wink catches me off guard. I scan our surroundings to make sure she's not being held hostage, trying to send me some kind of secret code, but the coast is clear. I guess we're winking now. My wink back is about thirty seconds too late, making the interaction even more uncomfortable. This is why I can't be around people.

Without another glance, I rush out the door and head for home.

Hollis is what you'd call my "ride or die". She gets me. We are studying very different majors, but our goals and ambitions are on the same level. The only reason we met was because she was struggling to find something in the campus library years ago and I was able to help her. We got chatting and realized she lived a block over from where I did when I was living with my sister, Angel. Hollis and I have both since moved, but our friendship bond has been forged forever.

Knocking at the door sends Nacho whipping across my condo, barking his high-pitched alarm bark, completely unaware of his size. I scoop up Nacho so he won't escape to terrorize other residents on my floor, then open the door.

Hollis doesn't wait for an invitation to walk inside. "Hey, stranger. Hi, Nacho." She rustles the fluff on the top of his head, undeterred by him trying to rip her hand to shreds.

I set Nacho down and tell him to go chill out somewhere. It surprises me when he listens. And my sister thinks I haven't trained him. Nonsense; he just has selective hearing. Once the coast is clear, I give my bestie a hug, noticing how tired she looks. She's still cute in her cut-off jean shorts, "All You Need Is Love" T-shirt, and her long, wavy blonde hair down to her waist.

She hands me a paperback copy of her cousin's sophomore novel, *Flat White Lies*. "Wow, a signed copy! Thanks." I flip through the first few pages, eager to read it, but return my focus to my guest. "How high is your caffeine intake these days?"

"Ugh. I don't even want to think about it. I've become such a regular at a cafe down the street from work, I don't even have to ask for my order. They just nod and hand me a *trenta*."

We chuckle together as we step into my living room, which looks out at the Gardiner Expressway. The Gardiner is largely built as an overpass with city streets running underneath, so my fourth-floor condo has a front-row seat to watch vehicles speed by, or rather, sit still because of traffic congestion. We opt to sit out on the balcony anyway, since it's a nice day out. We just don't expect to get any "fresh" air.

"So, what's new with you? I feel like we haven't seen each other forever." Hollis drops into the sling-style canvas beach chair.

"It has been a while. Your dedication is even putting me to shame." I squat down, but pop up before sitting. "Sorry, let me get drinks. What do you want?"

"Just water. With ice, if you have any."

Bless her. She knows how frugal I am, so I rarely have anything more than water or tea to drink. I go back through the patio door to fetch ice water and find Nacho having a dream on the armchair. He's yipping and twitching like he's trying to chase something. Probably trying to kill an innocent squirrel—the little warmonger. I love him so much.

When I step back outside with two glasses of water, Hollis is tying up what sounds like a rushed phone call.

"Sorry... my brother." She tucks her phone in her pocket, reaching for her glass of water.

"That's okay. Oscar or Ethan?"

"Oscar. He's living off campus for the first time. He's having an issue with his neighbour."

"Wow. From the few times I've met him, I got the impression he never has a problem with anyone. Must be serious." I sit in my chair and take a sip of water. "So, what does he want you to do about it?"

"Nothing." She releases a breathy chuckle. "He was just complaining. Mom didn't answer when he tried calling her."

We stick to nonsensical conversation for a while, then dive into the challenges and frustrations of pursuing a master's degree. She informs me her cousin Isla is releasing a new novel early next year and insists she'll send me a signed copy. As generous as that is, if she keeps writing at the pace she's going, her books will fill up my condo pretty fast. It's barely big enough to spin around in, so a book collection is a slippery slope. Plus, if I hadn't been in the habit of going to the library for my books, I never would have crashed into Holden.

"What's with the face?"

I blink several times and focus on Hollis, attempting to neutralize my facial expression. "What face?"

"The one that says there's something on your mind you're not telling me." For a chemistry major, she's phenomenal at reading into body language and facial cues.

"It's stupid." I proceed to tell her about the day I went to pick up *Catalyst* and met Holden, along with summaries of each encounter since—mentioning multiple times how infuriating he can be.

"Mm-hmm. Real irritating, I bet. Enough to get you all hot and bothered."

I scoff. "You are mistaken. I am *not* hot and bothered. Who even says that? It sounds like effects of an STD."

Hollis and I both laugh together. It feels nice to have a window of time to just be silly.

"Okay, maybe not, but you sound hung up on this guy."

"I don't know. There's no point, anyway. No one wants to play second fiddle to schoolwork. Eighty-five percent of my waking hours are spent reading and researching."

"That still leaves fifteen percent. And there's nothing wrong with taking time for yourself. I'm in no position to preach balance, but if he's piqued your interest, it might be worth pursuing. You'll find time for something that matters."

I contemplate her advice while I'm sipping my water, then fish out an ice cube small enough to chew on. That gives me pause to chew on her words too.

Obtaining a bachelor's degree isn't for the faint of heart. It takes commitment and dedication. The decision to pursue further education is reserved for masochists who don't care to have a social life. Or down time. I was fine with that. Really, I still am. I just wish I had the guts or the time to ask Dina to get together somewhere other than our unspoken meet up at the public library. The problem is, asking her out would be leading her on. Not because I don't have good intentions, but because it's unfair to expect her to understand my priorities. Studying for these upcoming exams is more than a full-time job. It's a lifestyle.

Regardless, I'm walking toward the library for a fourth Friday in a row. Smutty books and *War and Peace* in tow. I think I'm going to pick Phoebe up a copy of *Anne of Green Gables* or *Charlotte's Web* just to salvage my library credibility. She'll probably throw it at me, but it could be worth the risk to avoid another winking smirk from Julie.

Thankfully, when I walk inside, Julie is in her office, so I'm able to drop my books and sneak away without any awkwardness. I march up the stairs and look to the right, where I notice Ed sitting alone at a circular table with an orange plastic chair. He doesn't notice me—or at least, doesn't acknowledge me if he does.

Assuming Dina is on the opposite side of the stairs, I head left, but the area is virtually empty aside from a mom with her two children. The children's faces are bright with smiles as the mother reads them a colourful book with a fox on the cover.

Since Dina isn't here, I'll find something to occupy my time and wait for her to arrive. I search the stacks nearest the reading terrace and settle on a mystery novel that's set around the time of the industrial revolution.

I make myself comfortable on a vacant sofa near one of the large windows overlooking the intersection, giving me a view of the way Dina usually goes when she leaves. Not in a creepy way. In an intrigued, perfectly harmless, curious kind of way. No, this is creepy.

Instead of staying there, looming over the street, I switch to a different location beside a solid wall. As is my custom, I throw my feet up on an ottoman and lean back, diving into this novel. Twenty pages in, I'm gritting my teeth over how ridiculous the storyline is. I slam it shut and check the time; 2:34. Obviously, Dina isn't coming today.

After checking out my sister's requested reads, I walk home, then stop in to visit her and my niece, who is growing bigger by the day. Once Grace is down for a nap, I return to my office to get in some study hours—like I should have been doing all along.

Time with Dina is a mistake. It's like taking a loan I can't afford, only the currency is time. I can't afford to go bankrupt, either. With a finite "income" of minutes to spend, I have to be more mindful of my "expenditures". Waiting around at the library for no apparent reason isn't a sensible way to spend the too few hours I have in a day.

But I can't convince myself I should be anywhere else.

Fourteen days seems too long. Well, specifically, thirteen days, twenty-three hours, eleven minutes. I'm aware that's ridiculous after spending less than two hours total in Dina's presence—most of which I was making a real effort to irritate her—but the last seven days since my failed attempt to meet her at the library, she kept popping into my mind.

That's why I'm walking back to the library again—without any of Phoebe's books for an excuse. Here I am, abandoning my study schedule for a blind chance at running into Dina.

I enter the ornate building, and Julie's wink results in a giggle as she looks at me. Just as unnerving as the first time. She doesn't call me over and I have no books to return, so I give a pathetic wave and scurry past toward the stairs.

My ascent is occupied by thoughts of how I'll gently turn Julie down if her behaviour morphs into anything more than a passive wink.

To the left of the stairs, I find Dina sprawled out on a sofa like she's in her own living room, with Nacho in his bag on her lap, tucked in behind her book. She doesn't look up as I approach until Nacho starts to grumble.

"Hey, Killer," I whisper at the vicious beast.

Dina glances up from the pages of her paperback, entitled *The Gun in the Lake,* with a literal gun in a lake on the cover.

"Let me guess what this one's about," I say as I sit down by her feet.

She draws her legging-clad legs toward her, then turns to place her feet on the floor. "What brings you here, Dickens?" She adjusts Nacho on her lap and placates him with a pat on the head. "Back for another riveting romance novel for your 'sister'?"

It probably wouldn't go over well if I told her I came to see her. That I was here last week for the same reason and her not being here left me with a marked feeling of disappointment. So I play off the real reason I'm here by replying, "What can I say? You can never have too much romance in your life."

Blush creeps up Dina's tan skin, giving her complexion a glow that even the terrible fluorescent lighting can't dim. Not for the first time, it makes me wonder if perhaps she had a date or some other plans last week, which grips at my empty stomach.

"I didn't... uh... I didn't see you last week." I'm being a blockheaded moron. Just don't ask where she was. "Did you have somewhere more exciting to be?" Cue mental facepalm.

Dina stares at me for a second, closing her paperback and setting it on the sofa between us. "I guess that depends on your idea of excitement." Her dry delivery of that simple sentence confirms there was nothing exciting about wherever she was.

"So, let me guess the plot of this book." I'm desperate to change the subject before my traitorous mouth says anything else stupid—even though I have more questions than answers. "Starts out with someone discovering a dead body. Gasp!" I clutch my hand to my chest. "The person has been shot! One pragmatic, troubled detective joins forces with another stubborn, no-nonsense detective and they butt heads, but come together to create detectiving genius—the likes of which has never been seen before. Despite all the inevitable danger and roadblocks in the way, they eventually find the culprit. But not before... dun, dun, dun... finding the gun in the lake."

Dina's lips twist to one side of her face and her eyes narrow. "Well, now you've spoiled the ending, Dickens."

Nacho must pick up on Dina's mock displeasure, because he grumbles from his place on her lap. I've got to hand it to the little guy. He may be high-strung, but he always seems to have Dina's back. Regardless of how trivial her upset is.

"Sorry. None of the books I read have surprise endings, either." Non-fiction doesn't leave a lot of room for creative liberties. "What else is on the list this week?" I nod toward the stack of paperbacks she has on the table, impressed by her ability to read as much as she does.

"A YA fantasy, a memoir, a thriller with polarizing reviews, two romance novels on different ends of the spectrum, and a literary fiction novel." The way her face lights up when she talks about books is unmistakable. My sister might be a bookworm, but Dina is a voracious bibliophile.

"That's an eclectic mix. Are you going to read *War and Peace*?"

She sweeps her curly hair over one shoulder. "I already have. To be honest, I didn't think you'd read it. At least, not the whole thing."

"If *I'm* being honest, I would have preferred *Tales of a Grumpy Octopus*."

Without skipping a beat, Dina replies, "You'd probably benefit from the entire series. Not just manners. *Pick Your Battles* is a personal favourite, or perhaps, *Be on Time*." She levels me with a challenging stare, undeterred by my refusal to look away.

She's been a mainstay in my mind since the first day I met her. Every inch of progress I make with her feels like an epic battle. So, if she wants me to pick my battles, I choose this one.

I'll Be Waiting

Last week I had to meet with my thesis advisor, who insists I call her Sage, which ran later than I expected. Translation, I spent my afternoon having work I poured blood, sweat, and tears into—maybe just tears—ripped to shreds by a faculty member I admire. As if having my work critiqued and picked apart wasn't bad enough, my stupid brain couldn't stop reminding me I missed my implied library meetup with Holden. With my thesis well on its way to completion, I shouldn't be worried about arbitrary rendezvous or irritating nerds.

That didn't stop me from dragging myself to the library at 1pm after staying up all night to finish my latest thriller. I'm sleep-deprived and hungry because I rushed here without eating. *Hangry* Dina is not a happy Dina.

But even though Holden interrupted my reading, a silly thrill shot through me when he appeared. Nothing happening in this dark mystery novel is capable of reaching the same level of excitement I felt from Holden dropping into the seat beside me. That never happens. Reality has *never* been more exciting than fiction. Not in my life, anyway.

"Which book should Ed read?" Holden smirks, making it increasingly difficult not to return the gesture.

"*The Berenstain Bears Learn About Strangers*. Without a doubt. He invited me to live with him and his parents."

Holden's brows jump up his forehead. "I thought you just met him."

I hold in my chuckle because he looks as confused as I felt. "Mm-hmm. I guess he found me interesting."

Now one lone eyebrow remains raised. "Or maybe he's a serial killer and was hoping you'd make it easy for him to tie you up in his basement and skin you alive."

My eyes widen at his theory. "Well, that turned dark quickly. You don't think..." My words die in my throat as I picture myself tied up in Ed's basement, listening to him talk endlessly for hours without pause. Shudder. I mean, it's better than the alternatives, but still a situation I'd rather avoid. Maybe instead of my thought for him to read true crime books, he could be the subject of one.

When I blink and refocus, pushing aside thoughts of listening to Ed's endless diatribe against rent prices or the rising property taxes, Holden is staring at me with his lips tilted. "Why else would he invite you to come live with him?"

"I may or may not have implied that I was homeless." I grimace because I never want to make light of an unfortunate situation some people find themselves in. "But I didn't want to hint at where I actually live because... you know... stranger danger."

Holden shakes with silent laughter for a few seconds, then leans forward. "I'm glad he didn't lure you into his basement and skin you alive. That would have made my library time a lot less interesting."

It's obvious he's joking, but I still scoff and clutch Nacho to my chest in mock offense that Holden could be so flippant about my potential disfiguring. "Nacho would never let that happen."

"You know what? I believe that. He might be in need of an exorcism, but at least he's protective."

Again, I feign outrage at his comment. I don't think Nacho's behaviour is demonic, by any means. "He's misunderstood, but I love him."

He just isn't afraid to speak his mind when it comes to his hatred of people. If he were a CEO, people would fear *and* respect him. But because he's a chihuahua, he was born into a bad reputation that he's done nothing to change. Sometimes stereotypes are right, but I wouldn't characterize him as evil. He's passionate. Determined. Like me.

"I know what it's like to have people pass judgement on you just because of your appearance or an interaction taken out of context. It's human nature to base an opinion of someone on their first impression." My voice trails off as I finish, because that got a lot deeper than I intended it to. That's my cue to leave. "Anyway, I better get going. I've got a lot of work to get done." I point toward my stack of books, then rush to tuck them into my bookbag.

Holden hasn't spoken for at least a full minute when he stands and breaks his silence with, "Hey, Dina? Do you... uh... want to take my number?"

Holden has never been anything short of debonair—albeit nerdy, like Tony Stark—even when he's being irritating. Right now, he's looking at his feet, rocking back on his heels. If my years of reading about body language and physical cues were moderately accurate, he's nervous.

His uneasiness compounds mine, which is ridiculous. He asked if I wanted his number. It's hardly an invasion of my privacy. The problem is, it feels like it comes with expectations. Like we'll move from beyond library acquaintances to friends.

And I'd be lying if I said I thought about Hollis the same way I think about Holden.

Still, he has a way of making me do things I normally wouldn't. "Okay."

He pulls a small paper from his wallet, and for a second, I think he has an actual business card. That would be an ultimate nerd move. Thankfully, he flips over a card from a nearby kickboxing gym and writes his number on the back under his cursive *Dickens*. I study the card when he hands it to me, raising an eyebrow in question over how he ended up with it in the first place.

"They had a demo day in the park and a really muscular guy handed me a card as I walked past. I couldn't say no." He shrugs, making me stifle a laugh.

"Ah, the good old-fashioned ambush approach. Been there. One time I was walking through the mall and went past a hair straightener kiosk. The guy asked if he could demonstrate how it worked, and I didn't want to be rude, so I agreed. The guy straightened a three-inch-wide section of my hair, then sent me on my way. Do you even understand how awful that looked?"

Holden chuckles, which seems to melt the last of his nerves. It also eases mine.

"My sister made fun of me until we went past a skin care kiosk and she ended up with half of her makeup washed off."

We both laugh at that, which makes me remember we're in a library.

"I... uh... better go. I'll text you?" I say it like a question because I'm unsure what he wants from this exchange.

"Yeah. I should go too. I'll be waiting. Not literally. I'm not..." He pauses a moment, as if he's searching for the right words.

I try to help by adding, "I'm sure you have better things to be doing than waiting around for me."

That seems to startle him, which I find concerning. Cozy mysteries tell me I should read into that, because people don't usually make suspicious gestures without a reason. Lessons from contemporary romance tell me not to put stock in miniscule movements that will lead to misreading situations. I decide not to question it.

"Right. I... yeah. I've got plenty of other things to keep me busy."

I kind of want to ask what else he has going on since he seems to be able to carve out library time consistently on Friday afternoons, but I don't ask that either. I'll continue to speculate about what he does with his non-library time. Or maybe it will give me a topic to broach if I text him.

"Anyway, I guess I'll talk to you later." I give Holden a tight smile, then turn toward the stairs.

Nacho releases a grumble that tells me he's tired of being cooped up, so I better get a move on it. A second later, I realize it's Holden he's grumbling at, not the confines of his bag. Holden matches his stride with mine as I descend the stairs. We continue to walk toward the reception area, when I indicate I have books to check out.

Holden pauses. "Oh, right. Books." He snorts a huffy laugh, which seems to surprise us both. "Okay, I guess I'll talk to you soon."

For the final time, we say goodbye and part ways.

One thing I take note of regarding our latest encounter is that our silence has become as comfortable as our conversations are entertaining.

It's terrifying.

10

HOLDEN

Autonomy

So much to do. So little time. Therefore, there's no reason for me to be spending half of my Sunday morning staring at my phone, willing it to light up with an unknown number. I have six hours to get some research done before I'm supposed to be at my parents' house for our weekly family dinner. If I show up late or distracted, my mother will grill me until she uncovers the reason. Nothing escapes her notice when it comes to her kids. She even knew Phoebe was pregnant before she did. Most empty-nesters find a hobby; my mother has never had a hobby outside of being a mum and obsessing over the Royal Family. Her old country roots run deep.

Once again, glancing at the clock, I force myself to focus on the task at hand. Studying material for the four-hour exam I have to complete covering a variety of topics under the umbrella of social and economic history. The sheer volume of material in that category is mind blowing, but it best suited my intended thesis research. The other areas of study are equally broad and intimidating. Hence why studying takes months. There's no cramming for these exams at the last minute.

I get in the zone for several hours until my phone buzzes on the desk beside the thick copy of *A Commerce of Knowledge* I have open.

416-555-3462: *Guess what my latest book is about. I'll give you a hint.*

I glance at the screen, knowing exactly who the message is from, even though the number isn't saved in my phone. Correction: wasn't. It is now.

Holden: *What's the hint?*

Minnie: The title is…

What Happened in Vegas

I laugh as I lean back in my desk chair, distancing myself from the dry material I was trying to absorb about the diplomatic expansion of the British. Really, I could just ask my mother, who is a wealth of knowledge when it comes to all things related to her ancestors. Albeit, incredibly biased.

Holden: *That's a tough one…*

A single woman, recently dumped by the guy she thought was "the one". So she goes on a bachelorette trip with her friends. How am I doing?

Minnie: *So hot.*

I mean, so far, so good.

Like, not cold.

Another laugh escapes me reading her clarification. If Dina thought I was hot in any capacity, I'd be surprised. I'm not totally hopeless, but I'm hardly an adonis. I'm more like Dexter Morgan meets Spencer Reid, but with fewer homicides.

Holden: *Everyone gets good and drunk. An Elvis impersonator and a gumball machine ring are involved. They wake up the next morning with no memory of the night before.*

Egad! Turns out, they've unwittingly gotten married!

But instead of going to get an annulment, like a logical person, this enemies to lovers story has a happily ever after when they realize they're meant to be after all. Even though, two weeks before, they didn't know each other existed.

Silence. No bouncing dots to indicate a reply. No cry-laugh emoji at my sad attempt at a plot summary. Nothing. For seven full minutes.

Minnie: *You're scary good at this game.*

I'm assuming my guess was somewhat accurate again, which is a little embarrassing considering my fiction reading list is quite short.

Holden: *I blame my sister for sharing the entire plot of every book she reads.*

Oh, and I'm assuming that one or the other works through a lifetime of issues in those two weeks, so now they're miraculously cured.

"Hey. Are you almost ready to head to Mum and Dad's?" My brother leans into our shared office, his hair combed and styled in his typical mid-fade with a side part, giving his dark-blond locks a pronounced hipster barista style. His beard doesn't help change that perception either. Good thing he *is* a hipster barista.

I glance at my phone again before replying to him and note the time. "Uh, yeah. I just need a few minutes to change."

He levels me with the same stare he's been using for years. Ever since he made it clear that I was a perpetual disappointment to him. We may live together, and we may be civil, but our brotherly love has been lacking for a long time.

I rise from my chair and brush past Boyd without another word. No matter what I say, he's going to take issue with it.

Family dinner is meant to be casual, but our mum pulls out all the stops. Roast beef and all the traditional fixings. Homemade Yorkshire puddings, roast potatoes, whatever vegetable she felt inspired to cook, and finishes off with either Banoffee pie or sticky toffee pudding. We may live in the cultural epicentre of Canada, but my parents have not swayed from their roots in the slightest.

Once I've pulled on a clean charcoal grey polo shirt and dark jeans, satisfied I will pass Mum's scrutiny, I bound down the stairs to meet my waiting brother. I heard him stomp down as I was choosing my shirt, and could practically feel the animosity radiating from him with each step. The fact I took an entire three minutes doesn't help matters.

"Let's go. I don't want to show up late," Boyd grumbles as he heads for the door.

"You could have gone without me. I'm sure I can find my own way."

That comment earns me an eye roll and a deep sigh.

I spot Phoebe and her husband, Aaron, walking in our parents' front door as we approach, grateful for the distraction the baby will create. There's something magical about the first child in the next generation. Grace has been a bright spot for all of us. I'm no baby expert, but I'm pretty sure she's the cutest child to ever exist.

My phone buzzes in my pocket, and I'm curious how Dina replied to my plot summary. Since there's a strict no phone policy on family dinner nights, I rush to check it before walking through the door. Sometimes I feel like a child in a grown man's body because I'm terrified of my mother. Checking my phone inside is tantamount to treason in her eyes.

Minnie: *You've got to stop blaming your sister, Dickens.*

Your ability to nail a plot is way too accurate for second-hand knowledge.

I want to defend myself or at least send her back a joke, but my fingers stop short when I enter the foyer of my childhood home. The walk from our place is definitely not long enough.

"Hey, Dad," I greet when I see my father's beaming face cooing over his granddaughter.

"Ladies first, Holden. I've taught you better." His smile never wavers as my sister secures Grace in his arms. He stares down at his blue-eyed granddaughter. "You tell him. Gentlemen are a dying breed."

For as serious as our mother is, our father is the complete opposite, joking at every opportunity. He does have the uncanny ability to "joke" in a way that makes you question who you are to your core, though. This is one such instance.

I toe off my shoes and step toward Phoebe, giving her a side hug and a kiss on her temple. At some point in our teen years, I sprouted up and became her big brother. That's been our standard greeting ever since. Then I give Grace a peck on her forehead before shaking Aaron's hand. My mother isn't in the foyer, so I'm being a rebel when it comes to the ladies first rule.

My father turns toward the living room without another word to me or my siblings, only focused on the baby girl who has captured his heart.

Instead of following him, I beeline to the kitchen, where I'm sure to find my mother. She's dressed in her typical Sunday outfit—a pleated skirt and plain blouse, covered with a Union Jack apron. No one could ever see my mother cook and question her heritage. One look at the Will and Kate memorabilia in our china cabinet would make it pretty clear, too.

"Smells good in here." I stride toward my mother and greet her the same way I did my sister.

The woman rarely stops long enough to give her a hug or anything more than a brief greeting. So when she sets the meat thermometer on the counter and stares at me, it's unnerving.

"Who is she?"

I turn to check behind me, curious who "she" could be, but other than Boyd, no one is in my sightline. "Who is who?"

She wipes her hands on her apron, then plants one weathered hand on her left hip. "You're seeing someone." Her abrupt, matter-of-fact statement is void of any excitement or happiness. Almost as if she's disappointed.

"I'm not seeing anyone." My body betrays me and takes a gulp of air, swallowing it loudly. "When would I find the time?"

The fresh wave of disappointment oozing from my mother is practically tangible. As if each exhale from her five-foot frame is laced with irritation. "And she has you lying to your mother. She's no good for you."

11

HOLDEN

Next To You

What is happening here? My mother just guessed that I met someone based on what? My outfit? My facial expression? I don't even know. Then assume that said mystery woman is forcing me to lie about her existence? Sure, there's someone I'd be *interested* in seeing, but aside from chance meetups at the library and a very brief text exchange, we're virtual strangers. There is no "seeing", so I am not lying about it. However, her reaction makes me want to reconsider being honest in the future.

This situation requires a rapid shutdown.

"I'm not seeing anyone. Honestly. I'll let you know if that changes." After this exchange, it might take a while for me to fess up *if* that changes.

"Don't be daft, Holden. You can lie to your mother, but your face never could keep a secret. I don't want to hear you've lost the plot over some cheeky bird set on getting in your pants."

This is one of those moments in life, of which there have been many, when I'd rather eat my own pants than continue this conversation. "I'm going to visit with Grace." At least she isn't opinionated or judgemental. Just cute and gassy. I exit the kitchen without giving my mother a chance to continue on her irrational tirade, but instead of walking into the living room, I detour to the powder room down the hallway under the stairs.

I close the door behind me and pull out my phone to reply to Dina's insinuation I'm blaming my plot expertise on Phoebe.

Holden: *I've got a lot of second-hand knowledge. Trust me.*

Any big plans for the day?

Subtle. I scoff at myself, then remember where I am. Along with the powers of perception, my mother can hear a pin drop from a mile away, but only if it's one of her kids who drops it. The last thing I want is for her to stand on the other side of the door asking questions about my last bowel movement. I flush the toilet to keep up appearances, then turn on the water to wash my hands.

My phone buzzes as I turn the faucet off. A text message shouldn't excite me as much as it does.

Minnie: *Taking Nacho for a walk. Finishing this book, even though you spoiled the ending. Eating ramen. The usual.*

You?

My mother's overbearing nature may get on my nerves, but at least I don't have to eat ramen. I respond as quickly as humanly possible so I can exit the bathroom before anyone gets suspicious.

Holden: *Family dinner. I'll text you later?*

I tuck my phone in my pocket before I unlock the door and step into the hallway.

"Geez, Mum. What are you doing?" My heart jumps into my throat as I nearly crash into her just outside of the door.

"Thought I was going to have to repaint the lavvy." She stares up at me, which she somehow makes intimidating, and suddenly I'd give anything to crawl back into my office and dive into historical British commerce.

These Sunday dinners become less and less appealing after each interaction. But I respect my mother—my parents—so I comply with their one request to show my appreciation for all they've done for us. Even if I'd rather hide in the loo and text Dina about made up plotlines and how hot I am... or whatever.

"Your paint is safe." The olive green pedestal sink and matching toilet don't leave a lot of suitable colour choices, so it's a good thing. I need to steer this conversation elsewhere before she discerns anything else I don't feel like discussing. "Do you need any help?"

"Set the table." She dismisses me with a flick of her apron as she walks back into the kitchen. No matter how old I get, being in this house always manages to make me feel like a child again. Like I walk through the front door and I'm suddenly in the passenger seat of my own life. But instead of driving, I go set the table like a good boy.

Mercifully, dinner conversation is focused on Grace's newest accomplishments, like sleeping for four hours at a time and cooing—which is likened to the most intelligent sound ever uttered. Words can't express how grateful I am to not be the baby of the family anymore. Unsurprisingly, my mother is just as interested in Grace's bowel movements and has no qualms about discussing them over our roast beef dinner—with gravy.

Hours later, Phoebe and Aaron are the first to make their escape, reasoning Grace needs to get home for her bedtime routine. I never want to be the first to leave because it's always met with a guilt trip and reminders that I need to do more than study. A bit ironic, considering my mother stated earlier that she's worried I'll lose focus. After I help my mum clean up, I thank her, then Boyd and I leave at the same time.

On our short walk home, I pull out my phone and find a reply from my earlier message.

Minnie: *Sorry for bothering you. Enjoy.*

Shoot. She sent that three hours ago.

Holden: *You didn't bother me at all.*

I start to write about our family phone rules, but that seems like a lame thing to share.

"What are you so stressed about?" my brother asks as we walk through our front door.

Boyd and I do not have the kind of relationship where we share our woes. He doesn't express interest in my life, nor does he share anything about his. His question is unusual and makes me wonder if he's playing spy for our mother.

"Nothing."

Instead of sticking around to converse any more, I walk upstairs to my room, pick up the abandoned clothing I left on the floor earlier, and drop onto my bed. With one arm propped behind my head, I send a one-handed message to prompt a response from Dina.

Holden: *How's the book?*

I scan my calendar app while I wait for a reply, adjusting my plans for the week to shuffle things around and add in some more study time.

A response pops up a few minutes later.

Minnie: *You'll never guess what happened.*

Seeing her nickname pop up is like a breath of fresh air after dinner with my family.

Holden: *In the book? I bet they live happily ever after.*

Minnie: *You really like to spoil the ending, huh? ;)*

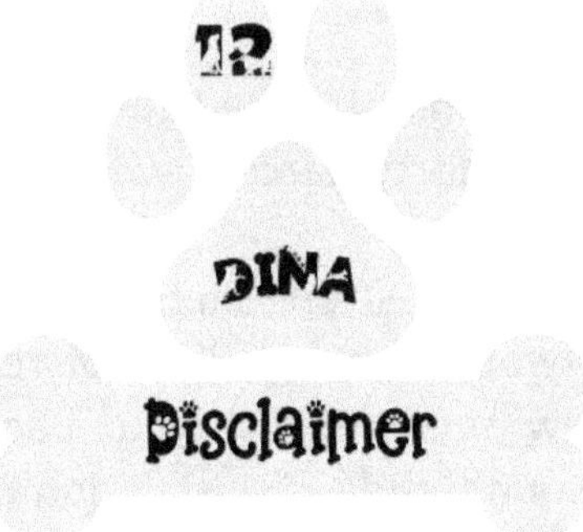

Whatever courage I had that possessed me to text Holden initially has disappeared. All the weeks we met on the reading terrace were informal, like two strangers in the same place at the same time, having a chat. But seeking conversations outside of the library changes our dynamic. At least, it does for me. We're no longer visitors who converge at the corner of Bathurst Street and Fort York Boulevard, Fridays at 1pm. We're two people who share text message exchanges that are nothing of substance, but still feel personal.

Holden texted me this morning, saying he had some free time this afternoon if I wanted to meet at the library. The funny thing is, even though it's Tuesday, saying no didn't cross my mind. Nacho even walked alongside me rather than riding in his carrier the entire way. He can't march through the library, though, so I tuck him in his bag and he curls up for a post-walk nap. He knows the drill.

As I reach the top of the stairs, Holden is waiting in what has become our usual spot, leaning forward over the coffee table, scanning a thick hardcover that looks like a textbook.

"Hey. What are you reading?" Books are in my comfort zone. If I have the opportunity, conversations always start there.

He tucks it behind him before I catch the title. "Hey, you made it." His smile is forty percent welcoming, sixty percent mischievous.

Math was never my strong suit, but I feel 100 percent nervous. "I said I would. Though I'm not really sure why." I stammer for a few seconds, trying to backpedal. "Sorry, I didn't mean to sound rude. I just... don't know why you wanted to meet, I guess."

Why has this guy turned me into a blubbering fool? I'm not a social creature, but I've always been confident. Able to speak when spoken to and engage in conversation—assuming I want to. My comfort zone may be the written word, but something about Holden turns me into a hopeless birdbrain with no grasp of the English language. And my degree is in English.

Holden's smirk grows more mischievous as he stands. Nacho doesn't make a peep until Holden is inches away.

"Hi, Nacho." He reaches out to touch my bag, but Nacho's grumbling gets louder. Holden wisely withdraws his hand, which silences my grumpy canine. "I thought it would be better to ask you in person."

I stare in his azure eyes for several seconds, waiting for him to continue, but he doesn't. "Ask what?"

"If you'll go on a date with me."

I know this is a library, but I swear, you could hear a pin drop in here. There are no murmuring teenagers. No parents reading inspirational tales to their children. No growling chihuahuas. I'm afraid if I look around, people will be staring, awaiting my response. The only person looking at me, though, is Holden.

"You want to go on a date? With me?" I'm struggling to keep my expression neutral and not gape at Holden with bulging eyes. It takes extraordinary conscious effort not to mimic a goldfish who's just discovered flakes dropped in its bowl. So much effort, I don't know what else to say.

"Nacho can come too… if he wants. Maybe we can take him somewhere he'll like? The… I don't know. The butcher shop?" Holden lets out an awkward laugh.

"The dog park," I blurt, then try to compose myself before saying anything else. "He likes to visit the dog park at *Canoe Landing*." I hook my thumb, gesturing behind me in the direction of the nearby park. "His favourite pet store is that way, too."

"So, is that a yes?"

My reply sure sounded a lot like a yes, even though I didn't say that specifically. Again, the possibility of saying no never crossed my mind. The only reason I hesitated was because I wondered why. Why, after how our first few encounters went, does he want to go on a date?

But in the interest of finding an answer to that lingering question, I reply, "Yes."

The smile Holden wears now looks like 100 percent happiness. "This Friday? Unless you need to stick to your library schedule?"

"No, Friday is fine. I can replenish my stash today." I glance down at the book he had tucked behind him when I arrived and read the title. "*A History of Commerce*?"

He turns his head toward the plain-looking textbook, then back to me. "Uh, yeah. Just some light reading." He bends down to pick it up, which requires two hands. It must be over 600 pages, and is a large trim size. It must contain humankind's *entire* history of commerce.

"*War and Peace* wasn't enough for you?"

"What can I say? I'm a glutton for punishment." He shrugs and sets the book back on the table.

Logic tells me that comment has nothing to do with me, but the panicked part of me that's grasping for a reason to back out of our date plan makes me doubt his intentions for a moment. "Am I part of your punishment?"

"What? No. That's... no. Nothing like that. Just when it comes to books. Trust me. You're the furthest thing from a punishment." One corner of his lip tilts up in an irresistible way. It's like the nerd equivalent of puppy-dog eyes.

Turns out I'm susceptible to both expressions.

"Oh." My face is far too warm for my liking. We need a topic change. "Are you picking up any books for your sister today?" Please say yes. Getting lost in the stacks will help my face return to a normal temperature.

"I'm sure she wouldn't mind a few extra choices. The spicier the better. Got any suggestions?"

Whelp. That doesn't help my blushing situation. "Come on. We'll find something for her to talk about over family dinner." I turn away from Holden to shield my burning face from his view and head to the rows of fiction.

Fifteen minutes later, we've chosen eight new novels for me, as well as *Southern Belle* and *Something Borrowed* for his sister's reading pleasure. Apparently, she likes the arranged marriage trope. It's one I've never been partial to myself. I'm more of an enemies-to-lovers or second-chance romance fan.

"Have you read these?" Holden asks as we head downstairs, holding up the paperbacks with his eyes smiling as intensely as his lips.

"Not those, no. I... I read reviews for them, though. They should be right up your sister's alley."

Holden pauses at the bottom of the stairs. "You read reviews? For books you don't read?"

My thesis research isn't a topic I want to delve into right now. Especially not with Julie staring at us with a cheeky grin on her face.

"Yeah, reviews help me choose what I'll read next. Sometimes a book is just not what I'm looking for, so it gets sidelined." Nacho and I continue toward the checkout desk and drop my stack of books to borrow. This should get me through until next week and get me close to completing my reading list for research. As much as I enjoy getting lost in a good book, I'm looking forward to reading just because I want to again. To pick up a book because it appeals to me for one reason or another. Or to put down a book I'm not enjoying.

Julie is exceptionally chipper as she chats with Holden and scans each book. She asks about his niece, and the sheer joy in his voice when he speaks about her is all kinds of adorable. It sounds like he has an active role in her life. I'm sure it will be years away, but I hope I can have a similar relationship with a niece or nephew in the future. It sounds exciting. Enjoy the cuteness, do the fun things, then ship them home for your sibling to deal with the sleep deprivation and poopy diapers. Pretty sweet deal, if you ask me.

Once everything is scanned and our return slips are printed, we say goodbye to Julie and exit onto the sidewalk.

"So... I guess I'll text you? We can make a plan for Friday." Holden stares at the exact section of concrete I was sprawled out on when we first met.

"Sure. I'm easy, just so you know." I freeze, internally berating myself for how idiotic I've sounded today. "With plans, obviously. Nothing fancy. You know?" A laugh spills out of me that would embarrass me if I wasn't at my limit already.

"Nothing fancy. I gathered that by the dog park suggestion."

We stand in silence for more than half a minute before Nacho shifts in his bag, catching me off guard. I grip It tighter to keep it from jostling. "I better get this guy home. He gets cranky if he's cooped up for too long."

That statement makes Holden laugh. "Is that what does it?"

"Well, that and... existing. He's a hard man to please." I really need to stop talking. "Text me whenever. I'll see you on Friday." I wave my hand and don't look back as I walk toward home.

13

DINA

One Fine Day

Anormal Friday consists of reading an entire novel, taking Nacho for multiple walks, texting back and forth with Angel and Hollis, and most recently, they've included a trip to the library. I'm not a creature of habit, but I am one who gets hyper-focused and struggles to take on anything else. Whether Holden will fit into my narrow field of vision is to be determined. He has broad shoulders.

I choose a pair of dark skinny jeans, a cognac crochet sweater with a white tank underneath, and brown ankle boots. I toss my phone and wallet in the pockets of Nacho's carrier bag and walk toward the library, where I agreed to meet Holden. I might have agreed to go on a date, but that doesn't mean I want him to know my address yet.

He's waiting out front when I arrive, and I almost laugh at his outfit. Not because he looks anything less than handsome, but because his outfit mirrors mine. He's wearing a blazer the same colour as my sweater, dark jeans, and shoes that match mine. I'm not sure what that says about us, but if he's wearing Mickey Mouse underwear, I might pass out. Not that I'm going to ask.

Holden smiles at me, holding his arms out to his sides. "Great minds think alike, I guess."

"One major distinction. You lack the most fabulous accessory of all." I glance down at Nacho, who is quiet in his bag.

"Are you ready?"

I consider asking to stop in the library to grab a book in case I get bored, but that would be rude. "Yeah, sure."

Our walk is awkward for the first fifty metres, which doesn't inspire a lot of hope. Our conversations until now have flowed well—even when painfully awkward—but as soon as "date" is attached to an interaction, there's a level of anticipation that impacts every exchange.

Mercifully, Holden sparks a conversation. "So, tell me a little more about the mystery of Dina Blake. Where did you grow up?"

Check that off on the list of 'last things I want to talk about'. I'd be more inclined to talk about my tampon preference or when thirteen-year-old me practiced kissing in the mirror. But again, it would be rude if I don't answer and I don't have a logical reason to deflect his question, so I try to be vague. "I've lived in the city my entire life. Grew up in Bloor West Village."

"Wow. How crazy is that? We grew up, what? Less than ten kilometres apart and never ran into each other before."

"It's a big city."

"Yeah. But I definitely would have remembered if I had seen you before." He smiles, which looks sincere. "So, do your parents still live there? In the village?"

Ah, snap. I stutter and stop a few times before I can produce a fluid sentence. "No, they're buried there." I cringe at how heartless my own words sound. I really do love my parents. It's just uncomfortable whenever the topic of them comes up. Dynamics change. People's behaviour toward me changes.

Holden trips over a crack in the sidewalk, then tries to play it off. "Dina, I'm so sorry. I didn't know."

"It's fine. Can we move on from that conversation? I'm just not…"

"Right. Okay." He exhales a long breath as we reach the dog park. "I'm sorry. Have I ruined our day now?"

"No, it's fine. It happened a long time ago. It's just… people always treat me differently when they find out, and I hate being the poor orphan girl everyone pities. So please don't treat me that way."

He studies me for a moment, and I'd love to be able to hear his thoughts.

"I get what you're saying, but is it really a bad thing if people feel sad that you lost your parents?"

Instead of observing the sheer joy of other dogs in the park, I freeze, staring at Holden. Several beats pass before I work up the nerve to reply. "Yes, Dickens. It *is* a bad thing when people only spend time with you because they feel guilty. Or they think you're a broken, fragile, little girl who needs handouts and shortcuts to make up for the crappy hand life dealt. But I'm not broken, and you know what? I'm tough as hell because of it. I don't need anyone's pity."

Every alarm system in my body is telling me to leave right now. Warning me against engaging in this conversation when I'm upset and frustrated. But I talk myself down. I understand where he's coming from and what he's saying, and I hope I've made my thoughts on the matter clear.

"Look, Dina. I'm sorry."

"Please stop being sorry. Tell me about your childhood." I take a few deep breaths, trying to curb the nausea flooding my system.

Holden nods as he leans against the chain-link fence. "Are you going to let Nacho out?"

"Oh, no. I don't need a lawsuit. He just comes to observe."

"That's smart." He chuckles and rubs a hand over his face. "Why did you suggest coming here? Just to watch the dogs?"

"Yeah, why not? Can a person ever have too much dog joy in their lives? I don't think so. Plus, I like to see if I can match the dogs to the owners. You know how they say dogs and owners look alike?"

Holden bursts with his uninhibited laugh that attracts attention in the silent library, but here, no one can be bothered. "I have heard that. Okay, let's guess." He watches a doberman patrolling the perimeter, sniffing along the fence. "I bet he belongs to that guy."

"Why him?"

"Because if I ran into either of them after hours in a wrecking yard, I'd run the other way."

Oddly enough, seconds later, the brawny bald man shouts "Cooper," throws a frisbee, and the doberman takes off after it.

"Good guess. Okay, my turn." I scan the crowd of about fifteen dogs and almost as many owners. "That guy belongs to that husky."

"Mm-hmm. I can see it. What makes you think so?"

"He looks like he lives in the drama department, and huskies are notoriously dramatic. Plus, I can see the dog hair on his black shirt from here."

"Cheater." Holden laughs again; the earlier tension disappears from us both. "Oh, that lady with the brown curly hair has to own that poodle."

"That's discrimination." I feign offense at his characterization of the woman's hair, placing one hand on my hip. "Curly-haired people don't have to have curly-haired dogs. Nacho doesn't have curly hair."

"No, but he definitely gets his spitfire attitude from you. You're kindred spirits."

I could be genuinely offended by that, but he's not wrong. "True. It's funny, because my sister has an American bully who gets along with everyone, and Angel is very friendly too. They look nothing alike, though. Unless we're counting that Genie is half brown, half white."

Holden stares at me again, as if he's processing something. "Half brown, half white?"

It didn't occur to me that comment would have us circling back around to family history. "My mom was Guyanese. Dad was Scottish."

He rubs the back of his neck with one hand, staring off into the distance. His silence is uncomfortable, but then he snickers. "I thought you just had a tan."

"Well, my tan doesn't disappear in the winter." I glance around at the other humans at the park, admiring the diversity of the downtown area. "Assuming I spent any time in the sun, I would be several shades darker. Angel and I aren't even in the same category. I have lighter eyes and skin. She's darker, but her hair is coloured lighter at the moment. She's stunning."

Holden steps closer to me, but keeps his distance when Nacho growls. "You're stunning, Dina Blake. In any shade."

Including bright red? Because I'm pretty sure that's what shade I am now. My face feels hot without needing to touch it for confirmation. This is not the first time someone has complimented my looks, but it's the first time I've cared. The first time I felt like those words were more than an empty comment made with ulterior motives.

When I snap out of the stupor Holden's words have landed me in, I blurt, "Should we go to the pet store?"

"Uh, yeah. Sure." Holden ambles toward the double gate that prevents dogs from escaping the enclosed area, and unlatches the first one for me to slip through. Once we confirm no covert canines have snuck out behind us, we exit onto the walkway and stroll side by side toward the sidewalk.

"Are you going to tell me about your childhood, Dickens? Or just leave a girl in suspense."

"The good ol' suspense novel, *Girl Who Knew Not of His Childhood*. What do you think?"

I giggle at the pride in his smiling eyes. "Instant bestseller."

"I think you're right. Okay… Childhood. Where do I start? I'm the baby of the family with one older brother, Boyd, and sister, Phoebe. My parents moved to Canada from the UK about thirty years ago. They planted roots and bought a triplex on Whitaker Avenue, where we still live."

"You still live with your parents? And your siblings?"

"Yes and no." He opens the door for the pet store, which rings as we enter. "The triplex they bought has three separate houses, obviously. Each has a one-bedroom basement apartment and three bedrooms upstairs. They were smart and rented the other units to pay down their mortgage. Now Boyd and I live in one, Phoebe and her husband are in the middle, and my parents live in the house we grew up in."

I imagine what that situation must be like and come to one conclusion. "Wow. You all must be close."

14

HOLDEN

Amazed

Dina's assumption my family is close causes me to stiffen. "Yes and no," I repeat, chuckling to mask my discomfort. "It's complicated. We are close, but that doesn't come without bumps in the road, I guess."

Her face twists, giving me the impression she's trying to stop herself from saying what she really wants to say. I feel like I owe her after my earlier question about her parents, but this is our first date. Diving into uncomfortable family secrets doesn't set a great tone to encourage a repeat. And even with the awkwardness, we've managed to wade through it and return to comfortable territory.

"Every family has their troubles, I guess. It's nice that you guys are close despite it all." Her voice loses volume as she finishes speaking and I worry that inadvertently, we are veering off course again.

We explore the pet store, aisle by aisle, and each time we return to the front, the young man behind the counter smiles and waves at Dina, then sends me a slight scowl.

I glimpse a stuffed baseball, which brings to mind a sharable memory. "I played tee-ball."

She glances up at me, giggling. "For some reason, I have a hard time picturing that."

"Oh, I hated it. Half of the kids on my team would be standing in the infield, building dirt piles with their feet, not paying attention to anything. Each kid at bat could have rounded home plate three times before the infielders looked up. It was torture."

"It couldn't have been that bad. There must have been some kids on the team who enjoyed the competition," she continues.

"They gave out a 'best sandcastle builder' award at the end of the year. There was no mention of best infielder. What does that tell you?"

Dina laughs again, which prompts a breath of relief to escape my nose. Hopefully, we get better at navigating these conversational landmines.

I scan the aisle of dog treats and toys, wondering what it would take for me to win Nacho over. Anything along the lines of a fetch toy is out. I have a feeling I'd be the one doing the fetching. A few items catch my eye, so I pick them up, one at a time, deciding on both.

Once again, Dina looks uncomfortable.

"What's wrong?"

"Oh, nothing. It's... uh, it's just that my budget dictates I not spend more money than necessary right now."

I look down at the items in my arms. "These are my peace offerings. My treat."

She looks confused, with her dark brows knit together, mirroring my expression. What kind of people is she spending time with that she'd assume I would pick up something and insist *she* pay for them? Who does that?

"You don't have to do that. He's pretty low maintenance," she insists.

That makes me laugh. "You carry him around in a purse."

She stares at me with her dark eyes, not saying a word.

"And a raincoat. Low maintenance doesn't apply."

"That's presumptuous of you." She turns herself and tucks Nacho behind her as if she's shielding him from my verbal assault. "He's easy-going when you get to know him."

Note to self: Don't say anything remotely negative about Nacho Dog.

"Well, he can still be easygoing with a plush squirrel tree trunk toy and an interactive treat dispensing dog chew," I read the tags aloud, confident in my choice. "Those sound like things a chill dog like Nacho would enjoy."

"You don't need to do that. Really." Dina worries her lower lip, drawing my attention to her full, pink pout.

I step toward her and hear a less intimidating growl from her overprotective Chihuahua. "I want to. He's left me no choice. At this point, I'll have to resort to bribery to make him like me."

We walk toward the checkout, where Dina is greeted by the short blond guy named Richard, according to his nametag. She returns the greeting, but doesn't engage in any further conversation.

I place the two items on the counter, ready to pay, when Dina snickers quietly.

"What's so funny?" I ask, sliding my debit card out of my wallet.

"Look at these dog cookies. There's one that says 'prince'."

I scan the display and see a more appropriate one. "I think 'bad attitude' suits him better." Another one catches my attention, so I pick it up. "Or 'bad to the bone'. I'm going to get him this... If that's okay with you."

"You don't have to buy him *anything*, Dickens."

"Once again, I want to." I slide the cookie across the counter, laughing at the absurdity of a six-dollar dog cookie.

But as the saying goes, the way to a man's heart is his stomach. I'm pretty sure the way to Dina's heart is through Nacho's. It's a two-step vetting process.

Richard bags my peace offerings, tears a receipt, then we're on our way. To where? I have no idea. If historical gender roles have taught me anything, now I should offer the lady a beverage or something to eat.

As we exit the pet store, I ask, "So, should we go get a drink somewhere? Or are you hungry?"

No snarky reply. No quick comeback. Dina appears to be glitching.

"We can go somewhere with a patio. A few are still open."

Nothing.

"Dina? Are you okay?"

"Hmm? Oh, sorry. I was just thinking. What did you say?"

Weird. She spaced out, and I can't help but wonder if she's bothered by my purchases.

"I just asked if you wanted to stop somewhere for a bite to eat." Before she's able to chime in with her budgetary restrictions, I add, "My treat."

"That's too much, Holden. You already spent money on Nacho. I can't ask you to do that."

I stutter step, and gently guide Dina to the front of a barbershop, so we're out of the way of other pedestrians. "If I didn't want to, or couldn't, I wouldn't have bought Nacho anything, and I wouldn't have asked you if you wanted to eat. Don't worry so much." My hand takes on a life of its own, rising up to stoke her jaw with my thumb. "If I was broke, I would have taken you to the hot dog cart or something."

She huffs a laugh, and once again we've navigated through an awkward moment. This has to be some kind of record.

"Okay. But I have a request."

"Name it." Please don't say Hibiscus. Please don't say Hibiscus. Smuggling an angry dog into a five-star restaurant doesn't sound like a fun afternoon.

"We grab something from the hot dog cart, then walk over to Garrison Common."

"That sounds perfect."

The grin that appears on Dina's lips is the most radiant I've seen to date. If a street vendor and a trip through a national historic site make her that happy, I can't wait to put in a real effort.

We reach *Weiner Winner*, which I will forever think is a terrible business name, and I gesture for Dina to order. She orders four hot dogs, which surprises me, and I wonder if perhaps Nacho has a ravenous appetite. I request one more for myself and two cans of soda.

Before I can pay, Dina rifles through her bag and pulls out some cash. "At least let me pay for the extra ones."

I close my hand around hers, tucking the cash into her fist. "No, it's fine. I got you."

The smile she had moments ago is quickly replaced by glassy eyes, which she refuses to look at me with. She just nods, and I notice a hard swallow.

It's not that I think our date is going poorly, but it's thrown several curve balls my way. And considering I never made it past peewee tee-ball, I'm floundering, unsure how to handle them.

When the vendor hands us our street meat, Dina takes three, leaving me with two. I expect her to dive in or throw a whole one in her purse for Nacho, but she just cradles them, careful not to drop any.

Not wanting to create any more awkward moments, I resist the temptation to ask her if she's going to eat them. We make it across the street and halfway through the park when she darts to the left.

"Be right back."

I stand in place for more than a minute, unsure where she even disappeared to. She emerges from behind the trees lining the pathway seconds later with empty hands.

Immediately my mind pictures her hiding behind a hedge, scarfing down three hearty portions of questionable pork, like a national hot dog eating champion.

She grabs one hot dog from my hands. "Thanks."

Confusion can cause speech paralysis. I'm proof of that fact; words fail me. I'm suffering from some kind of hot-dog-induced aphasia. So many questions.

Dina doesn't seem fazed by my silence. She nibbles on her hot dog like a civilized person. I don't get the impression that she'd stuff three in her face behind a tree, but I've been wrong before.

I can't resist asking. "Where did the other hot dogs go?"

She takes a sip of her orange soda before answering. "Um. There are usually a few homeless people in there. I see them a lot when I walk Nacho around here, so I try to bring them what I can."

My hand drops, because suddenly I feel guilty for eating my food. She implied she didn't have a lot of money to burn at the pet store, but would have spent what she had to feed other people in need?

This girl keeps throwing more questions at me than answers, and the more I get to know, the more there is to find out.

The mystery of Dina Blake is becoming more complex with each encounter.

15

DINA

Change the World

Why is he so quiet? I continue to eat my hot dog, even though it stopped being hot long before I took my first bite. Nacho is sniffing the mesh of his purse, so I open the top to let him poke his head out and break off a piece for him.

Time to change the subject. This whole first-date-small-talk business is not as fun as my novels make it sound. "Once we get up here, I'll put Nacho on his leash and walk him around for a bit. It's his spot."

"His spot? You come here a lot? I mean, I assumed that by the hot dogs…" Holden's voice trails off.

"I live right there." I point toward the condo building I've called home for the last three years.

"Oh, wow. You're really close to the library."

"That was on my must have list. I don't…" Nope, I'm not getting into that right now. "I don't mess around when it comes to books."

He chuckles. "I got that impression from the multiple threats I received for bringing a book back late."

I scoff. "There were no threats. You mistook my bookish passion for intimidation."

He looks contemplative for a moment, his eyes bouncing around everywhere but at me. "Okay, maybe you're right. But you were intimidating."

"Still didn't scare you away."

His gaze lands on me now, and he has a wide, toothy grin. "No. Nacho almost did." He crinkles up his hot dog wrapper and holds his hand out for me to give up mine, then he jogs over to the nearest garbage can.

Bonus points for not being a litterbug.

I decide, since there are no other dogs around, Nacho should get out to stretch his little legs, so as Holden marches back to where I'm standing, I hook Nacho's leash on and lift him out of his tote.

"Time to unleash the beast?" Holden quips as I set Nacho on the ground.

"There will be no unleashing. Who knows what kind of chaos he would cause." I watch as Nacho studies Holden's approach. To my surprise, Nacho remains neutral. Not even a single hair raised on his back. I nearly topple over when he walks up to sniff Holden's pant leg, then wags his tail. Nacho. Tail wagging. Never thought I'd say those two things together. He has rarely shown any level of happiness toward anyone other than me.

"Do you think he's trying to butter me up so I'll fork over the goods, then he can take me out? He looks calculating."

I snicker at Holden, who is staring at Nacho hesitantly.

"Don't turn your back on him, just to be safe."

Nacho continues to sniff, stretching his neck to inspect the hanging bag.

"Ulterior motives. I knew it." Holden chuckles, reaching his hand in the bag and pulling out the cookie he purchased. "Can I give him a piece of this?" he asks me.

"Sure. Watch your fingers." I say that as a joke, but Holden's fearful expression is what really makes me laugh. "Relax, Dickens. He's six pounds."

"You've never heard the phrase 'it's not the size that counts'?"

We both have matching raised-eyebrows and he appears to be suppressing a smirk, just as I am.

Holden is the first to recover. "The sentiment is the same." His ears flush pink, which is very noticeable on his alabaster skin. He looks like he got an instant sunburn.

"Right."

Nacho is patiently waiting at Holden's feet, his tail still wagging. I clutch his leash, shortening it as much as possible so I can yank him back if he tries to chew Holden's face. But he doesn't. He gently takes the small piece of 'Bad to the Bone' cookie and eats it like the regal chihuahua he is.

"Bribery works," Holden whispers and snaps off another piece of cookie; this time crouching down to put his face closer to Nacho. He gives my little terror another bite, which seems to seal the deal.

Nacho jumps up, propping his front paws on Holden's thigh, and bounces to reach his face. Not to eat... to kiss.

"This isn't what I had planned for my first kiss of the day, Nacho, but I'm flattered." Holden's ears turn an even more vibrant shade of pink, and I think mine may match.

I'm sucked into some alternate universe as I ask, "What first kiss *were* you planning on, Dickens?" What is wrong with me? I can read between the lines. I'm not ignorant to expectations on a first date. I've been on a few before and they all ended the same way. Each time, it just felt like I was fulfilling a duty in exchange for someone else purchasing dinner. I felt cheap and uncomfortable. Another date wasn't an option; the only thing I looked forward to each time was going home. Now I'm standing a few hundred metres from my front door and I'm not eager to get there. It doesn't appear that Nacho is either.

Holden avoids eye contact with me by scratching under Nacho's chin and stammering something unintelligible. I gather I'm not getting a response to my question.

"He… I think he likes me." Holden's smile is endearing as he stares at the creature I was sure would never tolerate anyone other than me. He digs through the plastic bag and tugs out one of the tiny stuffed squirrels that belong to the tree stump toy.

Nacho takes it, holding it in his mouth. He turns to look at me and I swear, he's smiling with the little stuffy in his mouth. When he clamps his jaw down, discovering that the new toy squeaks, his tail starts doing double time.

"Now we're in for it. He loves squeaky toys."

Holden stands, brushing his hands on his jeans. "The squeaking sound is supposed to mimic a dying animal. Makes sense he'd like that."

Yeah, that doesn't surprise me. "He's got killer instincts." My breath escapes me when Holden steps beside me, grazing his hand along my lower back. I don't know if it was intentional, but the brief contact stalls my lungs, and suddenly they lack the ability to function.

"Dina?"

Still struggling to breathe, I hum, "Mm-hmm?"

"Want to go check out the art installation at the museum?"

The unrelated, totally platonic question helps jumpstart my respiratory system. "Oh, yeah, sure."

I pick up Nacho and tuck him back in his bag. He is not forfeiting his new prized possession. The literal death grip his tiny jaw has on the brown polyester makes me giggle.

Holden and I stroll toward the museum, where an interactive art exhibit is displayed. The dark space and flashing screens displaying different imagery serve as a pleasant distraction. But standing next to Holden, not speaking, listening to a combination of the sound effects and Nacho squeaking his toy, makes all the awkwardness from the day hang over us like a dark cloud.

I could allow it to loom there, casting us both in a shadow, creating an overcast memory on this day, or I can try to focus on the bright points we've had. On how he went along with my weird date suggestion. How he didn't question my excessive food purchase in the moment. How he went out of his way to win over my dog, who, until today, I thought was unwinnable.

"What did you think?"

I glance to my left and Holden is now watching me, not the video art.

"I'm not sure I understand visual art. My brain doesn't work to process things that way, so I can appreciate pretty things, but I wouldn't say they evoke any kind of emotion in me. The Mona Lisa just looks like a grumpy lady to me."

"That's probably not the reaction da Vinci was going for, but I get it. I don't have any artistic ability at all." He holds an arm out, gesturing for us to continue walking down the pathway that cuts through the vast green space.

"So, what kind of abilities do you have?" I hope he doesn't take my innocent question the wrong way.

"Outside of studying, spending time with friends, and fetching books for Phoebe, I don't do a whole lot else. And even my fetching duties won't be needed much longer, so it'll be back to a hundred plus hours a week studying."

I stutter step, causing me to pull back behind Holden. He stops, then turns to face me, sliding his glasses up his nose with his pointer finger.

"What are you studying?"

He shifts his weight and grips the back of his neck "I'm working on my PhD in history."

So much about his personality makes sense. He has the lifelong student vibe. The perpetual learner, wanting answers to questions of the past. "Wow. So you already have your master's?"

He looks uncomfortable talking about this, which doesn't make sense. "Yeah, I finished it last summer. This past year has been dedicated to course work, then I've had from May until now to prepare for my comprehensive exams."

"I'm jealous you've already finished your master's, but if you've put the work in, you deserve it." I pick at a piece of fluff on my sweater, avoiding his eyes. "Sometimes I think I'll never get to the end of mine."

His mouth gapes, but he composes himself quickly. "You're getting your master's? In what?"

"Library Science." Normally I say that with a point of pride, but for some reason, knowing Holden has already achieved his master's, it feels less significant. Less impressive.

"That's... wow. You're still young, no?"

"Late birthday, so I started university when I was seventeen. And I didn't take any summer semesters off." I shrug my shoulders to play off my fast-tracked education. "It helps me stay in the zone if I never leave it. Hyper-focus."

"That makes a lot of sense. Are you doing a co-op type program?"

We continue strolling along, side by side, with Nacho murdering his squirrel. The relentless squeaking from my purse is drawing some strange looks from pedestrians walking past.

"My program gives some flexibility, so I had the choice for co-op or a thesis. I chose to do the thesis."

"You may be the only person I've ever known who would choose to put themselves through the thesis process when you had another option."

I'm not going to dive into the ridiculous reasons why I made that decision. Not right now. "It just worked better for me. The experience of the co-op would have been good, but I've learned a lot from my thesis research that I wouldn't have learned from hands-on experience. Pros and cons."

We reach the end of the pathway, leaving us the option to continue along the sidewalk in either direction or walk back through Garrison Common, which is often host to different outdoor concerts. Today, it's a wide-open space punctuated by horn honks, engine-revving traffic from the Gardiner Expressway buzzing overhead, squeaking squirrels, and awkward first date conversation.

Holden glances at me as if he's silently asking which way I want to go.

I ask, "Do you want to walk me home?"

15

HOLDEN

Get it Right

That question takes me by surprise. I've learned so much about Dina on this atypical first date, but for some reason, her allowing me to see where she lives feels like she's breaking down a wall. One she's carefully crafted that she doesn't often allow people to see behind.

"Yeah, I can do that."

Dina's smile is small, but so pure and definitely welcomed. The way the apples of her cheeks glow under the late afternoon sun gives her natural beauty a whole new dimension. She nods in the opposite direction, then starts walking south.

"Do you normally take guys home on the first date?" The words spill from my mouth without giving my brain a chance to catch up.

Before I can clarify the fact I'm joking, Dina retorts, "No. No one has ever… never mind. I can find my way from here." She strides a few feet in front of me, not sparing me a glance. Fury is a good alternative to stilts, because her legs seem to increase in length and tempo, making her walk at a pace I can't keep up with.

Why can't I get anything right today? Misinterpreted bad jokes. Inappropriate lines of questioning. One awkward conversation after the next. Yet, this has still been the most enjoyable date I've ever been on. She can't leave like this.

"Dina, wait. That's not what I meant. It was just a terrible joke. Not that I'd have an issue if you brought anyone home on a first date. That's totally your prerogative. I mean..." I scrub my hands over my face as I try to keep up, giving me pause to find the right words. "Please, let me start over."

She halts her steps before turning to face me. Her serious scowl is as intimidating as it is adorable. "Dickens, maybe this was a mistake. Obviously, we both have a lot going on and should stay focused on our studies. This..." She sighs, pulling her shoulders back to straighten her posture. "I can't let anything get in my way. This has been my only goal for the past nine years. I need to do this to prove..."

I wait for her to finish her thought, but she doesn't, so I prompt her. "Prove what?"

"That I can. That I'm not the damaged girl... No, you know what? Forget it. I just... this was a bad idea. Good luck with your PhD, Dickens. Maybe I'll see you around."

Instead of chasing after her, encouraging her to finish what she was saying, make peace before she walks away, or anything I should do, I stand on the sidewalk and watch her back retreat down the pathway that connects to Fort York Boulevard. A minute later, she's disappeared and I'm left holding onto a bag with half a dog cookie and a stuffed tree stump.

My walk home, navigating through late-afternoon traffic, feels like it's ten times farther than it is. I don't know why. It could be the disappointment of how our day ended. It could be my injured pride.

Instead of facing my own life, I dive into research on the cultural development of Eastern Europe in the seventeenth century, hoping to distract myself.

But as interesting as history can be, right now, it can't compete with the reality of my present, or the unknown of my future.

My thumbs hover over the glowing screen, itching to send Dina a message. I want to apologize for my stupid joke, but I don't think that was the entire problem. She's always been one to dish out colourful comments and insults before, always taking them in jest. There's something more to what happened on Friday, leaving me equal parts wanting to get answers and wanting to honour her wishes.

I resign myself to respecting her space, but if I don't hear from her within the next few days, I'll find a way to talk to her.

"What's wrong with your face?" my dear brother asks as he walks through the living room.

"Genetics. You're one to talk."

He stops behind the sofa, untying the apron he wears as part of his work uniform. "No. Why do you look like you just sat on a toilet seat that someone else warmed up?"

"That's... oddly specific."

"You know what I mean. You look like you're trying to decide between two uncomfortable situations."

I stare at Boyd as he starts to unbutton his white shirt, hoping he'll lose interest in my face and walk away. He doesn't. He continues until he's standing in front of me with his button-up undone, then tosses his apron over the back of the couch and takes a seat beside me.

"I know things have been a little weird between us, but I'm still your brother. I still care."

That's news to me. I thought we barely qualified as roommates, and even then, we make it work because we're both busy enough to limit our waking hours at home together. Even if I had gotten the impression in any of the last seven years that my brother wanted anything to do with me, there's nothing he can do to fix a failed first date.

"It's nothing. I'm just brain fried from studying and stressed about these exams. So I guess you're right. I have to choose between studying more, or staying here for this conversation." As soon as the words are out and I see Boyd's shoulders droop, I have a flash of remorse, but not enough to vocalize an apology. I walk toward the stairs, only glancing back to see my big brother lean back on the couch and cover his face with his hands.

I'm a jerk. But years of little brother shaming made me more resistant to guilt trips. Plus, it's not an untruth. My exams are next month, so it's understandable I'd be worried about them.

My familial relationships are just one other thing I can't seem to get right lately. So I'm better off focusing on something I can.

As I reach the top of the stairs, my phone chimes, and it wouldn't surprise me if it's my sister texting me to tell me Boyd tattled, and now she's angry with me. The walls between our houses are far too thin. Word travels fast.

The photo of a decimated stuffed squirrel brightens up my mood as much as the phone screen.

Minnie: *I have a sad boy on my hands.*

Holden: *You'd think he'd be happy. Mission accomplished.*

I turn right for my bedroom, rather than left toward my office, and throw myself on my unmade bed, awaiting a reply.

Minnie: *He's been moping around for hours. I don't think he's going to recover from this.*

Something about that message feels like maybe she's talking about more than just her dog. Or maybe that's wishful thinking on my part. If Boyd's reaction is anything to go by, I've been moping around, too, but that doesn't mean she has.

A photo of Nacho lying on a bed with a ratty-looking quilt and mismatched pillowcases makes me feel bad for the guy. He does look like his entire world has fallen apart.

Minnie: *Have you ever seen a sadder face?*

I contemplate how to respond, but ultimately decide to go for it.

Holden: *Yes. When I look in the mirror.*

I screwed up.

Once the words are sent, I tap the screen, wanting to take them back, but it's too late. For five minutes, I stare at the phone, wondering if service in the city has gone down or if I forgot to pay my phone bill and it's suddenly been shut off. I can't take it anymore, so I go to the bathroom to brush my teeth, leaving my phone on the counter.

What's the saying? A watched pot never boils? I think the principle applies to text messages, too.

Finally.

Minnie: *You didn't screw up. Promise. It's me.*

That's something I hadn't considered—the possibility that she thought any of our disaster date was her fault. I was under the impression it was pretty obvious the entire debacle was on me. But maybe she feels the same way.

Holden: *Can we try again?*

I rush to add, *No pressure.*

What is it about the words "no pressure" that seem to ratchet up the amount of pressure? The sentiment is the antithesis of its intention.

I brush my teeth with an intensity that will whittle them back down to baby teeth if I keep going, so I spit, rinse, set aside my toothbrush. Then I lean back on the counter, waiting for a response.

Minnie: *Meet me at the library on Friday?*

I reply quickly, agreeing to meet in our usual spot at 1pm. As I hit send, my pearly whites are on display in a way they haven't been since Friday—minus when Grace had a diaper blowout while Phoebe was holding her and my sister screamed like she'd been shot. I don't care how old I get; poop humour will always be funny. But this smile is genuine and long lasting. Right until I doze off to sleep.

Dina feelings

acho's poor little heart can hardly handle the devastation that came from the loss of his beloved squirrel toy, Squeakie. That's the only name we agreed upon, because Nacho didn't want to name him Slappy or Mr. Nutty. Even as he climbs into his carrier, he appears defeated. It's enough to break a fur momma's heart.

"Don't worry, you little drama king. I'll buy you a new one when I can afford it." I just don't know when that will be.

The temperature has dropped significantly this week, so Nacho is wearing his argyle sweater, which was a parting gift from his original owners who didn't appreciate his spunky personality. He looks dapper and depressed. Hopefully an outing will cheer him up.

I throw on my beloved university hoodie, scoop up my dog, and we're off. On our short walk to the library, I reminisce about my previous meetings with Holden and how we got from point A to point B, then totally derailed with our date. The second I asked him to walk me home last Friday, I wanted to choke the words back down. Something about knowing my street address changes a relationship even more than our transition from strangers to texters did.

Then he made his silly joke, and I did understand it was a joke. Had I not been so focused on my regret over asking him to walk me home, I would have laughed and snapped back. But the day was so littered with awkward conversations and moments, once we got to that point, I was looking for any excuse to cut bait and get out. Like I've done for years, I used my education as a crutch—as a legitimate sounding excuse to avoid letting anyone else in.

I arrive at the library, stop to return the books I've finished, and continue on to the reading terrace. Holden isn't here, so I pull out my phone to see if he's messaged me to cancel. I wouldn't blame him if he did.

Dickens: *Running 5 min late.*

His short, to-the-point message, void of Holden's characteristic playfulness, makes me run for the stacks—not an actual run; I'm not built for that. If this meetup is going to be a continuation of our awkwardness from last week, I'm going to need a book for cover.

Just as he said, five minutes later, Holden is huffing his way up the stairs, looking like he's just gone three rounds with a much tougher opponent. His hair is disheveled, as if he's been grabbing handfuls of it, and his stubble has grown into a short beard. His Offspring T-shirt is wrinkled, displayed under an unbuttoned plaid flannel shirt. He's carrying a small plastic bag in his left hand and a couple of paperbacks in his right.

"Hey, sorry I'm late."

"Five minutes is hardly worth holding a grudge over. Though my furry overlord here isn't as forgiving," I jest, trying to calm my nerves.

He holds up the plastic bag. "I brought a peace offering."

I immediately recognize the logo on the bag and the shape of its contents. "You're going to be his hero. He's never looked so heartbroken before."

Together, we walk toward one of the sofas, and I set Nacho's carrier down. Holden takes a seat beside me, then moves to open the plastic bag he carried in. I stop him, reminding him of the constant squeaking soundtrack we were subjected to last week.

"Good point."

A few seconds of awkward silence pass between us. I resist the urge to hide behind a book, but struggle to find something else to say. "The Offspring?"

He tilts his head down to take in the graphic on his T-shirt. "Yeah, you know? *Pretty Fly for a White Guy?*"

For a guy who has a collection of T-shirts featuring classic literature, the last thing I would have guessed is that he's an Offspring fan. If I had to place a bet, it would have been that he owned a Beethoven or Mozart T-shirt before the quirky punk-rock band.

"Are they your favourite band or something?"

"If I had to pick a favourite, I guess so. My friends and I were obsessed with that song in middle school. But I actually got this shirt because the lead singer, Dexter Holland, has a PhD in molecular biology. He's been part of some really great research on HIV, and I think doing that while running a charity foundation is pretty awesome." He smirks, melting away the remaining strain on his face he had when he arrived. "Plus, he has his own brand of hot sauce."

I think this is what fan-boying looks like. "Sounds like he's pretty fly for a white guy." I repeat the words in a sing-song tone, mimicking the famous tune. It's ridiculous and silly, but the resulting laugh from Holden is exactly what I was going for.

He relaxes and releases a long breath.

"So, what's got you all frazzled today? Everything okay?" I don't know why I'm asking. Actually, that's not true. I'm asking because I care, which is a scary realization.

Holden kisses his teeth, which makes Nacho's ears twitch. "These exams. I have three next month as part of my PhD qualifications. I can't even *get* to the dissertation part until I pass them, and they only run every November. If I don't pass, I have to wait until next year and that cuts into the time I'll have for my thesis defence, and I guess... I don't know. The pressure of it is weighing heavy today."

I have so much sympathy for him right now. Any advanced degree is a tough journey. Test anxiety is a real thing; especially when it could take another year to remedy. "What can I do to help? I'm terrible with history, but I'm an expert at research."

His timid smile is so anti-Holden, he reminds me of a small child. "Nah, don't sweat it. You've got enough of your own work to do."

"No, seriously. I opted to do my thesis instead of the co-op, so I could use that hands-on experience. I mean, the public library probably won't have what you need, but I can help you look in the university library. At least let me point you in the right direction."

Call me a mega-nerd, but that is my ideal afternoon. This is what I've been working toward. The ability to steer the course of someone's knowledge with the virtually endless amount of material on any given subject. Scientific journals. Biographies. Textbooks. Government documents. Maps spanning centuries. There is no limit to what a person can learn when they know how to navigate a library, which then provides them with more skills to set out and learn new things that can be added to the archives in the future.

"You'd do that?"

"Dickens, my name literally translates to 'angel of learning'... well, some resources say it means 'God has judged', but my parents wanted the angelic version. My sister is Angel, after all." I'm rambling; something I do when I get excited. "Sorry. Off topic."

"Is that why you read so much? Because of your name?"

"Not exactly. It started that way after my parents died. I spent hours in my room, reading anything I could get my hands on. Then I did my undergrad in English, which was a ton of reading. Now I'm reading for my thesis."

He studies me for a moment, finally settling on a reply. "What's your thesis topic?"

I make no attempt to stop the massive grin from overtaking my face. "It's kind of difficult to explain without repeating the entire thing verbatim. Essentially, I've noticed a difference over the years of how society perceives people differently based on their preferred genre. So if someone says they're a big reader, people jump to ask what they like to read. That can vary greatly from newspaper articles to erotica."

Holden nods, and his face looks genuinely interested.

"So often, if someone says they read classic literature, the perception from others is different than if they read romance novels. Or someone who reads fantasy is viewed differently than someone who reads biographies." I take a breath to calm myself because I get far too excited.

"I can see that. People tend to be judgemental. Even for myself, as soon as I tell someone I'm pursuing my PhD in history, they assume I'll be stuck up or boring. It's to the point I delay telling people for as long as possible, just so I can make a different first impression."

Again, that makes me sad for him. Plus, it makes me feel a little guilty for pegging him as the nerd type from the jump off. He's so much more than that.

"People, as a whole, will always be judgemental. And it's true that first impressions account for so much. Rarely do we have the opportunity to change someone's mind. But that's why I chose this topic to cover. To assess books as a whole—be it genre or speculative fiction, or nonfiction—then between online reviews, blog postings, and general comments, understand what kind of overall impression people have of both the book and its readers."

"That sounds like a difficult undertaking. How has your research been going?"

I smile as I lean back, grateful that he's listening to me talk about something that is a huge part of my life. Not many people are so inclined to hear about it. "What I can tell you is that the general population wouldn't think much of your 'sister's' reading choices."

"Society and I agree there. If I have to hear a recap of one more cheesy romance at the dinner table, I'm going to make like an ostrich."

"Run forty kilometres an hour or stick your head in the sand?" I giggle, picturing him sitting at the dinner table with earplugs in.

"Either or." Holden leans back, crushing the plastic bag he brought with him, releasing a slow squeak.

Nacho's ears perk up, but this time he doesn't lie down and go back to sleep. He starts whimpering, and I know from experience, it gets louder the longer his demands aren't met.

"We need to go." I mean me and Nacho, assuming Holden will stick around to finish whatever he came for, but he pops up, looking like he's ready to take off at a run.

"Sorry. That was my bad."

Nacho's whining is relentless as we descend the stairs, so I'm stressing that we're going to be busted by someone other than Julie. She's understanding, but I doubt the security guards will be. Before I can come up with a plan beyond 'walk faster', Holden starts whistling beside me. It takes only a second to realize it's the tune for *Pretty Fly for a White Guy*. I can't mask my chuckle as we beeline out the door without checking out a single book.

"That was close," I say, still laughing.

Once we're clear of the library's immediate vicinity, we stop, and Holden opens up the pet store bag. He pulls out a squirrel and gives it a squeeze. Nacho's tail starts beating either side of his carrier as he wags it with more enthusiasm than I've ever seen.

I unzip the top so Nacho can peek his head out.

"Here you go, little buddy. A fresh new squirrel to murder." Holden hands Nacho the new toy and everything is right in his world again.

"Thank you for that. It means a lot to us both." I smile to relay my appreciation since Nacho didn't even bother to say thank you.

"I discovered you can order replacement squirrels online, so I bought him four extras. He's got seven now. Should be good for at least a couple of weeks."

I open the bag after Holden passes it to me and see six more squirrels, a stuffed tree stump that's supposed to act as a hiding place for the squirrels—they'll need it—and the remaining half of the cookie from last week.

"You didn't have to do that."

"I know. But I wanted to."

Today will be my third library session with Dina at the university campus. Over the past two weeks, she's been instrumental in helping me find new peer-reviewed journals that fill in gaps in my studying, as well as new textbooks and even fictional works that have opened my eyes to things I never considered before. There's something refreshing about learning parts of history through a fictional story, then diving into a new direction of research to confirm or disprove it.

More than just helping me find material, she's renewed my zeal for studying. I was getting to the point of burnout and felt I had crammed my brain with everything that would fit. But she's opened up a whole new section, which she's filling to the brim.

I'm waiting outside for her to arrive, leaning on a concrete raised garden bed lining the front of the library. The courtyard it faces is becoming dormant for the winter, with scattered leaves and dying flowers. Still, there's something beautiful about the changing of seasons.

Not as beautiful as the woman walking toward me. Her curly hair is down, displaying its impressive length, all while framing her gorgeous features. Her arms are empty, meaning she's once again come without her usual paraphernalia, Nacho and books.

"Hey," she greets as she gets within speaking distance.

Something possesses me to step forward and wrap her in my arms. We met more than two months ago, and aside from once, we've seen each other at least weekly ever since. Yet, until she started meeting me here, she always had her guard dog on her shoulder.

She tenses right away, so I shift to let go, but in that split second, she returns the embrace. I pause, enjoying the warmth of her against me, which is a nice contrast to the cool autumn air around us.

"Sorry. I shouldn't have ambushed you," I whisper in her ear.

Instead of replying, she shakes her head, then loosens her grip.

Her face is inches from mine when I lean back, releasing her from my hold. A hug is one thing, but I feel like if I try to kiss her right now, she'd slap me and stop returning my calls. At least, that's what I think until I look into her eyes and see an unfamiliar expression. One Dina Blake has never shown me before. Vulnerability mixed with a hint of desire.

"We should get to work." She stops my thoughts in their tracks and takes a step back.

I agree and lead her inside to our usual spot on the second floor.

Once we get organized, she says, "Today, I'll show you how to use the online resources a little better. How to refine your searches so you're not sifting through pages of useless results."

"You're a lifesaver. That would save me a lot of time. I have a decent grasp of search techniques, but some of your wizardry would be helpful. Especially down the road."

She beams at me with a genuine smile that says she's found her purpose in life. One that shows her passion for her area of study and confidence in what she wants to do in the future. That might be the most beautiful thing about her.

We spend the next two hours refining my searching skills for both physical and online documents, using both the online catalogue and the library's in-house system. All these years, I *thought* I was doing a decent job, but that's quickly put in perspective. Dina's working knowledge of library systems is remarkable.

So is she.

I should stay here for a few more hours and make use of the information I've gathered, but as Dina shrugs on her coat and informs me she has to get back home to Nacho, I'm not ready to say goodbye. Especially knowing the next few weeks are going to be sheer chaos for me, and I won't have a spare moment between now and when my exams are completed.

What I should do and what I want to do are not the same thing, so I ask, "Do you want to share a ride? It is called a ride-share for a reason."

She pauses, buttoning up her plaid wool coat, and glances at the random papers with my chicken scratch writing on them. Her lips are parted and her eyebrows raised. It doesn't look like I'm ready to leave, but I don't think that's her issue. Packing up would take me less than a minute.

"Uh… no thanks. I'm just going to walk. There won't be many more nice days. Plus, you probably have a lot more to do, and I've got to meet my advisor tomorrow."

These tests are too important—too critical—to flake on just to extend my time with Dina by ten minutes. But logic has taken a backseat. "Really, I want to. You've helped me so much and saved me a lot of time. The least I can do is get you home."

"I've made it home every other time on my own. Don't worry about me, Dickens. I'll be fine." Her mouth says one thing; her eyes say another.

"I insist." I pick up my phone and open the app to order a car to campus, but a delicate hand covers the screen before I get the first few letters of our destination typed.

"No. Please."

The dark eyes I started daydreaming about weeks ago stare at me with a sadness I don't understand.

"Are you still mad about the joke I made on our date? Because I didn't mean anything by it."

She drops her gaze to the floor and releases an audible breath from her nose. "No. I wasn't even upset about that when you said it."

If that's the case, I'm not sure why she ran off in such a hurry. I reach out to touch her, hooking my hand around her forearm. "Then what is it?"

Seconds pass before she blurts, "I can't get in a car." She lifts her eyes to meet mine, then quickly redirects her focus to something on my left. "Ever."

That sounds so absurd, I almost laugh. But before I do, I think back to our previous encounters. Even the day she met me at the library to get her book back, she walked in a near monsoon.

"How do you get everywhere you need to go? You can't walk everywhere. It's a big city." I try to pound the pavement at every opportunity, but there are some scenarios—like days when the temperature drops to -30°C—when it's not possible.

Without breaking her focus on whatever it is she's looking at beside me, she drones on, "If I absolutely can't avoid it, I take public transit."

My first conclusion for her avoidance of cars was the germ factor. But given her penchant for library books, I dismiss that immediately. Taking public transit also squashes that theory.

My next guess would be the safety issue, but that doesn't make sense either. Not if she'd choose a giant tube full of strangers with no seatbelts over a vehicle with extensive safety features.

"So you won't go in cars. Ever. But you go on public transit? I can't work out how that makes sense." I realize how insensitive that sounds, so once again, I backpedal. "Not that it doesn't make sense; I just—"

"I get that it sounds crazy, but buses are big and slow, and… I just feel safer. Street cars drive on tracks. There's not a lot of deviation there. They all run on schedules, so they won't speed or veer off course. I know what to expect and…" She trails off; it doesn't look like she has any intentions of finishing.

That still doesn't explain a hard aversion to cars. I could understand limiting her time in them. Downtown Toronto is designed in a way that makes that possible. But never? Never leaving the city limits unless it's on a bus? Never having the freedom to strike out on a road trip and see where you end up?

"It doesn't sound crazy. You… I… It…" I stop talking to collect myself and try to find the right words that don't sound ignorant to her reasoning. "What is it about cars?"

Dina drops into the chair she was seated in earlier and pops the collar on her coat, shielding her face. "My parents died in a car accident when I was thirteen. I know millions of people drive cars every day and arrive at their destinations safely, but did you know that well over a million people die each year in car accidents?"

Fear, anxiety, and a traumatic childhood experience definitely make more sense than germs.

"I'm so sorry. I didn't know. That… it does make sense, knowing that. But they are very safe."

"Dickens, listen. I don't need you to convince me I'll be fine. Trust me, the rational part of my brain knows that. But an all-consuming, irrational fear grips me and won't let go as soon as I think about getting in a vehicle that's less than ten thousand kilos. It's part of who I am. Take it or leave it."

If those are my choices, it's a no-brainer. Take it.

She stands again, smoothing out her coat. "Plus, I don't have the budget to pay for car services to take me where I need to go. These trusty feet have managed just fine."

Instead of pushing the matter any further, I suggest walking her home. After some back-and-forth, she concedes and we head out.

Research techniques are not the most interesting information I learned today. And they're certainly not what my head is focused on as we stride down city streets.

19

DINA

She's Got Issues

This silence between us is uncomfortable. We were at a point in our friendship where our silent moments were tolerable, but this is torture. I had to go and make myself look like a bumbling idiot who's afraid of cars. I know it's irrational. I wasn't even in the car when my parents died and now, nine years later, I'm still holding onto that fear. In my defence, if they had been eaten by a shark, no one would think twice if I had a paralyzing fear of sharks. The scenario shaped me in so many ways and derailed the happy life I once had. Everything changed because of a car accident.

Plus, living in the city, I've enabled the fear by capitalizing on walkability and public transportation. It's been so many years now, the anxiety has multiplied and grown, allowing the wound to fester, rather than dealing with it when it was small. Now, short of a sedative, I don't think there's any way I'd get in a car.

Now that my quirk is out in the open, I wish I could reel it back in. We're a minimum four hundred metres from the library before I come up with a subject change. "So when are your exams, exactly?"

Holden hesitates, replying a few steps later. "The written exams are scheduled for November fifteenth and eighteenth. My oral exam is on the twenty-second."

"Woah. Three big exams all within a week. No wonder you're stressed about it."

He laughs as we side-glance at each other. "It's a lot, but I knew what I was signing up for. Just need to put in the work and get it done."

"That doesn't mean it's not hard. Just because we choose something doesn't mean we have to enjoy every second. That's classic toxic positivity. The whole 'good vibes only' mentality. It's okay to be human sometimes."

Holden slows his steps, making him trail behind a few feet until I slow to let him catch up.

"My brother is five years older than me. Seven years ago, he was working on his undergrad when our dad got sick. We… uh… doctors said he wasn't going to pull through. So Boyd dropped out so he could take care of our Dad."

In the few conversations we've had mentioning family, I got the impression his dad is alive and well, but I tread carefully. "That's admirable of him. That couldn't have been an easy decision."

"Sometimes I wonder if he did it just to have something to lord over me and Phoebe. Like he made some incomparable sacrifice. But my dad pulled me aside when I was graduating high school and told me I better not think about delaying university. That the sacrifices he made to provide a better life for us had to be worth it, but we had to put in the work, too."

My chest tightens because I miss that supportive parental relationship more than I could ever articulate. "That"—I clear my throat—"is an excellent point. He sounds like a wise man."

"I think because of that, I developed the mentality not to ever complain about school or anything related to it. Though, I guess I complained to you about being stressed. That was out of character." He tucks his hands in his jacket pockets, shrugging at the same time. "I chose this path and my brother sacrificed his, so the least I can do is shut up and deal."

"Sibling relationships can be complicated. Angel and I have our issues, too. I could have saved myself a lot of headache by living with her to finish my undergrad and get my master's, but I felt like I was holding her back. Like she was stuck in a job she hated just to take care of me. So I told her I wanted to be closer to the waterfront, took my insurance money, and bought the cheapest condo I could find. She still doesn't know the real reason I left."

This day should be marked on the calendar as National Overshare Day. It seems that's what we're celebrating.

"You and Boyd are opposites then. You made a sacrifice and kept it a secret. He made a sacrifice and continues to hate me for it, even though it wasn't my choice."

"I don't know your brother, but I know where making assumptions can get you. Someday, hopefully you guys can hash everything out. Maybe it'll help you understand his perspective."

This conversation has gotten much deeper than I intended. I'm sweating under my coat, growing more uncomfortable by the word. We round the corner onto King Street, and I recall Holden saying he lived on Whitaker Avenue, which is just up ahead. My place is another fifteen minutes from here.

"I guess this is your stop."

Holden stops abruptly, but a fast-marching pedestrian plows into him, knocking him forward so he crashes into me. I stutter step backwards, trying to keep my balance. Holden wraps his arms around my torso in a move much different from the unexpected hug earlier. He falls to one knee, but keeps me upright.

The offending pedestrian doesn't apologize, which isn't surprising, but both parties were at fault.

I look down at him clutching my waist. "Why does it feel like I'm always falling around you?"

Holden releases his arms from my waist, stands, and bends to brush off his one knee. "Are you okay? Should have checked my mirrors before I stopped there." He laughs at the lame joke, but I don't think he realizes that just encourages my fear of cars. Even people walking follow too closely and don't take responsibility for their actions. We're evidence of that, having crashed into each other before.

"I'm fine."

My breath catches when Holden moves closer to get out of the way of other people speed-walking by.

"I don't think I've told you enough how beautiful you are." He steps even closer, which I didn't think was possible. "I couldn't ever say it enough." He reaches his hand up and cups my jaw, caressing my cheek while biting his bottom lip.

But I don't want this here. In front of random strangers. After diving into each of our quirks and family dynamics. This isn't the moment I want to remember.

I duck my head away from his hand and turn in the direction we were walking. "Better get home before you cause any more accidents, Dickens. You've got studying to do." Then I walk away without looking back.

"I don't know what's wrong with me. Well, I do, but I keep taking off like a total coward."

Hollis sips her ice water as I relay my afternoon with Holden from two days ago. Lucky her, she's got weekends off from her co-op program. "You and I both know it's because you're afraid to let someone in. But, I just want to point out, you let me in, and it's the best decision you ever made."

That assessment is accurate. Since my parents died, my social circle has been limited. It was mostly just me and my books, hiding away from the world. That's still my preference, but is it so bad to try? Other guys I've gone out with have never crossed my mind once I left their company. Safe to say Holden has been the focal point of my thoughts the past few weeks—more so than my studies, which is probably what scares me most.

"You're right. Helping you find that scientific journal was one of my best decisions. But I can't get distracted. I'm so close to finishing my degree, and I don't want a stupid crush to derail everything I've worked for."

"So you admit you like him." Hollis smirks at me, while doing her best to hide it behind a sip of water.

I nearly choke on mine. After a brief coughing spell, I clear my throat to reply. "I don't know. There's potential there, I guess. He… makes me laugh, and I don't hate him."

"That's a start. That's more than we can say for Steven Seaman."

We both laugh hysterically at the mention of one guy I went on a very short date with. He was insufferable. He spent the thirty minutes I stayed talking about how he and his ex broke up because of their political differences, but he still loved her. I pretended I had diarrhea so I could leave. He didn't offer to walk me home.

"I totally forgot about him. That was a mess."

"It was. So all I'm saying is that maybe giving Holden a shot wouldn't be a bad thing. If you were willing to go out with someone like Steven Seaman, Holden can't be any worse. Some balance is good anyway. You can't just dedicate your entire life to studying. Once you get your degree, what's left?"

"You're one to talk." Though, I know she's not wrong about that, either.

"I promise I'll keep my options open if I come across someone I don't hate."

We spend the rest of our down time chatting about random things from her cousin Isla's upcoming book release, the latest update on Oscar's battle with his neighbour, co-workers who don't pull their weight, and Nacho's stuffed squirrel obsession. It's nice to decompress and get some perspective on this predicament I'm in.

She leaves just as the sun is setting, which always makes me a bit sad. We've both been so busy, our bestie time is limited. I don't know when I'll get to see her next.

But the least I can do is accept her sound advice.

Letting someone else in wouldn't be the worst thing.

20

HOLDEN

Spare Me the Details

Thursday was a disaster. I thought the moment was right. I thought she was feeling the same intense vibe as I was. But she shot me down before I could make a move it appears we both would have regretted.

Instead of coming home, I stopped by Sam and Phil's place to beg for some advice. Neither of them had any answers or easy solutions, but it was nice to talk things out a bit. I'm grateful they were willing to listen.

So I've spent all day trying to buckle down and get through some of the journals Dina helped me find. Her insight into my area of study is remarkable. She's got this knack for zeroing in on specific details in a search and coming up with materials that I otherwise wouldn't have found. Because of her, my confidence for these exams has increased exponentially.

Too bad my confidence in where I stand with Dina has decreased by the same margin.

Around 8pm, my phone chirps, but I ignore it, assuming it's either my friends or Phoebe. Aaron has been working nights, and she doesn't like being alone, so she keeps texting me to come over. I love my sister, but... actually, there is no but. If she needs me, I'll be there.

I pick up the phone to reply, only to be taken aback by the sender.

Minnie: *Hi.*

She's succinct; I'll give her that.

Holden: *Hey.*

There's so much more I want to say, like "I'm so happy to hear from you," or "I'm sorry," but I decide to let her lead.

Minnie: *About the other day...*

I'm sorry.

Sorry? What is she sorry for? I don't know what to say. You're forgiven? Should I consult Phoebe? I'm sure her billionaire boss romantic leads always say the right thing.

I'm not asking Sam or Phil again. Boyd would probably laugh. My dad would ask my mum, and that can't happen.

Guess I'm on my own here. I shake out my shoulders to pump myself up, then focus on my phone.

Holden: *You have nothing to be sorry for.*

This feels like the moment you turn in a huge exam and have to wait for the results. You know you've done your best, but without the validation of a percentage, you have no clue if that's good enough.

Minnie: *I do. Maybe you'll let me explain one day.*

I want to tell her she can explain now. That I'm not busy, so I'll come over and we can talk about whatever she thinks she's done wrong. But for once, when it comes to Dina, logic prevails. I just hope she understands where my priorities need to be.

My reply, no matter how I word it, sounds dismissive or short. So I opt to call.

"Hello." Her answer is tentative and lacking any enthusiasm. It's so anti-Dina, I check to make sure I dialled the right number.

"Hey. I thought it would be easier to call."

"Yeah, sure. Of course. Texting is my default choice, but it does lack context sometimes."

"That's… uh… I guess that's what I was worried about. Listen…"

She breathes a sigh into the phone. "It's fine, Holden. You could have just texted me. We don't need to make this a whole production."

Something about her not calling me Dickens stings. It may be because she says my name like it's a curse word. Or maybe it's the implication of what she's saying. Time for an instant redirect from my initial plan.

"No, I was just going to say, if you have any free time, I could really use a study accountability partner. Someone to grill me on critical information until I know it upside down and backwards."

She doesn't reply for a few seconds as Nacho squeaks his toy near the phone. "You have no idea what you've done to me."

An unexpected reply.

"You've had the same—"

"He squeaks this thing constantly, and I blame you for it. If I'm not paying attention, he climbs up on my lap to squeak it in my face. All. Day. Long."

Boy, am I glad she interrupted me or that would have gotten awkward.

"Sorry. Bribery was my only option to get on his good side. I'm not sure it's worth It If I end up on your bad side, though."

She chuckles as the squeaking sound fades into the background. "You're not on my bad side. Most of the time, it makes me laugh. Hold on while I go in my room." There is some shuffling before she continues. "Back to your question. What kind of grilling are you looking for?"

If I were less of a gentleman, I'd take creative liberty with that question. "Throw your best methods at me. What are you? The colour-coded flash card type? SQ3R? Making fun dance videos to illustrate a point?"

"I would dive headfirst into a tank full of ravenous sharks with a thousand oozing papercuts before you'd ever find me dancing on video. And it depends on your learning style. I prefer the PQ4R method."

"P? Four Rs? Teach me your ways, Dina Blake."

It sounds like she flops on her bed, then starts reciting her study wisdom. "With PQ4R, you preview, then you question."

"Mm-hmm. You're speaking my nerdy language. Continue."

Her giggle is the kind of sound that can roll the tension right off my shoulders.

"Then you read, recite, reflect, and review. Obvious addition being reflection. I don't know if it will be helpful for your material, but I always find that extra step of re-writing what I studied in my own words helps me retain the information better."

"Yes, this is brilliant. I propose a new, improved, 5-R system." I'm smiling wide; partly because I love nerd-speak, but mostly because I'm talking to her.

"What's the extra R?"

"Just like you said. Read, recite, reflect, review, and retain. That's the important part, isn't it?"

She doesn't reply for a second, but when she does, the joy in her voice is obvious. "We'd need a new title for this method. How 'bout AQ5R?"

I don't know what it says about me that I'm so enthralled and excited that we're having this conversation right now. "What does A stand for?"

"Analyze, question, read, recite, reflect, review, and retain. Sounds like a flawless method to me."

"You are one of a kind, Minnie. So what do you say? Will you grill me with the new, improved AQ5R method and help me *rock* these exams?"

"We're not adding rock as a 6th R. I'm drawing the line." She laughs again and I can't help but feel like she gets me on another level. Like no one else, not even my best friends or my family ever have.

Suddenly, a more interesting question dawns on me. "Do you have a middle name?"

The line goes silent again, but this time I know it's not because of spotty reception.

"That's a sharp turn in the conversation. I do, but I'm not telling you."

"Oh, now come on. It can't be that bad." I run through so many options in my mind, but none of them feel distinctly Dina.

"It's not that it's bad. A girl just has to maintain some mystery. I'll tell you what. If you *rock* these exams, I'll tell you my middle name. *But* you have to tell me yours, too."

"Fine. More motivation, I guess. Though I promise nothing can be worse than mine."

"Is it Morrisey?" There's a note of excitement in her voice as she rambles on that's different from her study method excitement. "You know? From *the Catcher in the Rye*? Holden Morrisey Caulfield. I figured since your sister was Phoebe, your parents were fans of the book." She chuckles into the phone as I lean back in my chair, absorbing her book nerdiness.

"They insist our names were a coincidence. Neither of them had read the book before. But I guess you'll have to help me *rock* these exams so you can find out what it really is."

"I said no, Dickens!"

My stomach sinks at her adamant refusal. How did I misunderstand this entire...

"I mean, no to *rock* being part of our new method. Yes, to the grilling… er, studying. I'll help you study."

Phewf. I was really confused for a second. "You're too good to me, Dina Something Blake. I promise I'll return the favour."

"You don't owe me anything. That's not why I agreed." I hear her tussle with Nacho for a minute, trying to take away his squeaking squirrel. "Just… drop it. Ugh." She laughs with a triumphant "Ha!" that I can only interpret as victory. Obviously, she returned to where he was or he made his way into her room. "When and where should we meet? Library? Your place?" She makes a hmm sound, then adds, "My place?"

For several weeks, since I first met Dina, I've been chiding myself for not maintaining my focus. For allowing myself to be distracted. But when the offer comes up, only one choice stands out as both the best and worst possible options.

"Your place would be perfect."

21

DINA

Want You Bad

The lobby buzzer number pops up on my phone, so I dial nine to unlock the door. I know from experience that gives me less than ninety seconds to prepare myself for this reality. Why I even suggested letting him come to my place is a mystery. Aside from my sister and Hollis, I don't let people in my space. This is my sanctuary away from the world. The place where I get my work done and relax with my dog.

Beyond that, it's nothing impressive. As a scholarship kid living on the dwindling reserves in my bank account from life insurance money, I couldn't exactly splurge on furniture if I wanted to eat, so everything in here is a hand-me-down that has seen better days. It's not a space that would be featured in any magazine, unless the title was *Poor Students R Us*.

Knocking forces me to blow out a breath and walk the few feet to open the door. I unhook the double locks, twist the deadbolt, and swing it wide to reveal a man who makes 'nerdy' the stuff of fantasies. His rugged scruff and chambray scarf would look out of place on most men, but Holden makes it work.

"Hey." He steps inside, looking in both directions like he's searching for a booby trap. "Where's the beast?"

"Oh, he's shut in my bathroom for a minute until you get settled."

He holds up a plastic bag, wearing a wide smile. "I brought more stuff to win him over."

"Gosh, your sister is going to have to watch you with your niece. Thank you, though. Nacho is happy to be on the take." I step back a few feet to give Holden room to move.

He slides off his tan blazer and scarf, hanging them on a hook behind the door, then pans the small room. The entire condo is maybe 600 square feet, and within that, there are two bedrooms, a bathroom, and a living space. It's the smallest footprint available in this building, and being on one of the lowest floors, the cheapest. Hence why I picked it.

"This is cozy."

"Tiny. It's tiny. But it's all I need."

He walks ahead of me, taking everything in. And by everything, I mean the eight-foot wide kitchen, the dated brown sofa and chair, an end table with an art déco lamp that works less than half the time, and a small wood dining table with two mismatched chairs. He stops and stares at the lone piece of artwork I own that hangs over the sofa.

"My sister made that. She designed it to match this lamp." I gesture to the faulty light source. "She hated it the second I picked it up, but I had this weird attraction to it. It's quirky and outdated. Reminded me of myself." I should have stopped at "this lamp."

Holden spins to face me, which lands him inches away. My small condo feels like it's shrunk by a factor of twelve since he walked in. Like we're fighting for the limited oxygen in the room, so all I can breathe in is him.

"The only similarity I see is that you're both beautiful."

That makes me laugh. "That's a terrible line, Dickens. Please tell me you don't think this thing is beautiful."

He chuckles in return, stepping even closer. "Okay, it's hideous." The man staring at me now is not the same one who walked through the door. He was carefree and confident. The Holden in front of me looks hesitant and unsure, but also has the unmistakable look of hunger. "But you are beautiful. Take my breath away, beautiful. And that's not a line."

I believe him. I believe him enough that the moment from the street five days ago replays in my mind, and this time, I don't want to run away. So I dive in instead. He seems to read my intentions, because as I inch toward him, he does the same and we meet in the middle, closing the foot-wide gap. He snakes a hand around my waist, but doesn't pull me in.

"Kiss me, Dickens." I grab two handfuls of his plain white T-shirt and rise on my tippy toes until my mouth reaches his.

As far as first kisses go, it's electric. Like an actual current flows from him to me as he expertly grazes my lips. It's just enough contact to make me desperate for more. I yank him closer until I have more control. So I can set the frantic pace my body is begging for. His stubble scratches the sensitive area around my lips, which adds to the thousand different sensations I'm feeling. He tastes like apple pie and smells more intoxicating than a library full of first editions. I could so easily get lost in him as he meets my demands, but we're interrupted by a loud whimpering.

I pull away, my chest heaving from my lack of breathing. "Nacho!"

What kind of neglectful fur mother shuts her dog in the bathroom and forgets him so she can have a make-out session? Someone needs to call the Humane Society, because this is a level of animal cruelty that cannot be tolerated. I sidestep to the bathroom door, not able to take my eyes off of Holden while he recovers just as much as I do.

I open the door just wide enough that I can bend down and scoop Nacho up, so he won't launch an attack on my houseguest.

Holden seems to compose himself and walks toward the door to grab the plastic bag he arrived with. He pulls out a 'prince' cookie, and waves it so a surprisingly silent Nacho can see it. "Look what I brought you, buddy."

Nacho squirms in my arms, so I set him down and hope he'll behave. He beelines to Holden, who breaks a piece of cookie off and hand feeds it to my little con man.

"I'm taking notes. Fresh baked dog cookies, stuffed squirrels…"

Nacho's ears perk up hearing Holden's words, and before either of us realize what's happening, he takes off into my bedroom and returns with one of his beloved squirrels.

I look at Holden as my shoulders slump. "Now you've gone and done it."

Sure enough, the squeaking starts before I finish my sentence.

Holden laughs, but I've listened to this incessant squeaking for three straight weeks, and the cute factor wore out a few days ago. On the plus side, at least he's distracted, and he's not trying to solidify his position as the man of the house.

With Nacho occupied, Holden drops the remaining cookie in the bag and sets it on the kitchen counter. Then he resumes his position in front of me, but we're spun around, so now he's facing the balcony and I'm facing the front door. Not that it matters. All I see is him.

"I hope you know this wasn't my plan when I asked for your help, but this is definitely my new favourite study method. You know about contextual effects?"

I shake my head, unable to form words with my suddenly dry throat.

"It's basically the connection between environment and recall. So I'd be willing to bet, if you let me kiss you while I'm studying, I can just think about kissing you during my exams, and I'll remember everything."

"If you are under the impression thinking of kissing me will help you recall historical facts, then I'm doing something really wrong."

He narrows his eyes for a second, then seems to understand my reasoning. "Valid point. I'd say it's more likely thinking about kissing you would make me forget the alphabet, which I memorized before I turned two." He smirks and shrugs one shoulder. "I was a child prodigy."

I swat his chest and laugh, then spin around before we get any more distracted. "Let's try our AQ5R method first, hmm?"

As distracting as that pre-study first kiss was for me, you'd never know by the way Holden buckles down and focuses on the material in front of him. He's scribbling notes, which I'm transcribing onto cue cards for a different study technique when he needs to switch things up. My searches even turned up a few documentaries that are endorsed by reputable sources as being historically accurate.

For more than five solid hours we work in relative silence, only stopping to take Nacho out for a bathroom break and grabbing a bite to eat, since I don't have much to offer.

"I've tried to read this journal twice before, but I couldn't get through it. I knew, in theory, the topics covered would be helpful, but I couldn't find the right way to approach it to *retain* the information. You're a lifesaver." Holden sets his pen down on his notepad, closes his laptop, and slides his knees out from under the table so he's facing me. "The AQ5R method is a success."

Watching him absorb the material and knowing I helped him get there. Seeing how my skills and effort can make a real difference in his future—as small or insignificant as my role may be—it's a feeling I can't quite describe. It gives me a sense of purpose that can't be replicated.

"I'm glad I was able to help."

"You know what would really help?" He stands from his chair and reaches a hand out to me.

I take the offered hand, stand in front of him, and shake my head.

"Another kiss."

22

HOLDEN

Bad Habit

I've kissed Dina exactly two times and I'm an addict. She's like the most all-consuming drug known to man, but instead of causing turmoil and chaos in its wake, she creates a calm. In place of destruction and heartache, she's filled me up with renewed purpose and a swell in my chest I won't put a name to.

My vantage point allows me to stare down at her brown eyes and pink lips, and I don't want to tear myself away. Selfishly, I wish I could stay all day, but I need to put in several more hours of study. Plus, she has her own work to do, so I can't monopolize her time.

"I hate to say this, but I should go."

Hurt registers in her expression, but she blinks it away. "Oh, okay. Sure. Got what you needed, I guess." Her eyes widen, then she stammers, "I didn't mean… I'm going to stop talking."

"Honestly, I'd stay all day and take advantage of your superb study methods"—I waggle my eyebrows to try to make her laugh; successfully—"but I don't want to take you away from your own studying. I promise, as soon as these tests are over, I will return the favour."

I close the gap that somehow opened after our last kiss and bend down to place a gentle kiss on her lips. At least, that's my intention. But she doesn't settle for that, which spurs me on. She wraps one hand around my neck, pulling me into her while teasing my bottom lip with her teeth. It takes everything in me not to growl like a wild animal... or Nacho, but in a totally different way. There's not an ounce of displeasure causing me to have that reaction. For too few seconds, I'm absorbed in her. Dina slows her movements and releases her hold on my neck slowly, until we break apart.

"You couldn't keep up with me, Dickens." The left side of her mouth curls up, creating a dimple I never want to stop seeing.

"I don't doubt that."

Reluctantly, I walk to the door and slide on my outdoor gear. Nacho is standing in front of me with a stuffed squirrel and a tilted head, looking like he's sad I'm leaving.

"He likes you now. If that wasn't obvious. He just takes a while to win over." Her words are obviously referring to Nacho, but the two of them have enough in common, I could match them together if I saw them at the dog park.

I glance at Dina as I shrug into my blazer. "It was worth the effort." Once I get my scarf secured, I pull Dina in for a final quick kiss. I'm not sure if I'll ever stop keeping count, but the fourth time, while short and sweet, is just as thrilling as times one through three. "Thank you, again. See you on Friday?"

"Yeah, we'll be here."

As hard as it is, I turn and walk out the door before I give in to every screaming primal urge begging me to stay. My feet feel heavier as I descend in the elevator and exit the lobby doors. Heavier still as I march toward Bathurst Street, all the way until I reach the Sir Isaac Brock Bridge. She stays on my mind the rest of the way home, but I know leaving was the right thing to do. If I don't respect her goals and ambitions, I have no business being with someone as remarkable as Dina Blake.

"She won't stop crying. It's a full moon, and honestly, I thought that was a bunch of hooey, but the women in my online mother's group may be right," Phoebe shouts through the phone to be heard over Grace's wailing.

"Have you called Mum? Maybe she has some tips? I'm not sure how I can help. If I could, I'd rotate the Earth a little to block the moon from reflecting as much sunlight, but that's out of my hands." I lean my head on the back of the couch and stare up at the ceiling. I had been trying to review the flashcards Dina created yesterday, then I was going to relax and watch a documentary she suggested, because my brain is fried after a full day of reading. That's all put on hold for the moment.

"You and I both know Mum is as affectionate as a cactus," she snaps. "She'll tell me some trick from 'the old country', which probably involves whisky or burning sage."

"Well, I say, don't knock it till you try it. Desperate times…"

"Holden. I swear, I'll drop her off at your door and ding-dong-ditch *so* fast. Don't test me." My dear sister is clearly not in the mood for jokes.

I set my flashcards on the table, knowing I won't be able to focus with my sister on the verge of a breakdown. "Fine, I'm coming."

"Have I told you you're my favourite little brother?"

I roll my eyes and hang up the phone, slip on my shoes, then walk the thirty feet to her front door.

She's already waiting when I arrive. "What took you so long?" Despite her frazzled hair, stained oversized T-shirt, dark under-eye bags, and screaming child in the background, she gives me a grateful smile and hug. "Thank you for this."

"Where is the little anarchist? Let me show you how it's done."

"Very funny. She's been crying non-stop for three hours. She won't sleep, eat, burp, fart, nothing. I tried a bath, tummy time, her swing, the baby carrier, singing—"

"You didn't. Tell me you did *not* sing to the poor child, Phoebe." That single word has me horror stricken.

She stammers before setting her face in an indignant scowl. "I'm not that bad."

I give her a side-eye glare as I walk past. That's a conversation for another day, but I make a mental note to secretly record her so I can play it back and prove my point. Her voice, which is simultaneously nasally and shrill, would no doubt incite Nacho to violence. It's the kind of sound you could play through a bullhorn to flush out terrorists from their hiding places. You could have prisoners praying for the death penalty. No wonder the poor kid is crying.

"Don't worry, Uncle Holden is here." I scoop up my tiny niece from her stationary swing and bring her to my shoulder. With a few gentle pats on her back, she starts to calm.

A few deep, shuddering breaths, and she's quiet.

"I don't know if I want to hate you or love you right now." My sister collapses on the couch in what I'd describe as the physical representation of relief.

I gently lower down on the other end of the sofa, but the second I hit the seat, Grace begins fussing again. She's the boss right now, so I stand and continue to bounce and rock her.

"You probably have so much you need to be doing right now. I'm so sorry." Phoebe doesn't lift her head from the throw pillow it landed on. "What can I do to help you?"

"Nothing. It's fine, really. I'm sure she'll settle and I can get back to studying."

Grace had other plans. Ones that included exam-prep sabotage. By 11pm, she's still refusing to sleep for more than five minutes, and that's only if I'm holding her. Phoebe suggested committing to the cry-it-out method, but I think that's meant for kids less determined than my niece. On the plus side, I was able to turn on a documentary while Phoebe caught a nap, but I've spent the first hour pacing around the main floor of my sister's house, trying to come up with an invention that can serve as an uncle stand-in.

Coming up empty.

This child is not going to fall for a warm bag of rice, despite what all the mommy message boards tout.

When the credits roll, Phoebe jolts awake. "How long was I out?"

"About two hours. Little Miss isn't giving up without a fight."

"Sorry, I was just going to rest my eyes, but my goodness, that movie was booooring."

I laugh at her dramatic facial expression. "It was a documentary. Not a blockbuster."

"Tomayto, tomahto." She stands and takes a stretch. "Let me run to the bathroom, then I'll take her off your hands. Thanks for letting me get some sleep. I'll be so glad when Aaron is done with this string of night shifts."

Phoebe's husband is a Toronto Police Officer, so I would guess little Grace is picking up on the anxiety Phoebe has every time Aaron is working nights. I don't say that though, because a helping of guilt won't cure her worries. They're justified.

A minute later, when Phoebe tries to reclaim her child, the tiny, twelve-pound blonde starts screaming like her world is ending. My sister looks at me with an expression that says, *she's yours now.*

Like a good brother and uncle, I get her settled how she was, and resign myself to doing laps until my legs give out.

"You sure there's nothing I can do to help you study while you cater to my drama queen?"

I can see from the twist of her lips and sad eyes that Phoebe feels guilty about this. Though there's no reason for her to.

In an effort to appease her, I say, "Can you run next door and get the flashcards off the table? You can quiz me."

Without a word, she hops up and dashes out the door in a pair of Aaron's running shoes. She returns a minute later, fanning the cue cards, inspecting them. "You didn't write these."

That much is obvious. Dina's loopy writing is a far cry from my scribbles.

"No, a… friend helped me with them."

"A friend, hmm?"

So, instead of studying, I end up spending the next ninety minutes telling my sister everything there is to know about Dina Blake. If studying *her* was a PhD program, I'd have no problem graduating with honours.

23

Denial, Revisited

Whether I'm helping Holden with his studying, I'm not sure, but his bi-weekly visits have become something I look forward to more than my library time, which I never thought possible. He's come each of the last two Tuesdays and Thursdays. Today will be our last study session before his exams start in five days.

From his perch on my sofa, Holden whines, "I've never been so stressed in my life. These exams are giving me an ulcer."

"Pretty sure it's the amount of caffeine you've been drinking that's giving you an ulcer." I walk over to Holden, move his books from his lap, and take their place. With my arms wrapped around his neck, seated on his thighs, I pepper kisses along his jaw. "Give yourself more credit, Dickens. You know everything you need to know. Relax."

His shoulders release some tension and he exhales a deep breath. "If you keep doing that, trust me, I won't be relaxed." He tilts his head to position his mouth on mine, so instead of the prickly feeling of his stubble, I'm gifted the soft caress of his lips.

Every one of his visits so far has turned into a make-out session at some point. It's a good reward for hard work and focus. The best reward, actually. Every time Holden slides his tongue into my mouth, I don't have the capacity to care about anything else. Only he matters. And that's still a terrifying truth.

"Phoebe wants to meet you," he blurts when our lips separate, his eyes still closed.

"Your sister? You told your sister about me?" I stare at him and wait for his eyes to open.

"She's been using your flashcards to help me study when I go over to help with the baby. Didn't take her long to realize I didn't write them myself. She's asked me no less than 900 questions about you, which I don't have a lot of answers to."

I try to dismount his lap, but he holds me in place.

"Don't run away. It's not a big deal, really. If you're not ready for that, then we'll hold off." His face melts from the supernova-level heat into the cool, calm Holden I've come to know. He looks at me with a gentle smile on his lips, his eyes now bright with concern.

"I... I just don't know how this is supposed to go. What we are or what the protocol is at this point. I'm out of my element and don't want to worry about labels or formalities."

His expression falls as the corners of his mouth droop. "There is no protocol. Right now, we don't have to label anything or make big plans. One day at a time. Okay?"

That reassurance helps me relax back into his hold. "Okay." I want to say that label or not, I care about him. That we'll figure things out as we go. That one day, I'll work up the courage to tell my sister about him and consider letting him meet the only family I have left. But all of that feels too official. Too real. It's a way bigger step than a first kiss or letting him into my home.

He kisses my temple and slides his book onto my thighs. "Can we go over this again?"

I kiss his cheek and twist myself off his lap, onto the cushion beside him. "Getting lost in a book, I can do."

Three times. Three separate times Sage had to snap for my attention because I was in dreamland, thinking about Holden. More specifically, his kisses, his soothing voice, and how I feel when I'm around him. If I wasn't convinced already, by my advisor's third snap, it's obvious having him in my life, at this point, is irresponsible. It's bad timing.

But it's also perfect.

On the bright side, aside from a few notes on what I presented, Sage is happy with the progress I've made, and I'm still on track to submit my paper within the next few months. The end is in sight. I need to maintain my hyper-focus and complete the task at hand. But I'm in too deep with Holden to back away.

On my walk back home, my phone buzzes.

Dickens: *How did it go?*

I smile, knowing he's eyebrow deep in studying for the most important tests of his life, but he still took a moment to check in.

Dina: *Fine, I guess. Minor tweaks.*
How's studying going?

I wait to cross at an intersection, staring at my phone. Some burly man who smells like pine trees and garlic grunts as he bypasses me when I don't rush across the street as soon as the light changes. Every time I leave the house, I'm reminded of why I prefer dogs and fictional people. Minus the few real-life humans who have become integral parts of my world.

Dickens: *Meh. I prefer studying with you.*

That makes me laugh as I reach the other side of the crosswalk, earning me a few funny looks.

Dina: *I'm not sure you learn anything with me.*

I continue walking down the north side of the street, passing by Nacho's favourite pet store that reminds me of Holden as much as it does my dog. He still doesn't reply by the time I pass the library, which also reminds me of him.

Finally, as I cross Bathurst, nearing my condo, my phone vibrates in my coat pocket.

Dickens: *I've learned I could live with only knowing how your lips taste.*

Did it suddenly get hot out here? No, it's November; it's barely above freezing. There's only one explanation why my core temperature has skyrocketed, and it's not a fever. I scan my surroundings, wanting to make sure no one else sees this message. This is a conversation I want to keep between the two of us. I want to feel like this is a side of him no one else gets to see.

Dina: ...

What do I say to that? I search my brain to recall every romance novel I've ever read to come up with something remotely cool and collected to say in response. How did this happen to me? I *never* used to struggle to come up with a quick reply. Even in situations I felt socially awkward and out of place. Now I'm a mute girl with no command of the English language.

As I step into my lobby, I finally form a sensible reply.

Dina: *Better get to work on the new AQ7R system.*

A quick ride up the elevator and I enter my condo to find Nacho lounging on the sofa. He lifts his head when I walk in, but beyond that, he doesn't put any effort into greeting me. I swear, I can almost hear the words "Oh, you're home" form in his little mind.

Dickens: *Seven? I'm intrigued.*

Unless the 7th R is riot. Count me out. I'm not man enough for jail time, Minnie.

He's such a dork. I laugh hard enough to startle Nacho, making him huff and walk into the bedroom.

"My apologies, Your Majesty. I'll keep it down."

Dina: *Read, recite, reflect, review, retain, rock... ;)*

Dickens: *I know math isn't my major, but that's only 6. I need to know if I should plan picket signs or at least design some T-shirts for a cause.*

And get my affairs in order.

Dina: *You are so weird. I laughed and annoyed Nacho. Now he's going to play his squirrel killing song all night.*

Dickens: *I'm glad I make you laugh.*

He does. Sometimes I think without trying. He just has a way about him that cracks me up. Maybe he's learned some tips from his best friend, the stand-up comic, but I'm more inclined to think it's just effortless Holden. That we just connect on a level other people aren't on.

Dina: *Reward.*

Sure enough, Nacho strolls out of the bedroom with one of his squirrels and plops himself on the floor at my feet. Within seconds he's got the toy wailing a morbid song. A mixture of short and long squeaks, to really make a point.

I get distracted scratching Nacho's head for a few seconds until I get a reply.

Dickens: *This might be the best method yet.*

Rather than continuing our nonsensical conversation, I insist Holden get back to studying. Breaks are important, and it's good to redirect your focus sometimes to prevent burnout, but I don't want to be a distraction. He's worked too hard and for too long for me to come in and ruin things for him. That's the last thing I want. I put my own work on the back burner to help him succeed. Now I'm wondering if that backfired, and he's only become more distracted.

As much as I hate to admit it, I need to keep him at a distance over the next twelve days for his own sake. We can both use that time to focus on the ambitious goals we've set for ourselves, and maybe after he finishes his last exam, our reward will be worthwhile.

Exams are finally over. Not that it gives me much reprieve, because I have less than six months to find an advisor, research not only what information exists on my chosen subject, but what doesn't, and complete a detailed proposal on how I'll fill in that gap.

But as I exit the campus building, instead of focusing on that next step, all I want to do is celebrate with Dina. Sure, I could go over to my sister's or parents' and they'd be happy to give me a hug or clap on the back and say, "Job well done." I could call up Sam or Phil to suggest a guys' night. But after weeks of burying myself in studying, that's not what I've envisioned as my reward.

Holden: *Are you busy?*

I eagerly await a reply as I walk to the parking lot where my ride-share is supposed to pick me up. Dina doesn't respond by the time I climb in the back of the dark blue Toyota Corolla that smells like cigarette smoke and BO. I instruct the driver to take me home, while my fingers hover over Phil's number.

A message bubble pops up before I can make a backup plan.

Minnie: *Just got in the door. How did it go?*

I've been so caught up in my stuff lately, I don't even know where she got home from. As much as I'd like to ask, I figure she'll tell me if she wants me to know.

Holden: *I think it was okay. Never talked so much in my life.*

Can I swing by?

I'm not sure if we're at that level yet where we can just swing by each other's places, but I'm about to find out.

Minnie: *There's nothing here to eat. But if you're ok with ice water, that's fine.*

"Excuse me, Warren? Would you mind dropping me off somewhere to get food in the CNE area?"

Without a word, Warren taps the screen of his phone, which is mounted on his dash for easy access. A few minutes later, he drops me at a cafe a few hundred metres from Dina's building. I thank him and jump out of the smelly vehicle, hoping the stench hasn't rubbed off on me.

The cafe isn't busy, but its location is a little off the beaten path, so I assume it's more of a neighbourhood hot spot. There are plenty of late lunch options, leaving me staring at the menu board for five minutes before I order.

With our food in one hand and warm drinks in the other, I walk the remaining distance to Dina's house. Someone is exiting as I enter, so I sneak in instead of having to fiddle with the buzzer with my hands full. But then I realize that's kind of shady, so I set our food down in the lobby, go back out to the keypad, and ask Dina to buzz me in.

She opens the door minutes later wearing black terry shorts and a loose white T-shirt, with Nacho cradled in her right arm. Dina welcomes me inside, closes the door behind me, then sets Nacho down. He runs in the opposite direction, so I take my opportunity to give Dina a quick peck. In the time it takes for my lips to connect with hers, Nacho comes tearing back around the corner, squeaking a tiny stuffed toy in a frenzy.

Dina smiles wider than I've ever seen her. "He brought you his favourite gift."

That gesture, as insignificant as it may seem, endears me to the little terror. "Thanks, Nacho. I'll keep 'em coming, buddy." Before I can set our food and drinks down to pat his head, he grumbles and runs off the way he just came from.

"He's so moody." Dina stands on her tippy toes to kiss me again.

Now I'm annoyed I didn't have the opportunity to set this stuff down. Kissing Dina is still new and intoxicating, but not being able to touch her feels like a rip-off. I don't get much time to mentally gripe about it, though, because she pulls away, swipes the drink tray from my hand, and giggles on her way to the kitchen.

"So tell me how the exam really went. I'm sure it wasn't just okay."

I walk over to the row of cabinetry and set our bag of sandwich options beside the sink, then lean back against the counter. "I have no idea, honestly. The adjudicators were like unfeeling robots. Not a single facial gesture. Not even a nod. They just asked questions and scribbled or typed as I spoke."

Dina stands in front of me, grabbing my shirt at either side of my waist, pulling herself against me. It's a good thing she didn't do that before my exams because my mind goes blank.

She nibbles on my lower lip as she says, "I have full confidence that it was the greatest oral exam they've ever adjudicated."

Now that my hands are free, I don't need to hold back. I place one on her hip and the other at the back of her neck, grateful her hair is piled high in a messy bun. I take my time, teasing her lips, but the second she whimpers, I have no desire to prolong the torture. Our tongues tangle together as I pull her closer to me until no air can pass between us. Our pace is so in sync, we could dominate the 90s boy-band charts. We break apart when we're both short on air, but I don't let her go.

"You're brilliant, Dickens. Don't doubt that. You and I both know how hard you worked for this, and it *will* pay off."

I never thought I'd find someone who understood the dedication, sacrifice, and level of insanity it takes to complete an advanced degree. Beyond that, someone who is working toward their own goals, but still did everything she could to help me chase mine.

"You realize I wouldn't have been able to do any of this without you, right?"

She steps back, still looking at me from hooded eyes. "Don't be ridiculous. You got through your undergrad and master's long before you crashed into me."

"Excuse me." I close the small gap between us, wrapping my arms around her waist. "You crashed into me, remember?"

She giggles and squirms, trying to work her way out of my grip. "That's not how I remember it."

"Well, you remember it wrong." I pick her up and twirl around in the tiny square of open floor space. "But it was the best thing that ever happened to me."

She waves off my comment, but she's blushing. "Did you bring food?" she asks, like she just now realized I brought drinks and a large paper bag.

I don't backpedal or readdress my confession because I've learned from our awkward encounters in the past. That may have been the one time I was a slow learner, but still, I think I've now figured it out. "Yeah, just sandwiches. I grabbed a few options because I wasn't sure what you'd want." I spin around to open the bag I set down moments ago and start digging out the contents. "Oh, and drinks. Cappuccino."

She reaches to grab one of the cups, giggles, and takes a sip. "Are you *trying* to keep me up all night?"

I drop the sandwich I was holding onto the granite, while Dina coughs and sprays cappuccino across her kitchen. She has a knack for saying things that have a double meaning, and I'm not entirely sure it's an accident. This time, however, she seems to have caught herself by surprise.

"Are you okay?"

She lets out one more little cough, looking away from me. "Yep. Great. Thanks for the drink."

Embarrassed Dina is adorable, even if I can't see her face.

I present her with the four sandwich options, and she chooses the classic ham and Swiss on a kaiser, so I take the roast beef on French bread.

We sit on the sofa, where Nacho promptly climbs into Dina's lap and receives a small piece of ham for his efforts. He looks at me next, so I feel obligated to give him a piece of roast beef or risk reverting to our previous relationship.

With two sandwiches left, Dina asks, "Want to take Nacho for a walk?"

I know exactly what she's asking. "Absolutely."

Once she changes into some pants, we venture outside and spend the next thirty minutes walking across Fort York Boulevard to the walkway that cuts through Garrison Commons. Dina takes no time at all to offload the remaining sandwiches, and Nacho does his business even faster. He may look ridiculous in his argyle sweater, but he struts around like royalty, then waits at Dina's feet to be picked up and carried home.

On our way up the elevator, Dina says, "Thank you for doing that. For the sandwiches."

"You don't have to thank me."

As the elevator dings and opens, she rushes out toward her condo. "You could have let me thank you properly."

My steps halt on the way to her door. "I could go for a proper thank you."

She snickers as she slips the key in her lock and opens the door. Now it's me chasing after her like an attention-seeking little puppy. I will not beg. I will not beg.

Safe to say, her thank you makes every ounce of stress I've carried over the last several months disintegrate. When her lips press against mine, she has one hundred percent of my attention. Not grades, research methods, thesis advisors, or future plans. Except future plans with her.

25

DIMA

Leave it Behind

It's hard to change habits that have been developed and held onto for nearly half a lifetime. My tendency to keep people at a distance has protected me from loving and losing, but I'm starting to wonder if losing out on love is worth the trade-off.

I love my sister. I love Hollis. That's easy for me to say conclusively because I'd give my life for either of them. I'd step in front of a bullet. Give them the last parachute. Wrestle a mountain lion. Whatever it took to make sure they lived a long, happy life. Their life and happiness matter to me more than my own.

But sisterly love, which I feel for both of them, is much different than the terrifying feelings I'm having for Holden. It's not obvious. Or maybe it is, and I just refuse to admit it. We've only known each other for just over three months. How is it possible that I would wrestle a mountain lion for him, too?

He left my condo five minutes ago and I've been spiralling ever since. Not in an out-of-control, losing-my-mind kind of way, but more of a rational this-is-too-much-too-fast kind of way. These feelings are too strong. I was supposed to hate him. Be annoyed by him. Keep him at a distance. Then I tried to be an adult and let him in and now look. I'm stuck with these big feelings that snuck up out of nowhere and consumed me.

These are the kinds of things girls should be able to talk to their mom about. Being robbed of my time with her makes this situation even scarier. She would have told me not to follow my heart because hearts are treacherous. Instead, use my head and my heart together. Don't jump and look later because falling in love only hurts when there's no one there to catch you. She'd tell me to be cautious, but not to lose out on a chance at happiness. And even knowing all of that, I still don't know where it leaves me.

I pick up my phone to text my sister because she's the closest thing to a mother figure I have, but before I can type out a carefully worded SOS message, another one comes through.

Dickens: *I just realized something.*

Dina: *?*

Dickens: *You promised when I rocked my exams, you'd tell me your middle name.*

Dina: *You didn't officially pass yet.*

Dickens: *Don't be like that. A promise is a promise, Dina ___ Blake.*

As stupid as it seems, sharing my middle name seems intimate. Like that's something private reserved for family... and government ID. But I want intimate moments with him. Silly nicknames, inside jokes, dreams and fears. I want to share it all.

Dina: *You first.*

Instead of texting back, my phone rings. I flop on the couch beside Nacho, trying not to disturb him, and swipe the screen to answer.

"Yes, Holden blank Edwards?"

"You're going to laugh at this." Traffic buzzes in the background, making it difficult to hear him.

"I won't laugh at your middle name. Hit me."

He lets out a signature breathy chuckle. "I have two. Ready for this?"

"Mm-hmm."

"Alastair Thomas," he says with a note of amusement.

"Those are noble names. What's wrong with either of those?"

He laughs a deep, rumbly sound as vehicles honk and people shout around him. "Say my full name."

I'm not sure what he's getting at, so I play along. "Holden Alastair Thomas Edwards. That's a nice name. I really don't get the Issue."

"My initials spell HATE. Talk about giving a kid a complex. My siblings teased me about it my entire childhood. I mean, Boyd's initials spell BONE, so I tried to dish it back, but it's just not on the same level."

He's right. I can't help but snicker. It quickly morphs into an unreserved, can't catch my breath, tears streaming down my face until my abs hurt laugh. I don't know if it's the unfortunate initials or my laughter provoking him, but Holden has joined in.

Once I can breathe again, I reply, "I'm sorry, but that's really awful."

"Told you. So now you owe me. If for no other reason than because you take pity on a poor first-generation Canadian boy who has English parents with no foresight."

"I'm sorry. Okay, a deal's a deal. My middle name is Unity."

"Unity? That's different."

"It's the name of the village my mom grew up in. Plus, clearly my parents had a thing for virtuous names."

"Dina Unity Blake. DUB. Not as cool as hate, but not everyone can reach the same status. And I still prefer Minnie."

Ignoring the embarrassing nickname, I cringe at his use of my full name. "I held up my end of the bargain, but please don't use my full name. It can just be a bit of unspoken knowledge you have that you never say out loud."

He's silent for a moment, but that could be on account of the door unlocking in the background. "What's wrong with your name?"

Since we're on the sharing track, I might as well explain. "After my parents died, my dad's estranged sister got custody of us. As affectionate and loving as our dad was, his sister was the opposite. So if she said my name, it meant she had an issue with something I had done or sometimes hadn't, and she just wanted to cuss me out. Anyway, long story short, my entire name is tied to those memories, and they're not pleasant."

"Shoot, Dina. I'm sorry."

"No! You don't need to feel sorry for me. It's fine. I told you because you asked." I release a deep breath, now irritated because he asked and angry at myself for being upset with him over something he has nothing to do with. "Are you home now?"

"Yeah. Just walked in." His voice is sombre and detached. Like he's answering me, but his mind is elsewhere.

That distance—real or not—creates enough of a fear in me, I revert to protection mode. "Okay, I'll let you go. I'm sure you're tired."

"Dina, wait." He sighs as he thumps his way up a set of stairs. "I'm sorry for bringing it up, but I didn't know. Now I do."

"I know. It's fine." That doesn't mean the memories just disappear, and the fear surrounding them certainly doesn't. "You should sleep, though. Good night, Dickens."

Then I hang up the phone, hopeful one day I'll stop letting my past strangle the joy out of my present.

Some days I feel like I've read every single book that has ever been written. I've found some incredible stories that will stay with me forever and others that were complete duds. So far, my research seems to validate my thesis, which will make my defence that much easier. The advisory committee doesn't want to hear about my opinion, though, so I need to get through these books and reviews so I can keep building my evidence and prove the point I'm trying to make.

I'm about sixty percent done a sweet romance when my phone startles me.

Dickens: *What does a person do when they're not studying?*

Dina: *I'm the wrong person to ask. Not a clue.*

Go to a movie? Plant a garden?

Dickens: *In November?*

Dina: *Point taken. Take a vacation?*

For no logical reason, the thought of him taking a vacation spurs a bit of concern. He's given me his attention while we're near each other, but would it be the same if he was off exploring some exotic corner of the world? When he'd no doubt have bikini-clad women at every turn? The bigger question is, why do I even care?

Dickens: *The only place I want to go is walking distance.*

Ambiguous. There are plenty of locations within walking distance of his neighbourhood. It's downtown Toronto. Scotia Bank Arena. The CN Tower. About a thousand restaurants or museums. I have no right to assume he means anywhere to do with me.

But I want to assume that. That after all of our snarky exchanges, awkward conversations, and unexplained personality shifts on my part, he still wants to be around me. I want to assume that I mean something to him, because he does to me.

Dickens: *I'm going over to see Grace. Call later?*

Oh. That's who he was talking about. Not walking distance to *me*. Walking distance to his sister's. If nothing else, that little guffaw makes it clear my attention needs to shift back to the task at hand.

Complete my master's.

Get a job.

Prove that I'm not a broken little orphan girl.

Do not get sidetracked.

I set my phone face down and dive back into my book with renewed focus. That's a lie. Holden slips into my thoughts at every mention of something sweet or romantic in the story. Every laugh-out-loud moment reminds me of an interaction we've had. Every smooth, perfectly crafted line, I imagine coming from his lips. Every mention of an enthralling graze or passionate kiss, I picture him.

My mind is its own recreation of *War and Peace*, which also reminds me of Holden. It's hopeless. He's woven himself into my every thought, and I can't shake him out.

Thirty minutes after his last message, I receive another.

Dickens: *Are you home?*

Because I'd really love to walk to the one place I want to be.

So maybe I wasn't wrong in my initial assumption. The surge of excitement that flows through me makes my heart stutter. I think back to our conversation when he first gave me his number and send a reply.

Dina: *I'll be waiting.*

How do you convince someone who has had certain feelings about something for so long that it doesn't always have to be that way? That our feelings and mindset can grow and change, just like we do. Our experiences shape us, but we can be in control of them if we open ourselves up to new ones, without letting old ones hold us back.

I understand Dina has been through hard things, and I can't even imagine how difficult they were to navigate as a child. But I care enough about her, I don't want her to get stuck there. To lock herself into a life in the downtown core, never experiencing things outside of a walkable radius. But I also don't want to make her think I'm trying to fix her.

She's been on my mind constantly since I saw her three days ago, and aside from a few short text message exchanges, we haven't spoken.

"Lady troubles?" Sam interrupts my brooding by tossing a flattened throw pillow at my head.

"Hey. What have I ever done to you?" I try to laugh off my spacing out because my best friends asked me here for my input on their professional endeavours, not for me to stare into space and tune them out. "What's on your set list for tomorrow?"

"That bad, huh?" Phil chimes in from his spot in his desk chair.

Sometimes, I think these two are on a totally different wavelength. "What?"

"Whatever you were daydreaming is bad enough you had to change the subject?" Phil raises an eyebrow, making it obvious he's goading me.

"No, nothing like that." I intend to stop there, but both guys stare back at me, waiting for me to defend myself. Their serious faces mimic what I expect to see at my future disputation. When I can't handle the deepening furrowed brows any longer, I blurt, "It's Dina."

Before I can continue, these idiots start cheering and high-fiving each other, saying "I knew it" back and forth. It's nice to know they don't find it necessary to sidestep my feelings.

Once they're done with their frat-brother demo, Sam clears his throat, schools his expression, and says, "Do tell. It's not often we get to give you advice, oh wise one. I can't say it will be any good, but we can try."

I give them both a small smile, hoping to relay my appreciation. "I really like her. *Really* like her. But she's an enigma I can't figure out. One minute she's opening up to me, telling me things about her past or dreams for the future, then the next, she shuts down and I barely hear from her for days."

Phil raises a hand like we're in Mrs. Adamson's fifth-grade class, not his own living room. "Have you told her you really like her?"

"Not in as many words, but she has to know. She doesn't need to be a mind-reader." Right? I've made it clear how I feel about her?

"Holden, my man," Sam says, sliding into the seat beside me and dropping his arm around my shoulders, "maybe it's not about you. Sometimes we react in a certain way to protect ourselves from things we've been through before, even when the people and situations are different."

I blink my eyes a few times, trying to figure out if I'm in some kind of twilight zone. "When did you get so philosophical?"

He hits me with the same flattened throw pillow he launched at me moments ago.

Phil and I both laugh at his faux outrage, which is a nice reprieve. These guys may not provide the soundest advice, but it means a lot to me that they always listen.

"Why don't you bring her to the pub tomorrow? Make it a date night. We can meet her or ask if she wants to bring some friends? Make it a casual group thing."

I contemplate his offer for a moment. I was planning to go see him play anyway, but it could be a good opportunity to introduce Dina to my friends or to meet hers. To make her see that I'm serious about having her in my future, regardless of her past. "Yeah, sure. I'll ask. As long as you guys promise to be chill. Don't do anything crazy."

Without warning, Sam whips with a pillow for the third time. I'm now understanding why it's so flat.

"We're always chill. I'm offended that you think we'd do something crazy." Sam's smirk offers no reassurance that he's taken my request seriously. It's an expression I've seen plenty of times before in our twenty years of friendship. It usually meant he was going to put a thumbtack on our teacher's chair or short sheet his sister's bed.

"Does she have any hot friends?" Phil waggles his eyebrows, but the question is so ridiculous coming from him. He makes jokes like he's some kind of Casanova, but you couldn't find a more loyal guy if you tried.

"Her best friend is some kind of chemistry master's student, and her sister is off limits."

Both of my friends groan, but quickly change the subject.

For the next two hours, I listen to Sam strum along on his guitar, fine-tuning his set list for tomorrow, and Phil perfect his deadpan delivery for some new jokes. Their presence grounds me and helps me see things from a new perspective.

When I finally walk home, trudging through the light snowfall dusting the sidewalks, I contemplate what Sam said. Maybe Dina's reactions have little to do with me. She could write an entire memoir about her life experiences before me. The short time I've known her isn't enough to rewrite any of them.

But I will try to prove to her that I don't give up easily.

I dial her number as I round the corner onto my street.

She answers after two rings. "Hey."

"Hi. Are you busy?"

"Um. I was just trying to get through this novel, but trust me, I don't mind taking a break."

"What's this one called?" It's been a while since we played the plot-guessing game. If I can make her laugh, I'll flex my skills.

"Oh… not one you're interested in." She dismisses our game without giving me the opportunity to object, and continues, "Why'd you call?"

"Now you have me curious." I march upstairs to my bedroom in the dark, realizing Boyd is either not home or sleeping.

"Well, we both are because I'm wondering why you called." Her voice is reminiscent of the spunky Dina who first captured my attention.

"Just tell me the title and I'll move on."

"Dickens," she grumbles. "Fine. *Texas Hold Me*. Ever read a poker romance before? Because I haven't, and this may be the first and last. Please don't make me talk about it." She huffs a soft chuckle I'm relieved to hear.

"You're right. That sounds awful. Okay, moving on. Are you busy tomorrow night?"

"That depends on what you're asking. I may have unbreakable plans with Nacho."

"My friend Sam—well, Michael, but we call him Sam—has a show tomorrow night at this bar at the corner of Queen and Spadina. Phil will be there too, so I was wondering if you wanted to join us. You can ask Hollis or Angel if you want. Or someone else. The more the merrier. We'll make it a group thing?" It's almost painful hearing myself speak sometimes.

Rustling sounds drown out whatever she's saying. "Sorry, I was readjusting. Uh… I guess I can ask if they want to come."

"Will you still come if they can't make it?" I roll my eyes at myself for acting so desperate and flop onto my bed.

She doesn't answer for a moment, but from the sounds of things, she's wrestling a dying squirrel from Nacho again. "Ugh. These squirrels will be the death of me. Every time I'm on the phone, he's got to come squeak it in my face."

I can't help but laugh at the exasperation in her voice; or maybe it's a nervous giggle because it seems like she's stalling. "Sorry. Well, not really."

"Sorry sounds like an admission of guilt to me." She grunts again, then I hear a relentless squeaking close to the phone. "Give me a sec." Seconds later, the sound is muffled. "Not safe in my own house."

"Just so you know, we have a law in Canada that makes apologies inadmissible in court. You can't hold me liable because I said sorry. Which, to be clear, I'm not."

Dina giggles, leaving me with a longing to see her. "I didn't know that, but I have no plans to take you to court because you bought my dog a toy. You're safe."

An awkward pause passes before I finally ask, "So, what do you say?"

"About what? Going to court?"

"No, coming to Sam's show." I hold my breath as I await her reply.

"Yeah. I'll be there."

This time, I won't leave things unclear.

27

DIMA

Long Way Home

Growing up with a big sister was kind of like having an entire closet full of things you wanted to wear, but never could. Like they were always just out of reach. But now that we're in our twenties, the script has switched, and the odd time I call my sister, freaking out over what to wear, she tells me to come over and shop in her closet. That's exactly what she does for me tonight, even though she's not home. Thankfully, I still have keys from when I lived with her.

I settle on a pair of distressed medium-grey jeans, a black blouse, a long open cardigan, and heeled black ankle boots. I also found a black trilby hat that my hair wouldn't have had a hope of fitting into if I hadn't tamed it with a straightening iron. A glance in the mirror confirms this is a cute, sensible, bohemian outfit for a friendly night out.

Hollis was too swamped between her studies and co-op, but said if she has more lead time in the future, she'll make it a goal to come. I guess I'll see how tonight goes before I hold her to that.

I walk toward the venue, knowing it would be faster to cut through Alexandra Park, but it's already dark, so I decide to stick to the busy streets. The detour to Angel's house has added an extra three kilometres onto my trek, but it was worth it to play out my teenage fantasies, shopping in her closet.

My phone buzzes in my clutch, so I dig it out, careful to keep my eyes on the pavement. Heels are a rarity for me, so I need to be extra careful—especially now that there's a dusting of snow on the ground that can't decide if it wants to come or go.

Dickens: *Want me to come meet you?*

Dina: *10 min away. Just coming down Ryerson.*

Dickens: *Why are you coming that way?*

He's quick. Didn't take him long to realize that's the opposite direction from my house.

Dina: *My sister's place. Turning on Queen now.*

I march down the north side of Queen Street with about 200 metres to my destination. Halfway there, a shadowy form that looks familiar walks in my direction. I don't need to see him in the light to confirm it's him.

The second he pulls me in his arms, I collapse against him.

"I'm sorry for being such a basket case."

"It's okay."

"No, not really. But I'm going to work on it." I lean back so I can look at his shadowed face. "It's hard to focus on a blind future when the past is so clear. I'm not trying to be difficult."

He tilts my chin to plant a quick peck on my lips, then focuses on my eyes. "I've spent a lot of time studying history, and one thing I know is that it always impacts the present and future. We can't ignore it and hope it doesn't. So, I won't press you to talk about it, but know that I'm ready to listen if or when you want to."

I nod, swallowing the lump in my throat. No, I don't want to bring it up again. Most days I feel like I should just get over it because it was a long time ago. Plus, compared to a lot of orphaned kids, Angel and I didn't have it so bad. So what if we lived with an aunt who tried to blow through our insurance money partying and bringing strange men home? Who cares that we've been disowned by our family because Angel decided enough was enough and got us out of that situation before we had nothing left? But it has a grip on me I can't loosen. My past has shaped who I am, whether or not I want it to.

"Come on. Let's get a drink to celebrate." He turns toward the pub, his hand finding mine without searching.

"What are we celebrating?" I ask as we march forward, assuming he's wanting to celebrate making it to the last phase of his PhD.

"The hopeless nerd getting to walk in with the gorgeous bombshell."

"Which one of us is the hopeless nerd?"

Holden laughs but doesn't reply. I guess he thought it was a rhetorical question.

We walk into *The Grand Ol' Lennox* hand in hand, and he leads me toward his friends, who I presume are Sam—or Michael—and Phil. They both smile at me, but their expressions morph into knowing grins when they look at Holden.

"You didn't tell us you were bringing a goddess." The taller of the two guys with slicked back red hair stands and reaches his hand out. "What are you doing with a guy like him?"

"Ignore him. He gets stage fright and loses his manners." The other guy reaches over to shake my hand next "I'm Phil."

"The comedian. Nice to meet you." I take in the clean-shaven brunette. He doesn't look like a comedian, but from what Holden has said, he's quite funny. I look at the first guy to greet me and realize he didn't give me his name. "Do I call you Michael or Sam?"

He gestures for Holden and me to sit, so we each take up one of the remaining chairs at the table.

"Everybody calls me Sam. Sometimes I forget my name is Michael until I have to fill out government forms."

"That's dedication to an on-stage persona. Like Slash. Could you imagine ever walking up to him and calling him Saul? Or calling Eminem, Marshall?"

Sam smirks at Holden. "She's a keeper. She didn't even hesitate."

Holden chuckles, pouring a beer from the pitcher. He looks at me and asks, "Did you read their biographies?"

"Yes, but I know their music, too." I narrow my eyes at him before returning my focus to Sam. "What time does your set start?"

"I've got to warm up in a minute. I just had to meet the mysterious Dina Blake we've heard so much about." Sam slides out of his chair and stands to his full height. He must be well over six feet. Yet, the most intimidating thing about him is the fact he has insider information about me, and I have none on him. He heads off with a promise to return after his set, leaving me, Holden, and Phil.

It's one thing to know Holden mentioned me to his sister. It's another to know he's been talking about me with his best friends. I don't get the impression he's talked about me in a bad way, but for all I know, Phil and Sam could be excellent actors. It's unnerving when I know so little about them.

After fifteen minutes of surface-level conversation, Phil excuses himself and disappears backstage, too.

"They seem nice," I say before taking a sip of my fruity cocktail.

"Yeah. They are."

Before he can say anything else, the lights dim through the pub and brighten over the stage in the corner. Sam walks out, holding a guitar, and introduces himself. He wastes no time getting into his first song, which Holden informs me is one of his originals. Typically, he plays a mix of originals and covers.

Judging by the reaction of the crowd, a lot of them know his music.

Holden and I make idle chitchat, listening to Sam, sipping our drinks. I wonder where Phil disappeared to right as Sam finishes one song and Phil walks out on stage. Both of them wear smiles that have me eager to see what's happening next.

"What is this guy doing?" Holden stares at the stage, anxiously spinning his near-empty beer glass.

"You guys know my friend Phil here," Sam's low timbre states through the speakers.

The crowd cheers and applauds Phil, who takes a dramatic bow.

Sam continues, "Our other good friend, who you may know, Holden, is in the audience tonight, and he reached a special milestone this week. He's two-thirds finished his PhD."

Again, everyone cheers, including me, making Holden smile and blush. He covers his face with one hand, still gripping his beer in the other.

"Anyway, Phil and I wanted to do something special for him tonight to celebrate. So, this one's for you, man."

It doesn't take more than two beats to recognize the tune they're playing. Holden and I both burst out laughing, listening to Phil and Sam sing the intro to *Pretty Fly for a White Guy*—Phil is alarmingly good at the high part. Sam shreds his guitar and starts singing, creating his amazing rendition of the song.

My face hurts from smiling, and I keep stealing glances at Holden, whose facial expression mirrors mine. We both lose it when Sam replaces the lyrics "go on Ricki Lake" with "go with Dina Blake."

When Sam finishes the song to a lengthy applause, my cheeks are frozen in a smile. I haven't laughed so hard or had so much fun in a long time.

That marked the end of Sam's set, so he and Phil disappear behind the stage curtains.

Holden slides his chair closer to mine and wraps his arm around my shoulder. He turns my head with a gentle hand on my chin and leans down to kiss me. "I love you, Dina."

I choke on my own saliva when I attempt to reply. That elicits a coughing fit, so I take a sip of my drink to help. That creates more of a problem than a solution. I cough again, sputtering out some of my drink into my hand. My eyes are watering from suppressing another cough. In a panic, I stand so I can excuse myself to the washroom, but forget I'm wearing heels. Faster than I can blink, I crumple to the floor and a sharp pain shoots up my leg. If alcohol helps to dull the pain at all, I can't tell.

"Ow!" I cry, then cough twice more.

Holden jumps from his chair and crouches down in front of me. "What happened? Can you stand?" He places his arms under mine and lifts me, but I can't put any weight on my right foot.

"I think I twisted my ankle." I scan the room and notice all eyes are on me. "This is so embarrassing."

Holden manoeuvres me so I can sit on the chair, then he unzips my boot to inspect my ankle. His delicate touch on the tender spot is a contrast of pain and pleasure. I stare down at him as he checks for any damage with concern etched on his face. Knowing what he just told me and watching him study my ankle like a priceless piece of art moves me to tears.

"Hey, what's wrong? Do you want to go to the hospital?" He stands in front of me, stroking my cheek.

I shake my head. "It probably just needs ice." That was a half answer, but I don't know what else to say. Nothing is really wrong, and that's what scares me. It cripples me with panic, thinking that someone else will love me and disappear. It's something I can't articulate. Especially not now, in this bar, half drunk and injured.

"Let's get you home." He searches the bar for something when his eyes finally land on his returning friends.

I'm embarrassed to look at either of them after causing such a commotion on what should have been an important night for Sam. Holden steps forward to speak to them before they're close enough I can hear.

The trio approaches me after a minute, all looking stressed and concerned.

"Let's get you home, little lady." Phil hunches over in front of me like he's waiting for me to hop on his back.

Yeah, that's not happening.

"Um. I appreciate the offer, but you can't piggyback me home."

"For a strapping lad like myself, that's not a problem, ma'am. We'll take turns. I'm on the first shift, so hop on. Your noble steed awaits."

I look at Holden, who looks like he's trying not to vomit. He's never looked so worried in my presence. Not even before his exams. But I can't let him and his friends carry me home. Walking isn't an option, either. And even if I take public transit, the bus stop is almost half a kilometre from home.

My bottom lip probably looks like it's been through a meat grinder by the time I make my decision.

"Dickens, can you call a taxi?"

28

HOLDEN

The Meaning of Life

This is not how I imagined this playing out. I was so hyped up from Sam's performance, watching Dina smile just did something to me. Like everything clicked into place and I knew, without a doubt, that I love her. But every second since the words spilled out has been a disaster.

When she asks me to call a taxi, I'm not sure if it's because she doesn't want to be carried home or she's that desperate to get away from me.

"You're going to take a car?"

She chews on her bottom lip again, which she's been doing non-stop since Phil and Sam joined us. "If… Will you come with me?"

That's a relief. I nod a silent thank you at my friends and step toward Dina, crouching down in the spot Phil just vacated. "Of course, I will. Are you sure that's what you want? The guys and I can carry you home."

Her brown eyes hold so much sadness and unsaid words. Whatever she wants to say, she's keeping it to herself. "I can do it."

I know she can, but I don't want her to unless she wants to. Unless she's ready to take a step that she hasn't felt ready for in the last nine years. "Are you sure? Phil would be a magnificent steed."

She chuckles, which alleviates some of the sadness on her face. "I'm sure he would, but I can't ask him to do that. Just… can you make the call before I lose my nerve?"

I slide the last of my beer toward her. "Here. Drink this. I'll order a car."

Moments later, we say goodbye to Phil and Sam. Then, with one arm over my shoulders, Dina hops out of the bar as we wait for our ride. I'm on her left side, and I can feel her heart pounding in her ribs. We stop at a bench outside, where I help her get situated with her bum leg raised on the seat.

I'm not even sure what to do or say right now. Acknowledging what is happening will draw attention to it. But not saying anything feels like I'm ignoring her genuine fear. People don't actively avoid things for close to a decade if it's just a mild concern.

Before I can do anything, the white Toyota RAV4 quietly pulls up in front of us. I had hoped that an SUV might make Dina less afraid. If I could have found a hummer or an army tank operating a ride-share tonight, I would have chosen that. This was the best I could do.

I hold my hand out to her, which she hesitantly takes and stands.

She tries to step forward on her bad ankle, but winces the second it touches the sidewalk. "Looks like this is happening."

I open the back door and pause for a second to wrap my arms around her. "Try to relax. I'll be right here the whole time. Luckily, it's a short trip and there isn't much traffic. It's a good practice run."

She nods and slides into the rear passenger seat, clutching her hat to her chest so tightly she's crushing it. I can feel her shaking until I let go to close the door and run around the other side. When I hop in, tears are leaking down her cheeks, but she's silent. I realize she hasn't even done up her seatbelt, likely because she's paralyzed by fear, and she's not used to safety measures on public transit. I reach across, click her belt on, then secure myself in the narrow middle seat. Buckles dig into my hips on either side, but that minor annoyance disappears when Dina leans into me. She lays her head on my shoulder, so I lean over to kiss the top of her head.

The driver pulls out onto the street and heads east. Each shift of the vehicle's engine or change in direction makes Dina gasp. The driver pays no attention to us, which I'm grateful for so he can focus on the road.

"Almost there. See. We're already on Fort York."

She doesn't lift her head to see where we are. Whether it's because she trusts me or she's too scared to look, I don't know. The only thing I'm worried about is comforting her.

Minutes later, we pull up in front of her condo. Dina seems to be paralyzed when I shift to unbuckle us both.

"We're here. We made it. Wait there; I'll come around." I don't want to be presumptuous and assume she wants me to come up, but there's no way I'm leaving her to hobble upstairs by herself. Plus, Nacho will need to go out.

I rush around the SUV and pull Dina's door open. She's frozen, aside from her blinking eyes. I ease her out, thank the driver, close the door, and usher her inside.

Nacho is at the door when we enter and wags his tail when he sees me. It's a major boost to my ego. I take Dina right to her bedroom and set her on her bed. It's the first time I've ever been in here, but I've seen pictures of Nacho on her bed or the background when we had video chats, so it doesn't feel unfamiliar.

"What do you need? Pyjamas? A shower? A drink?"

She stares off into space, not paying attention to my questions. "You know why I decided to do a thesis?" She doesn't wait for me to answer. "Because I was afraid that they'd assign me to a co-op on the other side of the city and I'd have to drive there. That's the real reason."

Her confession causes an actual pain in my chest. Knowing this woman I love was so stricken by fear, it prevented her from taking on a great opportunity. "Hey, you did what you needed to do. And like you said, you've learned a lot from your thesis."

She finally blinks, focusing on me. "Yeah, I guess. I just feel like a coward."

"You're one of the strongest people I've ever met."

"Ha! You're just saying that. Trust me; I'm a coward."

I step between her legs, careful not to touch her ankle, and she automatically tilts her head to look at me. The words I said earlier almost spill out again, but I reel them in before we have another disaster. "I meant every word." Our eyes stay locked on each other as I try to make it clear I'm talking about everything I've said tonight.

Nacho paws at my leg, which surprises me and Dina.

"He needs to go out." She attempts to slide off the bed, but I stop her.

"I'll go. You rest your leg."

She opens and closes her mouth three times before speaking. "Are you sure? You don't mind?"

"I'll come in for another thank you when we get back." I wink at her, then call Nacho as I walk to the front door.

His Empress takes his sweet time finding the perfect spot to claim as his. Or should I say spots? By the time we head back inside, he has conquered the entire neighbourhood.

Dina's bedroom door is only open a crack when we return, creating a slant of light across the dimly lit living room. That hideous lamp does little for light. Ugly and impractical. The fact Dina said she resonated with it is a little depressing.

"Dina?"

"You can come in."

I inch the door open and poke my head around once the gap is wide enough. She's sitting at the head of her bed with her legs tucked under the blankets. It's only now I realize her ankle needs ice.

"Do you have frozen peas or something? For your ankle."

"No, but I have ice cubes." She grimaces, and I'm not sure if it's because she's in pain or she feels bad for not having frozen peas.

I assure her I'll figure something out, then pop into the kitchen to make good on my word. She has ice cubes, but no sandwich bags or anything to seal the ice in. I find a pair of plastic bags, so I dump a tray of ice cubes in one, use the second to make sure it doesn't leak, tie a knot at the top, and wrap that in a clean dish towel. It'll have to do.

Nacho is curled up on the bed beside Dina when I return. He doesn't even lift his head.

Dina, on the other hand, puts down the book she's reading and greets me with a smile. "Thank you for this. For every-thing."

"Of course." I walk to the head of the bed and pull the blankets back to place the ice on Dina's swollen ankle. It's looking angry and purple, which worries me more than I thought possible. "Are you sure you don't want to get this checked out? It could be sprained."

She shakes her head as she bites her lip again. A move she hasn't done since we left the bar. It drove me wild then, and even more so now.

"I want to say thank you." In a fluid movement, she reaches up to grab my shirt and pulls me toward her.

The jolt surprises me and I nearly topple over, but keep myself standing, bent over her as our lips collide. I've lost count of how many times I've kissed her now, but I will say it never gets old. Every stroke of her tongue, graze of her teeth, little whimper-moan she makes, all of it gets imprinted in my mind. I accept the spectacular thank you until I worry I can't keep myself upright.

As I pull away, Dina asks, "Will you stay?"

29

DINA

Something to Believe In

I ask him to stay in a totally platonic way, but I can tell by the widening of his eyes, he doesn't take it that way.

"I have a guest room. It's just a twin bed, but I can sleep in there. Totally fine if you need to get home," I rattle out clarification before he thinks I'm asking something I'm not. My concern is if Nacho needs to go out or if I wake up and my foot has fallen off. Maybe a little that I'm not ready for him to leave.

He leans down to give me a sweet kiss. It feels like a goodbye kiss. My stomach sinks, feeling the sting of rejection.

"You stay here. I'll go in the other room. Do you need anything before you sleep?"

I can't stop the smile from overtaking my tingling lips. "No, I've got everything."

The smile he returns replays in my mind long after he leaves the room. Finally, I drift off to sleep.

I'm awoken by a full bladder and the smell of frying eggs. I shift my legs under the blanket and also discover the ice melted in my bed, so my sheets are wet. Awesome.

With considerable pain, I hobble to the bathroom. Turns out, it's really difficult to stand from the toilet with an injured ankle. Plenty of noises echo through the bathroom as I "ow" and "ah" my way to the sink. I quickly brush my teeth, not wanting to confront Holden with offensive morning breath, then hop my way to the kitchen.

"Morning. How are you feeling?" Holden chirps, focusing on whatever is on the stove.

"Fine. Sore, but I'll live."

"I refilled the ice last night before I went to sleep. If you want to go put your feet up, I'll bring it in a minute. Just making eggs and toast. You didn't have much."

Yeah, that's the broke student life. I never have much, but I have enough. "Thank you. Did you sleep okay?"

"I can sleep standing up when I'm tired enough. Nacho woke me up early, so I took him outside. Then he conned me into giving him some kibble. I couldn't risk telling him no and end up back where we started."

"That's smart. You never know what he's planning in that nefarious little brain of his. Thanks for taking care of him."

Holden clicks off the stove, slides the beat-up old frying pan—that stopped being non-stick two years ago—to the back, then walks toward me with a determined gleam in his eye. "Last night, things didn't go how I imagined, but I do love you."

I gulp a loud swallow. There's no doubt in my mind that I love him too. I knew that before he admitted it, but was too scared to admit it. To him or myself.

But something about the reciprocity of 'you say it first, then I'll say it' makes it feel like a transaction. An exchange out of obligation, and I don't want it to lessen the meaning of the words. That, and the fact I'm afraid to admit my own feelings because that moves us to another level of serious I wasn't sure I'd ever find.

Instead of saying the words he deserves to hear, I reply, "Thank you." As if his declaration is no different than taking my dog out or making breakfast. I hate myself for not replying how I should as soon as his shoulders sink along with the corners of his mouth.

If I can't get the words out, the least I can do is show him he means something to me. I wrap my arms around his neck, still trying to keep my balance on one leg, and as soon as my hands are clasped behind him, I feel steady. Unmoveable. Like it's okay if I only have one leg, because he'll give me the support of his. It's an overwhelming emotion, and I pour every bit of it into a kiss.

He melts into me in response. Relief floods through me as I realize he's not holding back—unlike me, who is holding back those four words on the tip of my tongue. *I love you too*. My tongue is otherwise occupied as he explores my mouth with his, grips my hip with his gentle hands, and lifts me so my legs wrap around him. He walks us over to the couch, where he backs into the seat, placing me in his lap. I wince as my ankle folds underneath me, making Holden pull his head back.

"Did I hurt you? Are you okay?"

"Shh. Just kiss me, Dickens."

Having Holden here should feel suffocating. Two people and a dog inside 600 square feet *should* feel like he's cramping my style. But after thirty-six hours, I'm convinced we could live in a tiny home, and it would still be comfortable.

The only problem is, I haven't gotten any work done for my thesis, and I've got a strict schedule to keep. Losing two days to play domestic bliss shouldn't have happened. My ankle is still sore, but I can walk. There's no reason for me to ask him to stay. I can't find a good enough reason to ask him to leave, either.

His phone rings from its spot on the end table beside the sofa. Since I'm closer, I reach to grab it and hand it to him, without looking at the screen. As soon as I hand it to him, the content expression he was wearing disappears. He turns two shades lighter in an instant.

"Hello?" He hums and nods along with whatever the other person is saying, then thanks them and hangs up. He taps his phone screen a few times, scrolling and waiting. Without looking up, he says, "That was my TA. The... uh... exam results are up."

My own heart starts racing because I know how anxiety inducing those moments are. "Are you ready?"

"Now or never." He sinks into the cushion beside me and holds the phone so we can both see as the student portal loads.

It's painful watching as the information pops up, one thing at a time, with his name, student number, major, underwear size, takeout preference—I swear, everything except his grades. The information he's anticipating slowly appears on the screen. We both look at it, at each other, then back at the screen.

"This can't be right." Now he's staring at the screen, not blinking.

I grab his arm and squeeze, trying to contain my excitement. "It is right. You rocked those exams, Dickens."

He's silent for several seconds, then repeats, "This can't be right."

I turn his head to face me. "You deserve this. You put in the work, and beyond that, you're brilliant."

"Wow." He slouches back against the couch with his forehead creases reaching new depths. "I'm pretty sure I would have passed on my own, but this—passing with distinction—this is because of you."

"That's not true, but I won't argue." My smile is so wide I can feel the bulge of my cheeks. "Safe to say the AQ5R system is a resounding success."

"You *rock* my world, Dina Blake." Holden practically dives on top of me, making me squeal and lean back to accommodate him. His smile is as bright as I've ever seen it.

"Time to implement the AQ7R system."

We laugh together as Holden props himself up above me.

Here, in this moment, my heart is so content—so happy—I can't stop myself from saying, "I love you too. Just so you know." The words tumble out and it doesn't feel transactional. It doesn't feel like a tit-for-tat moment, like I'm saying it just because he did. It feels true. Like the real reward.

We don't need any other words. It's so easy to get lost in him and how fulfilled his presence makes me feel. Every time I've read a romance novel where a woman gave up who she was or her goals because a man came into her life, I've rolled my eyes so hard and grumbled at what I perceived as stupidity. But now I understand. I can see how easy it would be to get caught up in these all-consuming emotions and abandon everything that once felt important.

I *could* see it happening, but that doesn't mean I'll let it.

We spend thirty minutes cuddling on the sofa, peppering each other with kisses, getting lost in one another's gaze, until I finally work up the nerve to say, "I've got so much work to catch up on."

Though my words come out little louder than a whisper, they seem to spur Holden into action. He pops up from the couch like a spider crawled in his pants. "I'm so sorry. I wasn't even thinking. Let me take Nacho out one last time, then I'll leave you to it... Unless you need my help with anything."

"Dickens, wait." I sit myself up and reach for his hand. "I'm not trying to kick you out. There's just a long list of things I've put off for two days, and I need to get caught up. It's all things I have to do myself."

"I don't feel like you're kicking me out. Your studies are important to me too, and I want you to focus on them. What kind of terrible boyfriend would I be if I took up all your time with super hot make-out sessions?" He smirks and winks as he turns toward the door.

The rattle of Nacho's leash wakes him from his slumber, and he trots over to the door after a big stretch. Seeing him take to Holden makes me almost as happy as being loved by them both does. My boys. I pause for a second, realizing Holden called himself my boyfriend. It felt so natural, it didn't stand out to me at the moment.

I love being Angel's little sister, Nacho's mom, and Hollis' best friend. Those are all important titles to me. But the one that's defined me the most is 'orphan'. Being Holden Edwards' girlfriend doesn't remove that title, but having his love makes it more bearable.

If only I could tamp down this dreadful feeling that his love is temporary. The fear that he'll leave me, too.

"Be right back." Holden beams at me before walking out the door.

I can't help but think that is foreshadowing for what the future holds. An excellent literary device, but a sickening feeling when it comes to your own life.

30

HOLDEN

Living in Chaos

After spending two days with Dina, returning home feels ominous. Like swimming in dark waters with creatures lurking beneath the surface. Boyd asked where I was, but didn't bat an eye when I said I stayed at my girlfriend's place. He either doesn't care or he wasn't surprised. I haven't talked to him about Dina, but I have with Phoebe, so the rumour mill has likely spread the word. I just hope no one said anything to our mother, because I'm not ready for that confrontation yet. A few days of peace—post exams, but more importantly, post 'I love you' exchange—is all I want right now.

That's not what I get, though. My phone chimes with an SOS message.

Phoebe: *Help!*

A one-word message and I know exactly what she's hoping for.

Holden: *Be there in 2*

Like a good little brother, I arrive at my sister's house to rescue her from her own child. Aaron has been working double shifts a lot lately because the police force is short staffed, and as a result, Phoebe's anxiety level has been at an all-time high.

Most of the time she asks for help, I'm sure it's just because she wants some adult interaction.

"So, are you going to tell me where you've been for the past two days? I had to tell Mum you were doing the night shift with Grace and sleeping all day. Do you understand how hard it is to lie to that woman? She knows something."

Grace is fussing in my arms, so I hush my sister, acting like I don't want to disturb the baby. Really, I just need a second to school my features, so I'm not grinning like an idiot and giving away the answer before I can say it.

I clear my throat to make sure my voice sounds like a man and not a prepubescent boy. "Thanks for doing that. I didn't mean to put you in that position."

"What are siblings for?" Phoebe beams at me, new creases forming around her tired eyes.

Knowing Phoebe stuck her neck out for me to lie to our super-spy mom, I decide it's time to fess up. I know my sister will be happy for me, anyway. "My girlfriend twisted her ankle, so I stayed to help her with her dog and stuff." That's it. Calm and cool. Well played. I mentally pat myself on the back for keeping composed.

Phoebe, on the other hand, instantly loses her mind. "Girlfriend? You mean Dina? The girl with the flashcards? I knew it. Tell me *everything*, Holden. Everything." She sits down on her red sofa and pats the seat beside her.

"You know your daughter isn't going to let me sit."

"Good point. Okay, so when did this girlfriend thing happen? How did you ask her?"

With my eyes locked on a decorative glass bowl on the coffee table, I think back over the past couple of days. "I didn't. It just kind of happened." That realization makes me worry a little. "Should I have made some grand gesture? Does that sort of thing matter?"

After adjusting herself with a decorative pillow atop her crossed legs, Phoebe imparts some wisdom on me from the pages of her favourite books. "Woo the woman. This isn't a caveman romance. You can't just walk in and declare she's yours. Whack her on the head with a club... or a dictionary, or whatever you'd use."

My brows furrow of their own accord. "I wouldn't whack her on the head with anything."

"Not the point. My point is, it's an important foundational moment of a relationship. If you want her to take you seriously, you have to show her *you're* serious."

Part of me thinks I would have gotten better advice from my friends, but a tiny fraction sees her point. "Fine. Will you help me come up with something that's not straight out of a cheesy rom-com?"

"I can't control where my inspiration comes from."

Twenty minutes later, I have a plan in place. Tomorrow, I'll put it into action.

Maybe it wouldn't have been a bad thing if I replicated a romance novel. This feels next-level corny. But I'm already at Dina's door, pizza in hand, so there's no turning back.

She answers a moment after I knock, dressed in a pair of small shorts and a tank top, just like last week when I showed up after my exam.

"Hey. What are you doing here?"

"Study food?" I hold up the pizza like a peace offering. "I thought you might be hungry."

She holds out her arm to welcome me inside. "Oh, sure. Come in."

"I should have called, but I wanted to surprise you. If you're busy—"

"Dickens, get in here. I have time to eat."

I step inside, shifting the pizza box to balance on one hand so I can lean in to give Dina a kiss. She tastes like orange pekoe tea, and I'd be perfectly fine getting my caffeine fix this way for the rest of my life.

She pulls away and swipes the pizza box from my palm. Her apartment is so small, she's at the kitchen counter in a couple of steps.

I'm worried she'll open it before I'm ready, so I try to stall. "Where's my little buddy?"

"Preventative measures. He was in the bedroom when you knocked, so I shut the door." She nods toward her room, giving me the go-ahead to open it.

The little fluff-ball comes whipping out of the room as soon as I set him free. He tries to do a hairpin turn, but his feet are slippery, so he runs in place until he gets some traction. Now, when he comes running for me, I don't fear for my pant legs. He jumps up to greet me like we've been best buds forever. "How's my little Cujo?" I rustle the long hair along the side of his face, which he enjoys, because he leans into my hand.

"Cujo? Really?"

I chuckle at Dina's deadpan expression.

"The first time I met him, I thought that would be a better name. Nacho sounds too cute. He needs a name that strikes terror into people's hearts."

"Hate to break it to you, but most Torontonians would think of Curtis Joseph, the old Maple Leafs' goalie. Not Stephen King's rabid dog."

She has a point.

"Fine. Hellhound it is."

Her lips tilt in an irresistible smirk as she turns to grab plates from her cupboard. "What kind of pizza did you get?"

I'm almost embarrassed to say it. "Double cheese."

"Hmm. Can't go wrong with extra cheese. Do you want to eat now or wait a bit?"

I *want* to cut bait and run back home to tell my sister what a terrible idea this is. It's far too late for that. I can only hope Dina maintains her sense of humour and takes pity on me for being so ridiculous.

"Whatever you want. I can eat." I hold my breath and wait as she turns around to open the box.

She lifts it open at a painfully slow pace, giving me ample time to berate myself a little more. We both pause when she spots what's inside. A glorious double cheese pizza and a note taped to the lid. One that says, *This is extra cheesy, but will you be my girlfriend?*

I imagine my sister at home, busting a gut over this scenario right now. She couldn't have possibly thought this was a good idea. Is this what her novels are touting as romance? Why did I listen to her?

"Is this for me?" Dina asks. She's as confused as I am embarrassed. "I thought we were already…"

I walk over so I can wrap my arms around her. "We were. Are. I let my sister convince me I had to make a gesture. This was the best I could come up with."

Dina starts shaking in my arms, making me afraid she's sobbing into my chest. When she takes a gasping breath a few seconds later, it becomes clear she's in a fit of giggles. Though, it looks like she is crying, too. Her unreserved laughter prompts mine, and soon we're both in hysterics, which seem to renew every time either of us stands upright and sees the pizza box again.

"Dickens, this is… I don't even know." She puts in a good effort to rein in her hysteria, but we're at the point now, once it's started, it's hard to stop. "Cheesy. Oh my gosh. That's hilarious."

"I'm glad my embarrassment is entertaining for you. Remind me never to take advice from my sister." I wipe my eyes because even I teared up from laughing so hard.

"It's perfect. I love it."

Now that we've both caught our breath, I hold her tighter. "I love you. So what do you say? Do you want this level of romance all the time?"

She guffaws into my chest, telling me she thinks I'm joking. "I love your level of romance. And you."

It may have been a really, *really* stupid idea, but it created a moment I'll remember forever. And that, I am grateful for.

31

DINA

fire & Ice

Life is a balancing act. It's a challenge to keep up with things we need to do and still make time for things we want to do. A level of self care is necessary to survive this world that can catapult you into a series of to-do lists. Learning to strike a balance between my studies and being Holden Edwards' girlfriend has been tricky.

His schedule is a bit more relaxed now that his exams are done. His thesis progress can't move too far ahead until February, when he submits his application for a thesis advisor. He's been doing all he can to help me when the opportunity presents itself, and I'm grateful for that.

I, on the other hand, am barrelling toward completing my degree in March, and can't take time to slow down. I'm in the final stages of the process, reading over my conclusion for the fifty-eighth time. With three months to go, I feel a mix of anxiousness and relief that the end is in sight.

The only part of my goals that has changed is that now Holden factors into my future. We've been an official couple for less than a month, but I can't imagine moving forward without him. He's given me no indication that he doesn't feel the same way.

"Are you sure you don't want to come by for the holidays?" he asks, putting the washed dishes back in my cupboard.

We've had this same conversation six times now, but he doesn't seem to grasp what I'm saying. "I'm sure. I've never celebrated the holidays; being alone doesn't bother me. Not to mention, I'm broke and I've never met any of your family, so it'd be uncomfortable showing up with nothing or with cheap gifts no one wants."

"Fine. I'll stop asking." He sighs and hangs the dish towel on the front of my oven, then makes his way to where I'm seated on the sofa. "To be honest, I don't enjoy them either, but Mum insists on family time. Like the fifty-two Sundays we spend together each year aren't enough."

A sensation that's a lot like a punch to the gut and a fist around my heart incapacitates me for a moment. I take a deep breath before I reply, "Poor Dickens. Must be tough having a family that loves you." The words drip with anger and jealousy, coming out a lot harsher than I mean them.

Holden's entire demeanour changes. "I'm sorry. That's not how I meant it. I just... I wish you'd join us."

That irritates me a little more. "We've been over this. Stop asking. I'm not comfortable going, and guilt tripping me isn't going to change my mind. I'm not trying to be harsh, but you've asked me *seven* times now. At some point, you're going to have to respect my answer."

He leans forward with his elbows on his knees and drops his face in his hands. "You're right. I'm not trying to pressure you."

"Could have fooled me. Asking seven times feels a lot like pressure. But I won't change my answer. I'll support you in literally anything else, but I'm not comfortable with this. Not now, and maybe not ever."

My mom was raised in a Hindu household and my father in an Anglican one, so once they got married, rather than choose one way or another, we had a completely neutral upbringing. They told us we could decide for ourselves when we got older. This is me making my decision, and if Holden can't accept that, I'm not sure where that leaves us.

"I'll support you in this. Sorry for… all of it." He leans back, wrapping an arm around my shoulders.

"You don't need to be sorry for asking. Honestly, it means a lot that you wanted me to meet your family. But we're just not there yet. And not under these circumstances."

He nods, and that's the end of that. It's our first real argument, so now we can check that off of the 'new couples' bucket list. Relief from navigating that potential snare makes me collapse into Holden's embrace.

He twirls a lock of my hair in his fingers and asks, "Are you going to introduce me to your sister someday?"

That makes me nervous for no logical reason. "She's got a weird schedule because of her job, but I can ask." An awkward laugh bubbles out at the thought of Angel scrutinizing my boyfriend. Not that I don't think he'd hold up to her grilling. It's that the connection—welcoming him in to meet my family— will be one more thread tethering us together. Holden will be woven into every aspect of my life. I guess that's what's supposed to happen when you love and commit to someone, but that doesn't make it less terrifying.

"One sister can't be as intimidating as an entire family. I guess I get off easy."

I snort-chuckle at his assumption. "You obviously haven't met Angel. She's the epitome of small but mighty. Plus, I'm her only family, so she won't let you off easy."

"Good thing I've never been one to go for things that are easy." He pounces on me, in what has become his signature move, making me lie back so he can hover over me. "I love you so much. I hope you know that." His tender kiss alleviates all the upset and anger from earlier. Plenty of opportunities to compromise will happen in the future, I'm sure, and I don't expect to always get my way, but I'm relieved he's accepted my choice this time, even if he doesn't understand.

Angel and Hollis both agreed to meet Holden as soon as I suggested it. Despite the semi-heated conversation Holden and I had last week about meeting his family, the decision for him to meet mine was less dramatic. Less official, I suppose. Angel, Hollis, and I are at a gourmet bagel cafe in the heart of downtown. We're awaiting Holden's arrival, sitting in a booth by the window. The atmosphere is casual and comfortable, which I hope will translate to our introduction.

"Is he normally late for things?" Angel asks, raising one dark eyebrow.

"No. He's only been late once before, but he texted me to let me know. And it was like five minutes. Not... eleven."

"Maybe he chickened out," Hollis adds, unhelpfully.

"So help me, if he stands us up, I'll—" My threat stops in my throat as I see Holden round the corner on the other side of the street with his laptop bag draped over his shoulder.

The bell on the door jingles as he walks inside and makes eye contact with me right away. A smile transforms his face as he strides toward me. "Sorry I'm late. Baby emergency." He's out of breath and unkempt—so unlike typical Holden.

I stand and lean in to give him a quick peck. "Angel, Hollis, this is Holden." I present him like a grand prize on a game show, then reverse the introductions for my sister and best friend.

Holden offers a handshake to both of them, which they each accept. While he shakes Angel's hand, Hollis sends me a wink. The gesture makes me blush. Angel, on the other hand, levels me with a serious scowl, and I don't think it's because he's late.

"Have you ladies ordered yet?" Holden glances up at the blackboard menu, then back at me.

"No, we were waiting for you." Angel's no-nonsense tone makes the hair on the back of my neck stand.

"Oh, I'm sorry. Not the best first impression."

Angel only replies with "Hmm," before stepping forward to place her order. She turns back to ask what I want, paying no mind to Holden.

Once we've all ordered, he insists on paying. Instead of appreciating that offer, it seems to make Angel more annoyed.

We finally sit down—Holden and me on one side of the booth, Angel and Hollis on the other—but I have no appetite. I'm too busy trying to rationalize why Angel's friendly personality has disappeared.

Angel doesn't even wait for our food to be unwrapped. "So, Holden, tell me about this baby."

32

HOLDEN

Come Out Swinging

My niece made me late for the one thing I didn't want to be late to this week. She's lucky she's adorable, because otherwise, I may hold a grudge. I thought Angel was a little frosty because I arrived thirteen minutes after our scheduled meeting time, but when she inquires about my niece, I realize she's just being a protective big sister.

"Grace is my sister's four-month-old baby girl. I live next door, so sometimes when my sister needs a hand, I go over to help. Her husband is a cop; she's on her own a lot." I won't mention that I was eager to go over when Phoebe texted because I was desperate to get her input on this little meeting. She wasn't helpful.

Angel's scowl relaxes and morphs into a small smile. I feel the tension release from Dina as she watches it happen in real time.

"I'm sorry. Here I thought Dina had found one of the many guys in the city who have sowed their wild oats and have more baby-mama drama than anyone needs in their life." Angel's smile grows a little wider. "That's nice of you to help your sister. Brownie points."

Helping with my niece has never been something I've done for credit. I do it because I love her and my sister. Still, I'm pleased to earn a little favour with Angel.

"How's your PhD coming along?" Hollis asks around a mouthful of bagel. Her long blonde hair is tucked under a knit toque, and her cheeks are flushed pink from the cold.

I finish chewing the small bit of my sandwich, then respond, "I'm on hiatus at the moment. Still doing research, but until I get my advisor in order and submit my proposal, I don't want to get too deep."

She nods toward my laptop bag standing upright on the bench seat. "Not long now until you'll be Dr. Dickens."

Knowing Dina has mentioned me enough to share my nickname makes me smile. It's as if each aspect of her life is coming together. Family, friends, school, dog, me. Not existing as separate entities with one common denominator. Rather, all integral parts of Dina Blake's life.

We fall into comfortable conversation, and by the time we're finished our food, the dynamic between the four of us feels familiar. Both Angel and Hollis ask questions about my studies, family, and friends. Dina lights up, telling them about Sam's rendition of *Pretty Fly for a White Guy* and how she twisted her ankle. She can barely breathe as she explains the pizza box fiasco that is clearly a memory she cherishes as much as I do.

I get up to order us each a coffee, and glance back to see them leaning over the table, discussing something and laughing. One can only hope that means I've met Angel's standard for approval.

I return with drinks moments later, and we all discuss how much we've come to rely on caffeine in our twenties. Angel from long working hours, the rest of us from long hours of study.

When everyone slides on their thick jackets and gloves to leave, Angel pulls me in for a hug; there's no mistaking the strength she surrounds me with. Small but mighty, indeed.

"Thank you for making her happy." She releases me and pats me on my arm. "And good for you for winning over Nacho, because that is *not* an easy task."

We laugh about Nacho's "misunderstood" personality quirks as we walk out the door, say our goodbyes, then Hollis and Angel travel north on foot. Dina and I are left standing outside of the bagel shop, so for the first time in over a week, I pull her in to give her a proper kiss.

Kissing her feels like coming home. She wraps her arms around my neck to hold herself up on her tippy toes. Her eagerness to kiss me is the hottest thing about it. She wants it as much as I do, and being able to communicate our love for each other without needing to say it makes me happier than I've ever been.

"What are your plans for the rest of the day?" she asks, not releasing her arms from my neck.

"I was going to go to the university library to search through a few things, but it's nothing that can't wait."

She looks a little disappointed in my answer, which is confusing.

I redirect the conversation, hoping to replace the happy expression she wore seconds ago. "Do you have plans? I'm down for something else. Want to go to the aquarium?"

"During every school board in the country's winter break? I don't think so. I don't want you changing your plans, either. If you've got stuff to get done, go do it." She gives me a sad smile that I desperately want to kiss away.

Instead, I ask, "Do you want to come with me?"

"You sure know how to romance a girl, Dickens." Her lips turn into a genuine grin, confirming the love she has for libraries. "I'd love to." She hesitates for a second before continuing, "How do you normally get there? It's kind of cold to walk."

I run through different scenarios. "Normally I grab a rideshare, but we can take the bus. I'm not in a big hurry."

Dina stays silent as her eyes flick from one spot behind me to another. Her breathing accelerates, creating an endless cloud of condensation to form in front of her. "We can grab a ride… If you want."

To say I'm surprised is an understatement. Beyond that, I'm proud. Grateful that she's willing to face her fear. "Are you sure?"

"Not really. But if you're with me, it doesn't feel as scary."

That sentiment causes the love I have for her to explode in my chest even more. To know she trusts me to help her through hard things—to tackle her fears—makes me feel ten feet tall.

Dina handled the car ride like a seasoned veteran. She was breathing heavily and kept her eyes closed the entire four kilometre journey. She squeezed my hand with an intensity likened to Phoebe when her contractions first started and I was the stand-in until Aaron arrived, but we made it. Unscathed—minus my tender fingers.

The library is bright and warm as we enter, but there's virtually no one here. They were closed for a week over the holidays, but opened up a few days before the next semester starts. I'd bet most of the people here are master's or PhD students whose semesters aren't as clear cut as they are for undergrads.

We have no trouble finding a table to get settled at, so I set out my laptop, tie into the Wi-Fi, and Dina drops into the chair beside me.

"This is really none of my business, but I'm curious about something."

I pause, expecting her to ask about ex-girlfriends or an outlandish topic we haven't discussed yet. "Okay…"

"It's no secret I'm broke. Not that I'm broke, but if the money I got from my parents' life insurance is going to last, I have to stretch every dollar. So I'm just wondering how you always manage to have spending money when you haven't worked—at least, you've never mentioned working. I didn't think PhD students earned much."

Some people may find finances an awkward thing to discuss, but I don't want any secrets with Dina. "My parents had their triplex paid off fifteen years ago. Until my siblings and I moved into the extra units, they had renters who were paying downtown rates for over twenty-five years. With two three-bedrooms and three one-bedrooms, they made quite a bit."

She nods without turning to look at me.

"They saved that money for our education. At least until Dad got sick, then they had to use some of it to survive. Whatever they had left over, they divided up between us."

She nods again, this time turning to face me. "That's incredible they were able to do that. That must have taken a lot of dedication on their part."

"It did. It was a lot of sacrifice." I run through many of the concessions my parents made while my siblings and I were small, and continue to make to this day. "I was a scholarship student too, so most of what my parents gave me, I put into savings. Boyd and I split the rental income we get from the basement apartment, plus the bit I get for my PhD. It's enough to get by."

"Wow." She stares off into the distance. "So they gave you a house and a bundle of money, no strings attached?"

I almost laugh at that assumption. "Not exactly. The house comes with stipulations and they own everything. We're really just squatters they allow. And the money had to be put toward our future. Either education, savings, or investments. In my mother's words, 'If I so much as catch a whiff of marijuana on any of you, I'll make you wish you were never born.'"

Dina shares a smile that looks more sad than happy. "They just want what's best for you."

I place my hand over hers, understanding that talk of my parents must make her miss hers. After the events of the day, I try my luck and ask, "You're what's best for me. They'd really love to meet you."

The stress of this day is causing me premature hair loss. Holden has given me some insight into his family relationships, but I still feel like I'm going in blind. Not that more preparation would have eased my anxiety at all.

"How am I going to do this, Nacho?" This is so out of my depth, I'm questioning whether anything is *within* my depth. I'm struggling to hook my bra. Skills I mastered long ago have all disappeared, along with any confidence I once had.

Once I finally secure my undergarments, I slip on a sweater dress and black tights. It's the only presentable outfit I have for the weather, and even then, my tights have seen better days. I hope they don't judge me for being thrifty because I don't have time to visit Angel's closet again.

My phone chimes, and I know who it is without looking.

Dickens: *Are you sure you don't want me to come pick you up?*

To be honest, I'd love for him to meet me, but I can't bring myself to ask.

Scratch that. I need some kind of familiarity. If I can't bring Nacho as an emotional support dog, I'm going to need Holden to step up.

Dina: *Please. I'm freaking out.*

I'll come up Bathurst to King. Can you meet me?

Once he replies he's on his way, I give Nacho a proper goodbye snuggle and pick the fur off of my sweater dress, I throw on my wool coat and walk out the door. I met Phil and Sam, and that was perfectly fine. The few times we've seen each other since have been fun and comfortable. This could go just as well—minus the twisted ankle. Deep breath.

My worn leather boots pound along the pavement as I trudge up Bathurst. I don't even make it as far as the library when Holden comes into view. He must have jogged. Or I'm dawdling.

"How did you make it this far so fast?"

Holden smirks as he pulls me into his arms and warms me with a tender kiss. "Training."

All of my anxiety from moments ago dissipates as I stand in his embrace. I don't want to move. "I'm not going to ask." My breath evaporates into the air and I dread how cold it's going to be later. "Can we just stay here? Will they notice if we don't show up?"

The laugh that bubbles out of Holden tells me he's not going to agree. "My mum can probably hear this conversation from her kitchen. She'd notice. But don't worry. They're going to love you." He kisses my forehead and swivels beside me to start walking northbound with my hand clasped in his. "What's the worst that can happen?"

Instead of answering that rhetorical question, I run through different scenarios in silence.

"How mad was Nacho that you left him alone?"

I heave a deep exhale in an attempt to redirect my thoughts. "He was fine. I gave him a couple of squirrels to hang out with. Again, thank you for ordering more."

"We can't let that supply run out. I have it worked into my budget for eternity."

Our conversation is complete fluff the rest of the short walk. We take less than ten minutes from where Holden met me. It's not nearly enough time.

The three red-brick homes look well maintained and spacious—as far as downtown houses go. Holden explains that the first unit we pass is where he and Boyd live, and the middle is Phoebe's. Then he squeezes my hand a little tighter as we walk up the concrete step to the farthest unit, and he opens the door without knocking.

Inside is quiet as we enter, but we're quickly greeted by an older man with light grey hair and the same blue eyes as Holden. As he gets closer, I notice he's so fair, even his lashes are blond.

"Dad, this is Dina."

The older man reaches his hand out to me. "Dina, lovely to meet you. Forgive my son's manners. I'm Alfie."

His warm smile and kind welcome ease my mind a little. Until I glimpse a figure a few feet behind him staring at me like I'm her mortal enemy. I've read about mothers who thought no woman was ever good enough for their son, but can't say I've ever run into anyone that delusional. The way she's glaring suggests she's my first encounter.

"Mum, this is Dina. Dina, this is my mother, Imogen."

The greying auburn-haired woman doesn't acknowledge me beyond a sour nod. She spins toward the back of the house and marches forward with intensity. Alfie called Holden out for his improper introduction, yet doesn't say a word about his wife's reaction. Now I'm more nervous than ever.

I glance at Holden, pleading with my eyes for him to make up a plausible reason that explains why I have to leave. I'm not above using diarrhea as an excuse again. Other scenarios run through my head, like pretending to faint on the spot or coughing relentlessly until they're convinced I have an incurable plague.

But Holden doesn't budge. It appears none of the men in this house will confront the matriarch.

The door behind us opens and a less nerdy version of my boyfriend walks in. He's got the same style of facial hair, but hazel eyes and no glasses. He also dresses more like an executive than a history nerd.

"Dina, this is my brother, Boyd." Holden utters the words with little enthusiasm.

Boyd's eyes flick between Holden and me, settling on me as he juts out his right hand. "Nice to meet you, Dina. Welcome to the fun house." His crooked grin makes the physical similarities between him and Holden even more clear. And their obvious sarcastic humour.

I smile at Boyd and shake his hand, returning his sentiment. Then I turn my attention to their father. "Thank you for having me, Mr. Edwards."

We move to the right, into a cozy living room, where I sit on an elaborate Victorian sofa with a dark wood frame and red pinstripe fabric. It's not the kind of furniture you sink into to get comfortable; nothing about this is comfortable. Holden steps beside me, but instead of sitting down, he kisses my temple and says he's going to help his mum. I flash another look at him that I hope he interprets as 'don't leave me.'

He doesn't catch my desperation this time, either.

Before he leaves the room, the door opens again, and a couple with a baby enters. It's easy to conclude this is Phoebe, Aaron, and Grace. Holden detours to greet them, first kissing his sister and niece on the forehead, then shaking Aaron's non-baby-holding hand. His father and brother follow suit. I tentatively walk over, unsure if I should also greet them or stay put, but Holden snakes his arm behind my back as he smiles proudly at his adorable niece.

I stay silent, not knowing the protocol, but as Phoebe slides her jacket off, she locks eyes with me and her smile triples in size.

"Dina?" She jumps up and down, then dives across the room, throwing her arms around my neck. "I'm so happy to meet you. Come, I want to know everything about you."

I send a meek wave to Aaron as his exuberant wife drags me back to the lounge and sits on the sofa, gripping my hands. Something tells me this isn't Aaron's first experience with this level of extra.

"I can't believe you're here. Holden is so stingy on details, I feel like I barely know you," she says with a resounding sigh, flashing a disapproving look at her little brother.

The literal part of my brain wants me to say, 'Actually, you don't know me at all,' but I keep it in. "There's nothing exciting to tell. I'm just a nerdy bookworm with a chihuahua."

"I've heard all about Nacho." She smirks, and I see the similarities between her and her brothers. Her fair skin, light hair and eyes, and trim figure make her fit right in. Her sense of style is far more relaxed though, because she's wearing yoga pants and a baby-blue off-shoulder sweater.

Phoebe and I fall into comfortable conversation, covering everything from book suggestions to Grace's latest milestones.

Imogen never enters the living room until she calls everyone for dinner. Even over a heaping plate of dry roast beef and potatoes, she doesn't seem any happier. I'm not sure if this is typical Sunday dinner behaviour, but if it is, I don't know why her kids come back week after week. The food is a little bland, so it can't be that.

Holden keeps reassuring me with a gentle hand on my knee, but it doesn't quell my nerves. It doesn't matter how much everyone else attempts to engage in polite conversation with me, the fact his mother won't acknowledge I exist is paramount right now. It's the *only* thing that matters. Not knowing how to appeal to her is demoralizing. I feel less than human sitting at this table. Even if I were the family dog, sitting on the floor, begging for scraps, I think I'd garner more attention.

Before dessert, I'm fighting the urge to excuse myself and run home to the safety of my own space. I don't know what I've done wrong, nor how to fix it. It could just be that she's having a bad day. But my gut says this is personal. Her problem is with me, not with speaking.

I swallow the last bite of my dessert, decline a cup of tea, which doesn't seem to earn me any favours, then excuse myself to the washroom. When I exit, Holden is waiting in the hallway.

"I'm so sorry. She's not normally like this."

Hearing that doesn't help the number of questions playing in my head. "Is she normally warm and fuzzy?" I whisper.

He lifts a hand to rub the back of his neck, then drops both arms to his side and releases a sigh. "I'll talk to her. I don't know what's wrong. It's not you, though."

"It's kind of hard to believe that. Seems I'm the only thing that's different from every other week, right?"

He says nothing.

"I should go. I don't belong here. That much is clear."

He stays silent, staring at his feet.

"Okay, then. Thanks."

Despite Holden's obvious cowardice, I feel some sympathy for him. Still, *I'm* not going to be a coward and sneak out while no one is paying attention—as much as I want to.

I start with Phoebe and Aaron, since they were warm and receptive all evening. Phoebe pouts when I say I'm leaving, which makes me laugh, but I explain I don't want to wait any longer for the temperature to drop more. An early January late-night stroll isn't appealing; though I'd prefer frost-bitten toes over the frosty reception from Imogen.

Boyd is indifferent, but polite, seeming distracted by something. Alfie assures me it was nice to meet me, not saying a word about his wife. The same wife who actively avoids me as I try to thank her for dinner and her—lack of—hospitality. After I circle the main floor for the third time, I give up.

Holden doesn't even see me out, having disappeared somewhere, and I can say resolutely, I've never been so disappointed in him or our relationship. This evening made me question if we were walking through the forest and were confronted by a bear, whether he'd just feed me to the creature to save himself. And here I was, ready to fight a mountain lion for him.

I walk home, feeling a cavernous crack forming in my chest.

Like the tides have turned and after months of convincing myself that letting someone in could be a good thing, it's about to backfire.

Like the bullet has been fired and I won't be able to dodge it in time.

I have a feeling I'm about to get shot right in the heart.

34

HOLDEN

Take it Like a Man

After Dina and my siblings leave, I stay at my parents' house to have a chat with my mother. She may not be the most affectionate woman around, but her abrasive, cold demeanour toward Dina was inexcusable. She was downright rude. I need to understand what the issue is, because I felt like an idiot standing before a dispirited Dina, not having any answers.

Imagine my surprise when I walk into the dining room and my mother blurts, "You can't date her," from her position at the end of the table.

I pull out a chair to sit beside her, despite my better judgement telling me this conversation is bound for disaster. "For years, you've been telling me not to get too caught up in my studies. To find a nice girl because there's more to life than a degree. Now that I do, you're telling me *not* to date?"

"I don't care if you date. I said, you can't date *her*!" My mother's accent appears when she's angry, and right now, she sounds like a typical cockney lass.

My stomach sinks. "And what, exactly, is wrong with Dina?"

"Do I need more of a reason than she had you lying to me about her for months, and even had your sister lying to cover your illicit affair?" She draws a long sip from her tumbler of whisky.

"Dina had nothing to do with that. *This* is why I didn't say anything when we started dating. There's nothing illicit about it. So you can't blame her for that." I move to stand, hoping that's the end of this unwarranted Dina headhunt, but drop back in the chair when my mother continues.

"She's… dark."

I stare at her for several seconds, blinking, trying to convince myself I just imagined those words. "Excuse me?"

She slams her glass on the table, her temper on full display. "Don't make me say it, Holden. You know exactly what I mean."

"No, Mum. I don't. Because I refuse to believe what you said is what you actually mean."

The only time she's ever mentioned anything remotely racist was during the most recent royal wedding. It surprised me when I heard it then. Now, I'm disgusted.

"I meant what I said. You cannot date her. Break it off and find someone else. Someone who suits this family. She wouldn't even come for the holidays. What does that tell you? She'll never fit in here, and I will not allow a girl like her to tear our family apart."

"Suits this family? That's what you care about? Not that she's intelligent, she understands me, she makes me happy, or how strong she is? Your issue with her is her complexion?"

"Don't be dramatic, Holden. Your father and I did not work as hard as we did to leave everything to you and a mixed-breed orphan."

My jaw drops and my eyes pop open wide enough they nearly fall out. I love my mother, but at this moment, I'm so ashamed. How this woman who has spent thirty years in the most populated, diverse area imaginable can harbour such ignorant thoughts is beyond me. I could make excuses for her because she's old-fashioned or misinformed. But there's no excuse. She's acting like our royal blood line is at stake.

"For the past several weeks, I've told you about her and how important she is to me. I said I wanted you to meet her so you could see firsthand how special she is. And you're telling me *now* that this is a problem?" I take another breath, but it does nothing to calm me. "Mum, I respect you, so I'm not going to say what I'm thinking. What I *am* going to do is walk away and come back to have a conversation when I'm not so angry. Whenever that might be."

Without waiting for her reply, I exit the dining room and storm out of her house. My knuckles are white from how tight I'm clenching my fists as I stomp toward my front door. Anger prevails when I walk inside—into the home my parents own and let my brother and I live in—and slam the door.

Boyd is nowhere to be found, which is a small mercy. I have no idea where he disappeared to, but I have no interest in being lectured by the golden child.

All I want to do is call Dina, make sure she got home okay, and have her voice tell me this is all some sort of warped fever dream. To tell her I love her and let that be enough for my family to love her, too.

Or maybe my mum sees something I don't. That small seed of doubt takes hold in my mind and I spend a full hour replaying every encounter Dina and I have had over the last five months. Am I missing something? Have I been blinded by my intense connection to her? Distracted by my studies and swayed by her study prowess? I don't think that's possible. What we have is too real to be a mistake.

But how do I go against my mother's demands?

My family has always been in close proximity, but not exactly close. It's just how we operate. My parents were married at nineteen in England, then moved to Canada shortly after. Neither of them had education beyond high school, but they never let that stop them. My dad worked his entire life as a welder, starting out sweeping floors, and eventually becoming a specialized welder, which had him travelling across the country to do work few people had the skill to do. My mum started as a mail clerk in an office job and worked her way up to senior case manager. I'm proud of my parents. I appreciate their sacrifices. Their hard work has set my siblings and me up with opportunities we wouldn't have had otherwise.

It's for that reason, I feel like I owe them. My loyalty, my devotion, above anything else. But I can't be loyal to ignorance. That being said, as much as I love Dina, I can't bring her into a family where she wouldn't be treated as an equal. She deserves better than this. After all she's been through—losing her parents, living with her neglectful aunt, and still persevering through it all—I can't ask her to tolerate anything less than mutual respect. Nor do I want her to live with the thought she separated me from my family.

It's not a matter of me or my mother winning this disagreement. There is no winner.

I lose Dina, or I ask her to commit to me, knowing this issue will exist in the background. I've never known of a happy relationship existing with a shadow looming overhead. If I choose Dina, I'll drive a wedge between me and my family. If I choose my family, it's possible I'll resent my mother forever. I'd exchange every sacrifice she's ever made for this one. For *her* to sacrifice her ignorant way of thinking and open her eyes to a person's character above all else.

My mind drifts back to *War and Peace*. When Emperor Alexander was informed he would either lose Moscow or he'd lose his army *and* Moscow, he was pragmatic. He thought things through. Either way, he would lose the city. So even though in his case, his army was willing to fight, knowing they faced impossible odds, I can't ask that of Dina. I'm losing my target either way.

This isn't a war I can win.

As I agreed, I return to my parents' house to discuss the issue further, now that I'm not so furious—though I'm equally upset as I was last night.

But as soon as I see my mother's hate-filled hazel eyes, my anger returns.

"I hope you're coming back here to tell me you've taken what I said seriously."

My shoulders slump and I stare at the floor. I can't look at her right now. "Unfortunately, I have."

"Good. You'll see that I only want what's best for you. That *girl* isn't good for you."

I drag my eyes upward and narrow them at the woman who raised me. The same one who always told me to be a decent person and put others first. The same one who told me not to allow anyone else to make decisions for me. To always be my own person. "Dina. Her *name* is Dina. And if you cared what was best for me, you wouldn't put me in this position."

"Oh, please, Holden. You're blinded by some pretty bird who gave you the time of day. She's done nothing but distract you from your studies and your family. Did she shake her tail at you and suddenly you lost all self-respect?" She scoffs, standing with her hands on her narrow hips.

Listening to my mother accuse Dina of seducing me into abandoning my studies makes me even angrier. Not only does that imply I'm some simple-minded oaf, operating on primal urges, it implies Dina is no more than an inconvenience with ulterior motives. That couldn't be further from the truth.

"She has done nothing but support me, and it's because of her I did as well as I did on my exams. I love her, and—"

"You're too young to even understand what love means."

I stare at my mother's appearance, wondering if I missed the spitefulness before, or if it's just now appearing. Her vibrant red hair has morphed into a mass of greying auburn strands, each hinting at hard work and dedication. All of which has directly benefited me. So whether she's right or not isn't the determining factor here.

"I'm not a foolish little boy! You and Dad were nineteen when you got married, so that excuse doesn't work for me. This is because of your hatred for someone who doesn't deserve it. And if you ask me, which you don't, because you don't seem to care about anyone's opinion but your own, my love for *her* is the only thing motivating my decision."

She stares at me for a beat, then steps forward to pat my cheek like I'm every bit the little boy she implies I am. "You'll find someone else. Someone better."

My blinding rage is drowned out by the crushing defeat of my broken heart.

35

DINA

Hurting as One

Holden didn't call last night, so I didn't get to debrief him on the evening. To be honest, I was too angry with him to discuss it. Phoebe was lovely; we had great conversations about books, during which I was able to make some recommendations based on books I know she's enjoyed. Grace is as adorable as Holden said, and sweet as can be. Aaron, Boyd, and Alfie were all friendly. The only wildcard was his mother. Though, not that wild, because it's pretty clear how she feels about me. The uncertainty I've been wrestling with is entirely because Holden's thoughts on the encounter are still a mystery.

His name lights up my screen as I'm stepping out of the shower, so I grab a towel to wrap myself and dry my hands, then answer on speakerphone.

I'm nervous, so I start the conversation by avoiding the elephant in the room. "Good morning. You didn't call last night. What if I was trapped in Ed's basement while he skinned me alive?"

"I'm so sorry." He releases a loud breath that makes it obvious he didn't think my joke was funny. Not that one should joke about being skinned alive. "Can I meet you later?

Are you busy?" Suave, confident Holden isn't on the other end of the phone. I don't recognize this Holden.

"What's wrong? Why do you sound like that?"

He clears his throat before repeating himself.

Realizing I won't get an answer, I agree to meet at Garrison Commons in thirty minutes. I have to take Nacho for a walk, anyway.

I tug on an oversized hoodie and leggings, dress Nacho in his cold-weather gear, then grab my outdoor stuff so I don't freeze. Not until I'm fully dressed do I realize I have to pee. Nerves. Bladder. They're sworn enemies. I rush to the washroom without taking everything off and struggle to relieve myself while holding up my long, bulky sweater and coat. By the time I go to wash my hands, I'm sweating like I just finished a 10K.

On account of my clammy skin, walking outside feels even colder than the eight degrees below zero it really is. My heart pounds faster and harder as I walk down the catwalk into the open area where we agreed to meet. Nacho goes about his business, so I scoop him up once he's done to spare his paws from the cold. Holden appears five minutes later, holding two coffee cups, wearing a forlorn expression.

He hands me a paper cup, but doesn't greet me with a kiss or even a hug. The distinct lack of his usual greeting causes nausea to swirl in my stomach. My shaking hand struggles to grip my drink. My heart is beating an irregular staccato that would alarm most doctors.

The sigh he releases as he avoids my questioning gaze makes me want to vomit. He doesn't even need to speak. I know what's happening.

"Dina, you know I love you. I've never met anyone so perfect. You're incredible, and I want you to always believe that." His voice cracks, confirming my fears.

I choke out an instantaneous sob, shaking my head. "Don't say it. Don't even bother saying it."

He steps forward, now looking like he wants to give me a hug, but Nacho growls, and I push Holden away with my shaking coffee cup.

"No. Don't you dare. Don't you dare ask me to come here so you can break my heart, then act like you're trying to make it better. You don't get to be the hero and the villain at the same time."

"Dina, I—"

I'm using all of my emotional fortitude to stop myself from crying. "For almost a decade, I kept people at a distance because I was afraid they'd leave. That I'd learn to love, only to have it ripped away like my parents were." I sniffle and use my scarf to wipe my face. "But you walked into my life, and against my better judgement, I let you in. I fell. Hard." I turn to walk back toward my house because I can't keep my tears at bay much longer. I also can't handle looking at him right now. Before I'm too far away, I turn back to add, "This is it for us, Dickens. The love I had to give wasn't enough for you, and I'm not foolish enough to try twice. This is how our story ends, and it was a plot twist I never saw coming."

A tear trickles down his cheek as I walk away for good.

My own tears come so hard and fast, when I enter my condo, I can barely see. I could call Hollis or Angel, but I can't admit what just happened out loud. Now is not the time to talk through the tsunami of feelings I'm drowning in.

Instead, Nacho and I crawl into bed after I change into comfortable pyjamas, and I sob myself to sleep.

I have no idea what time it is. It's dark outside, but I don't want to check the time on my phone. For no reason other than I'll see Holden's number, a string of text messages that once made me smile, pictures of us being silly and in love. Reminders of everything that's now gone. And what's worse, I don't really know why.

Sure, I could have given him a chance to explain earlier, but I couldn't bear to listen to another word. I'm confident his abrupt termination of our relationship had to do with his mother, but what her issue was specifically, I don't know. Not that it matters, because we're through. I'd never ask him to choose me over his family.

Before I know it, I'm sobbing on my pillow again. It takes a minute for me to realize Nacho isn't in the bed anymore, so I croak out his name, hoping he hasn't gotten into anything that would make this day worse. He comes trotting in, seconds later, and launches himself onto the bed.

"Hi, baby boy. What are you up to?"

He comes closer and even through my tears, I see a gold-coloured thread hanging from his mouth.

"What did you do?" I wipe my eyes with the backs of my hands and swing my legs out of bed. Reluctantly, I walk into the living room to see what Nacho destroyed while I was unconscious.

He darts in front of me, glancing back to see if I'm following. His tail is wagging like I've never seen it before. He jumps up on the couch beside a pile of shredded fabric and fluff. More specifically, shredded stuffed squirrels. Plural. The lot of them. He sits beside his mess, proud as can be.

"You killed your squirrels?" I'm so confused because he loved those things. He'd never bothered with more than one at a time. For him to rip them all up is weird... I freeze as I stare at my cavalier pup. "You killed your squirrels because they were from him?"

If anyone ever tries to tell me dogs are not intuitive or intelligent, I will repeat this scenario to prove how wrong they are. I was pretty confident Nacho loved those squirrels more than anything—even if he kept slaughtering them. But looking at his wagging tail and perked up ears, now I'm certain he loves *me* more than anything.

I collapse on the couch beside him, and he wastes no time crawling on top of me. I cradle him in my arms, kissing the top of his head. The love I feel for him might not be normal, but I never was one to go with the flow. Nothing about who I am or the life I've lived has been 'normal.'

Suddenly, I feel guilty for loving Holden as much as I did. Rather, do. Even after he shattered my heart, I can't just stop something that has become an integral part of who I am.

My eyes well up with tears again. I thought they would have run dry by now, but a new wave of emotion overtakes me and I sink into the pits of despair. I never should have gone to retrieve *The Cracked Curtain*. Never should have taken his number. Never should have texted him and agreed to let him into my world. I was fine before he came crashing into my life, and now I'm what?

Broken.

And it's a lot harder to put something back together when it's been broken twice.

DINA

Intermission

When my parents died, I felt a kind of heartbreak few people ever have to. The subsequent years were full of plenty of more crushing experiences because of my aunt. My coping mechanism then was to dive into books and try to learn as much as I could. To escape into as many fictional worlds as possible, so I didn't have to face my own. To live up to the name my parents bestowed upon me, just like my big sister did.

Faced with a new heartbreak, that's exactly what I've been doing for almost two weeks. I have to submit my final examination form for my thesis defence in eight days, and the thought of nearing the end of my school career has my stomach in knots. Suffice to say, I've had enough of things I love ending too soon.

Before I can set my plan for today in motion, it's derailed by a knock at my door. My stomach sinks, both hopeful and afraid it's Holden coming to apologize. To tell me he made a horrible mistake, and he wants to get back together. But I don't know if I'd say yes. Isn't the definition of insanity doing the same thing time and time again, expecting the outcome to be different?

"Dina, open the door!"

I guess I don't have to make that decision today, because that's my sister shouting. Nacho goes tearing into the entryway, ready to attack. I scoop him up before I open the door, and I'm surprised to find Angel, Hollis, and Angel's American bulldog, Genie.

"What are you guys doing here?"

The trio steps inside, closing the door behind them. I release Nacho so he and Genie can go running off to play. Though he seems a lot more excited about it than she does.

Hollis holds up a large paper bag. "Ice cream, chocolate, and"—she gestures toward my sister, who proudly holds up a bottle—"wine!"

Angel squeezes me in a tight hug and says through gritted teeth, "I'm going to beat the nerd out of this jerk, so help me."

I may not be able to see her expression, but I can hear it. She's not kidding. Hollis and I both know what she's capable of when it comes to putting people in their place. We recently watched her get kicked out of a club for assaulting a guy who wouldn't leave her alone. I'm not even sure what he said to her, but he underestimated her dainty five-foot-one-and-a-half frame. I chuckle at the memory.

"You should know by now I'm dead serious. No one gets away with breaking my baby sister's heart. I know Hollis will have my back on this." Angel glances at Hollis as we walk into my living room. "Hey, can you make some sort of biological weapon? Nothing serious. Just something like an intense itch cream or... ooh, an anti-anti-wrinkle moisturizer?"

I hear Hollis laugh as I stop in my kitchen to put the ice cream in the freezer. I grab a few glasses and walk into my living room. Once I set everything on the side table, Angel wastes no time popping the cork on her favourite budget wine, and pours a little in each glass. To make things easier, I take the hideous art déco lamp I no longer have any affection for and set it on the floor, then move the table in front of the sofa. I plop myself on the middle cushion between the two people I have left in the world.

"Okay, dish. Tell us everything," Hollis requests. She grabs the chocolate, holding it out for me to grab a piece, so I oblige.

Chewing this chocolate-caramel nougat sticks my teeth together, so I have an excuse to delay sharing what happened. Something I've actively been doing since Holden dumped me in the park. Because the truth is, I don't really know. Nights of analyzing and questioning where it all went so wrong haven't given me any answers. How do you explain being in love with someone one day, then being dismissed the next?

I clear the candy from my teeth, resigning myself to explaining as best I can. Angel and Hollis both listen intently for as long as it takes me to get it all out. Everything from him crashing into me in the blazing summer heat to the look of regret on his face as I walked away in the snowy park. It's been thirteen days, but every time I close my eyes, I see that face.

"What a jerk. I don't care if he looked sad after he broke your heart. I oughtta break his face. At least his glasses. Or steal his stupid pocket protector so his pen ink will stain his shirt." My sister is riled up, even as she scratches the top of her snorty dog's head.

"Cool it on the violence. I appreciate it, but I just want to move on. It was stupid anyway because I have my thesis defence in two months and then I'll need to get settled in a job. Having to consider another person is foolish. This way, at least I can keep my options open." I've recited this to myself at least 299 times over the past two weeks, but it sounds even less convincing out loud.

"I get what you're saying. There's no way I could even consider a relationship until I finish my master's and find a job. But it sounded like you guys had such a good connection and a lot in common. He made you laugh. I really thought he was one of the good ones." Hollis pops a chocolate in her mouth and appears to have the same sticky-teeth struggle I did.

"Well, you guys are the only ones who have come into my life and not left. If either of you dump me, I'll never recover, just so you know."

Angel wraps a dainty arm around my shoulders and pulls me into her side. "I love you, Dina. Nothing and no one could ever break us apart."

That's reassuring. Not that I had any worries about my sister ditching me, but if I'm being honest, I didn't have those fears with Holden, either. If someone had asked me flat out, I would have said he was it for me. The one. My person. But in the end, I wasn't enough for him. Nothing I could do or say was enough for him. *I just wasn't enough.*

I don't even notice I'm crying until both Hollis and Angel have their arms wrapped around me, squeezing me tight.

"How could I be so pathetic? Do you even know how much time I took away from my own work to help him study? I never thought twice about it. I loved him, even when I didn't realize it yet. His success was so important to me, I sacrificed my own. And for what? So he could decide I wasn't worth the effort?" Saying it out loud turns my tears from ones of sadness to anger. "How dare he take advantage of my generosity. What kind of person does that? A jerk! That's who. A big, nerdy, handsome, kind, funny jerk." My voice loses serious enthusiasm as I work my way through that list.

"Oh, Dee. You're not the problem. If he doesn't see how incredible you are or appreciate the sacrifices you made, then forget about him. People like that make me so mad. Taking what they can get, then turning their backs. I have no sympathy for them when all of a sudden no one wants to help anymore." Hollis says that entire spiel while staring at the opposite wall with narrowed eyes.

"Holl, is everything okay?" Suddenly, wiping away my tears, my focus isn't on my own problems anymore.

She shakes her head, returning her focus to me and looking unfazed by whatever zone-out just happened. "Totally fine. There are just a lot of people like that."

"Yeah… okay." I'll leave that question for another day. "Whatever. It is what it is. I'm telling you guys, that family dinner was so painfully awkward, he just called it quits because he couldn't bear to sit through that again." Remembering the uncomfortable evening makes me shiver.

Angel clutches my left hand. "There's no valid reason for anyone to behave that way. I'm sorry, Dina, but it's the truth. If you're going to invite someone to your home as a guest, you treat them as one. That woman sounds wretched. And I hate to say it, but Holden is no better if that was his reason."

I can't come up with an argument in Imogen's defence. At the same time, she raised three kind, considerate kids, so she can't be all bad. If she was able to teach them how to be decent people, I have a hard time believing there wasn't some other reason for her behaviour. "I'm pretty sure it's me who's the problem; not her."

Angel practically throws my hand back at me because she lets go so fast. With wine in her left hand, she rotates so she can look at me. "Don't make excuses for that woman. You showed up and were polite. I know that for a fact without you even telling me, because I know *you*. Don't you dare tell yourself her miserable attitude is your fault. You, little sister, are a freaking ray of sunshine." She chugs the remainder of her drink and sets it on the table. "So, what do we say about some ice cream?"

What's that saying? Ice cream will fix all that ails you? That's not a real saying, but I'm going to pretend it is while I have a girls' night and drown my sorrows in a bowl of cookies n' cream.

37

HOLDEN

Let's Hear it for Rock Bottom

I'm fortunate I've never suffered through a bad breakup before now. When I was in high school, I had a girlfriend for three months, but we parted on good terms. She was pretty and popular, so I got the impression she was more interested in Phil, anyway. Then I dated a sociology major during my undergrad. She found someone she was more interested in after about eight months. Neither time was I in love, so there was no heartache. No self-loathing or questioning what to do with myself.

This time around, I feel like I've been gutted. My stomach has been an endless well of anguish for twenty straight days. I have barely eaten, haven't shaved, and haven't given a thought to my thesis beyond thinking that I *should* be thinking about it.

Sam and Phil have both tried calling for days, but I can't bring myself to answer. That's probably why the two of them are barging into my house right now and finding me sprawled out on the sofa watching reruns of *Brooklyn Nine-Nine*. If Captain Holt can't make a person laugh, they must be dead inside.

"He's aliiiiive!" Sam jests as he pokes me in the ribs. "At least, I think he is."

My parents' request to have keypads on the door with four-digit codes is just another one of their demands I resent right now. Another way for my mother to exhibit control.

"Oh good, he's breathing," Phil chides as he walks past me. "But he needs a shower. You look like rock bottom if it had a face."

Looking down at my Offspring T-shirt, I try to recall which day I put it on. Pretty sure this is only day two. "Not in the mood, man."

"For jokes or a shower?"

I shake my head as I prop myself up in a seated position. "Neither."

"Yeah, I figured. We brought beer. In the mood for one of those?" Phil smirks, but it disappears quickly.

"No."

For a comedian, Phil can flip to serious mode like a light switch. "I'm not going to ask what happened, but I'll just make it clear that when you're ready to talk about it, we're here to listen."

These two have been the best support system a guy could ask for, all through public school, until now. They were both the good-looking cool guys who had charisma and flair to spare. They took me, the quiet little nerd, under their wings and always watched my back. Most people assumed we had an arrangement where I did their homework for them, but they're both as smart as I am. They were just good friends and continue to be to this day.

That may be why I feel so pathetic right now. I'm supposed to be a grown man and I've let my mother destroy the best thing to ever happen to me. My time with Dina made up less than one percent of my life, but somehow she consumed the entire thing. Like my life didn't start until she was in it.

Phil hands me a beer as he drops onto the loveseat to my right. "You love her."

I nod my thanks for the beer, crack it open and take a sip. If for no other reason than to delay confirming that. Not past tense. I didn't love her. I *do* love her. "Yeah."

"Then it's not over. If she's important to you, figure it out."

"I can't." I set my beer on the coffee table and mimic Phil's slouched posture in my own seat. "It's not about me."

Sam clears his throat and adds, "When it comes to who you love, it should only be about you, man. It's not up to anyone else."

Phil and I stare at Sam, who has been virtually silent until he drops a matter-of-fact statement out of nowhere.

"You guys need to give me more credit. You know musicians are deep thinkers. Stop being so surprised."

Sam's mock outrage makes my chest rumble with laughter, and I realize it's been nearly three weeks since I heard that sound. It's a nice change; something that even Detective Jake Peralta couldn't achieve.

But I'm not ready to dish all the details of what happened. Not ready to confess what a coward I am. Or how I let Dina slip through my fingers because I didn't want to offend my mother—who, in all honesty, doesn't deserve that kind of sacrifice right now. But it's so much more than choosing one over the other. A future with Dina, against my mother's wishes, means tension and conflict. Things that often overshadow love and respect. As ashamed as I am over Imogen Edwards' mindset—which is largely because of the Royal Family drama—I can't turn my back on my family. I can't ask the rest of them to pick sides, so I have to.

Every rational thought tells me to let Dina go. Give her the chance to find someone with a family who accepts her for the incredible person she is. Someone who can fill that gap she's been missing for the past nine years. But that thought turns the beer in my stomach sour.

So instead of diving into the situation further, I dismiss it and move on. "Thanks, guys. Should we order food?"

A short time later, we're diving in to Bajan food, while Phil and Sam laugh at something on the TV. I force a chuckle to make it seem like I was paying attention. I appreciate their offer to talk, but there's nothing anyone can say to fix this.

For now, I'll just take comfort in knowing they have my back, even when I smell like a donkey in a compost heap.

Nothing on social media ever interested me before. I have various accounts because that's how people keep in touch these days and it helps connect with family still living in the United Kingdom, but I never found myself scrolling for hours, drawn to the content. Not until seeing the odd picture of Dina and Nacho pop up is the only bright spot in my life.

I could delete my account and spare myself the torture of seeing her but not being able to talk to her. Touch her. Kiss her. All things I miss. But I'm a bit of a masochist because the pain of seeing her is at least a reminder of the thrill of loving her—which I still do. I'm not sure I'll ever be able to stop. Our relationship was quick, intense, and life changing. Problem is, now my life has been changed, and I can't change it back.

She posted a picture of her and Nacho in their cold weather gear, down at the waterfront earlier this morning. Her cheeks are pink, and her eyes look sad, but she's plastered on a smile for the selfie with her beloved pooch. Nacho is rocking his signature angry eyebrows, looking unpleased he's been forced into his sweater again.

Is she trying to appear unaffected? Or has she just moved on? It's been four weeks. That's more than half as long as we were officially together. I can't expect her to stay hung up on me forever. Or at all. I don't deserve that kind of commitment.

My finger hovers over the like button. Would it be wrong to click on it? To let her know I see her and I'm not indifferent to her striking brown eyes or soft pink lips? It feels rude to see it and not acknowledge it.

Even Napoleon sent a letter to the Russians in *War and Peace*, trying to come to a resolution. Granted, it seemed he wanted them to surrender, but he still tried. If he could reach out in the middle of war, would it be so bad if I did?

So many unanswered questions.

I'm desperate for an interaction with her, but worry that reminding her of my existence would only disrupt the contentment she seems to have found. Or at least it could get me blocked. If I lost my lifeline to seeing her photos, I'd be completely adrift in a sea of unresolved feelings I can't navigate.

So I remove my finger, only to click on the photo and save it to my phone's memory. Nothing says you're moving on like a collection of your ex's photos in your gallery to pull up at random moments. She can have her peace, and I'll keep battling my internal war.

I set my phone face down on my desk and pep talk myself to get back to working on this paperwork. The weeks are ticking by, and once I submit my advisor request in three days, I will be full speed ahead on my thesis. This is the last phase of the nine-year-long process, but it doesn't feel like an accomplishment anymore.

38

HOLDEN

Kick Him When He's Down

Two weeks ago, I submitted my forms to request a thesis advisor and now have less than two months to complete my proposal. It's crunch time. I had a brief reprieve after my exams, but it's time to bury myself in history again. Something, anything, to keep my mind off of the gorgeous brunette staring at me from inside my phone. The part of my history I want to keep reliving.

I find myself wondering if she's still going to the library every Friday at 1pm. Is there a chance she'd go to try to see me? Does she want to see me as much as I want to see her? I wouldn't blame her if she hated me. After how we ended things, she probably suspects it's something to do with my mother, but I doubt she'd guess the entire reason. In all honesty, I hope she never does. It still floods me with shame when I think about it

"All right, I've let you wallow for weeks. Now, we're going to sit down and talk."

I lift my head when my bedroom light turns on and find my big brother standing in my doorway.

"What are you doing here?" I ask, draping my arm over my eyes to block the light.

"Well, I live here. I'm questioning whether you're living or dying here. It's time for an intervention."

I roll my eyes under my forearm. Captain Obvious is here. "Specifically, what are you doing in my bedroom?"

"Technically, I'm still in the hallway. It would never hold up as a trespassing claim. Get yourself up. We'll be in the living room." Without giving me time to debate, Boyd walks off down the hall.

We?

I check the time on my phone, taking a moment to stare at the photo of Dina, me, and Nacho in front of the red canoe feature the last time we went to observe the dog park. Again. Our smiling faces gave no indication that we'd be in this situation a few weeks later. I wish she knew if I had it my way, we wouldn't be here.

Once I'm somewhat presentable, I plod downstairs to find the sibling duo who have taken it upon themselves to disturb my silent brooding. I sit in the lone armchair without acknowledging either of them.

Boyd leans forward so his elbows rest on his knees, drawing both my and Phoebe's attention. He may irritate me, but my brother has a natural ability to command a crowd. "You can't keep going on like this. I get it. She dumped you, but it's time to move on."

I blink at him, trying to determine if I'm annoyed or angry. "She didn't dump me." I cringe as the defensive words spill out because it sounds like I'm trying to protect my pride. I lower my voice and start over. "She didn't dump me. I... I broke up with her because..." Words fail to form. Nothing can make this scenario okay, and saying it out loud feels like I'm ratting out Mum for her ignorance.

"Spit it out, boy. Because what?" Phoebe prompts, gesticulating with her hands. Based on her tone, she's trying to resist wrapping them around my throat.

I glance at my siblings, harbouring guilt over this secret I've kept in, not wanting to change their perspective of our mum. But the truth is the truth, even when it sucks. "Mum told me I couldn't date Dina because she's 'dark'. She also said her and Dad didn't work as hard as they did so they could leave everything to a 'mixed-breed orphan'." I practically choke on the words as I say them; a renewed fury building.

"She said what?" Boyd stares at me, eyes narrowed.

"Don't make me repeat it." I take a deep breath and continue. "So I broke up with Dina because I wasn't going to build a future with someone who would never feel welcomed. She doesn't have anyone other than her sister. She deserves better than that."

Boyd releases a long, low whistle and collapses into the back of the sofa. "Wow, I never would have imagined her saying something like that."

"Me neither. I honestly don't know if I can forgive her." I've been trying, but I can't.

"When you first started moping around the house after that family dinner, I assumed Dina either broke up with you because of how uncomfortable it was, or Mum encouraged you to call it off because Dina was distracting you from your studies."

"No. The opposite. She's done everything to keep me motivated and helped me more than I can even explain. The way that girl can find her way around a library? Whoo." I blow out a breath and chuckle, recalling our library sessions. Then I feel suffocated by guilt because I promised if she helped me study, I'd help her, and I didn't. Another way I failed her.

Boyd and Phoebe laugh and exchange a look before my sister adds, "You are such a nerd." Phoebe, who has been uncharacteristically quiet, levels me with a serious look. "Now I get why you haven't been coming to family dinners." She stares at me with so much anger in her face, but I don't think it's directed at me. "Are you going today?"

Really? That's what she's worried about?

"No, I'm not going. And if Mum can't figure out why, then she's more ignorant than I thought."

My sister's face relaxes, giving way for a more sympathetic expression. She tilts her head, which reminds me of Nacho when he was confused. "You know, for the last few weeks, I was angry with you for disappearing. I thought you were just being dramatic because, let's face it, Dina is ah-mazing. But if that's what happened... Why didn't you tell us?"

"Because I don't want anyone picking sides. This is between me—"

Boyd cuts me off. "But it's not. It's not between you and Mum. It's between right and wrong. She's wrong, Holden. I know you think I don't pay attention, but this girl made you happier than I've ever seen you. That has to be worth something."

The determination in his voice surprises me. He's speaking like he's giving a closing argument, or ready to launch a revolution.

In *War and Peace*, when the troops failed to assemble when they were supposed to, no one could recover to create an appropriate battle plan. Then again, that didn't seem to matter in the big picture. The big picture changed because of that failure, and what was their initial plan wasn't the focus anymore. There was a plot twist, and that made the ending a mystery.

Truth is, I don't know how mine and Dina's story ends. It doesn't feel like it's over. Too many plot holes and unresolved questions.

But not every story gets a happy ending.

I'm fidgety now, from too much pent up frustration. I get up and start pacing around our main floor.

Boyd and Phoebe whisper to each other when I'm at the far point in my circle, so I can't make out what they're saying. Whatever it is, they're both experiencing the same waves of emotions—from outraged to calm and collected.

The clock strikes 3pm, which is normally the time we'd be walking into our parents' house. Boyd returns from the kitchen after making a phone call, so I expect him and Phoebe to walk out the door to avoid being late. Instead, Boyd sits back down on the sofa and kicks his feet up.

He shrugs when he catches me studying him. "I'm not choosing sides between you and Mum. I'm choosing between right and wrong."

"Me too. One way or another, she'll have to realize she was wrong. If that means we have to show some tough love, so be it." Phoebe takes a sip of the coffee she's been nursing since this conversation started. "And if I don't have to eat her dry roast as a result, I'm okay with that, too."

Boyd and I both laugh. We've all suffered through far too many overcooked roasts over the years. There's a reason we always have gravy.

Someone pounds at the door a short time later, in the middle of a conversation about Grace, who is next door with Aaron. The tempo of my heartbeat speeds up, worried it's our father coming to fetch us. He'll lay on a guilt trip like the expert he is. There's no limit he'll reach when it comes to defending or supporting his wife. I used to admire that about him, but in this case, he's guilty by association. There's such a thing as being too supportive and enabling toxicity.

But Boyd answers the door, and on the other side is a young man holding a pair of pizza boxes. Once he's tipped the delivery driver, Boyd shuts the door and brings the boxes to the coffee table before walking through the dining area into the kitchen. The sight of a pizza box turns my stomach. It's one of the many things that reminds me of Dina. Along with books, specific internet searches, documentaries, coloured pens, dogs—in any shape or size—street cars, hot dog carts, Minnie Mouse, and happy couples. But perhaps pizza most of all.

Boyd returns with plates, handing one to each me and Phoebe. "Dig in."

My sister opens the top box, elated Boyd ordered Hawaiian. The two of them love it, but I'd rather eat gravel. She spins the other box toward me, and I silently pray it's not double cheese. I open it, looking inside the lid before glancing at the pizza itself. No cheesy notes. No extra cheesy pizza. I lift a slice of Canadian onto my plate, with no desire to eat it.

"What's wrong? Not hungry? You've barely eaten," Boyd states, with a piece of disgusting pizza halfway to his mouth.

"I don't know how to move on. I think I'm just stuck in this permanent state of fearing she'll never forgive me. Like some kind of breakup purgatory. Can't go forward; can't go back."

And neither of my siblings, no matter what they say in support, are able to fix it. I'd give anything to be able to go back. Unfortunately, the only choice is to move forward.

39

DIMA

Let the Bad Times Roll

Fallout with Holden derailed my thesis momentum. Something I swore I'd never allow to happen. My degree is too important to me to throw it away for someone who threw me away. From now on, I'm going to trust Nacho's judgement though, and if he tries to shred someone's pant legs upon first meeting, I'll take his opinion seriously. It's not his fault he was swayed by delicious cookies. Who wouldn't be?

Thankfully, Hollis and Angel have helped me through my first romantic heartbreak over the past two months, and now I'm ready to defend my thesis next week. Despite the bad weather, I've got no choice but to venture to the library so I can double check to make sure my bibliography and direct quotes are correct. It's a last-minute task I have put off for far too long.

Nacho is ready in his layers, with a knitted sweater underneath his raincoat, then tucked into his carry bag. With me in my sweater and raincoat, umbrella in hand, we're on our way to the library.

The entire walk is miserable. The wind off the lake, coupled with the tunnels created by the tall buildings in the downtown core, makes the rain pelt my face and body with ferocity. Not to mention, the temperature is hovering just above freezing, so the rain is ice cold. Nacho is not pleased, but at least he's dry. I could have made him walk like a normal dog.

"It's okay, baby boy. Momma will get you there as fast as she can." I try to pick up my pace, but the wind is head on.

Could this day get any worse?

The library door, which usually slides open like every other automatic door in existence, apparently doesn't recognize me as a human. I stand at the entrance, waving my hands, doing jumping jacks and irritating my already angry dog until finally the door inches open enough for me to slip inside. The dark grey carpet in the lobby is a couple of shades darker from the water tracked in by other visitors, and everything smells damp. No one is at the reception area, so I just wave at the security guard and continue upstairs.

It takes about twenty minutes to find the books I need. One was misplaced and took three-quarters of that time to track down. Instead of finding a comfortable place on the reading terrace, I go to the right and find a lonely couch set along the walls with only a few small, round windows almost at the ceiling. The artificial light is sufficient to complete my task, but this space doesn't compare to the bright light and comfort of my usual spot. Unfortunately, that space has been ruined forever.

For over an hour, no one disrupts my work and I make good progress with Nacho snuggled up beside me, still in his open bag, but his outfit removed. The rain hasn't let up enough to head home yet, so I dive back in after setting an alarm on my phone to come back to the real world in thirty minutes. The forecast is brief periods of cloudiness, but the chance of showers decreases as the day goes on. Even if it slows to a drizzle, I'll make a break for it just to be safe.

I skim through one book I read a few months ago, *Once Upon a Desert Isle*, because I vividly remember it making me laugh so hard, I had tears streaming down my face. I could use a few laughs. The author of this book seems to have written the nonsensical comedy with me in mind. It makes me chuckle and boosts my mood. There's nothing like the right book appearing in your life at the perfect moment.

My phone buzzes from my alarm, so I get up to stretch my legs, leaving Nacho on the sofa while I check the weather situation. I step a few feet around the corner when a loud alarm starts blaring. It's a stark contrast to the otherwise silent space.

I look around at other people in the vicinity, wondering if we should run for our lives or if it is a false alarm. That question is put to rest when the security guard rushes up the stairs and starts shouting at everyone to leave the building in an orderly fashion through the back emergency exit.

Nacho! I rush over to where I left him, which is less than five metres away, only to find my baby has disappeared. I resist the urge to crumple on the ground in a panic. I have to find him.

"Nacho! Nacho Dog? Where are you, baby?" I shout as I walk away from the stairwell. Surely if he ran that way, people would have noticed. "Nacho Dog. Come to Momma, please. Please, Nacho. I can't leave without you." My words get stuck in my throat because I can't imagine walking out of here without him. He's my entire world.

"Ma'am, you need to exit the building immediately!" the stern security guard shouts. "Please, head for the exit."

There are sirens blaring outside, which further confirms this is not a drill or false alarm.

"My dog. He was just right here. I have to find him." At this point, I don't care if I get banned from the library for life. I'm not leaving without him.

"Dog? You brought a dog to a public library?"

"Now is not the time, Ronald! I need to find him. He's a little chihuahua, about yay big"—I hold my hands several inches apart to demonstrate Nacho's size—"and he's a textbook ankle biter, long hair on his ears, white and caramel colour. Please, help me find him."

"Ma'am, my responsibility is to get you out of here. The firefighters can find your dog. We need to leave."

"Firefighters? Is there a fire?"

"Afraid so. Smoke is coming from the main entrance." Ronald performs a visual scan of the top floor, then steps over and grabs Nacho's carrier. "I have to cover the rest of this floor quickly. You get to safety, and if I find your dog, I'll bring him out. But please, you need to go."

The thought of leaving Nacho when he's scared and needs me the most makes me feel sick. "I can't leave him. Please, just let me find him."

"Ma'am, you need to leave... before we all wind up dead."

I close my eyes, which forces the pooling tears to run down my cheeks. It's starting to smell like smoke up here. I can't be responsible for Ronald losing his life because I was stubborn. With no other choice, I nod.

Firefighters are filing in as I descend the stairs through the thickening smoke. I stop one who is rushing past me to inform him of my missing dog. He promises he'll relay the information and do what he can. That doesn't sound encouraging, but I have to hold on to the glimmer of hope that offers. Before I reach the bottom floor, the sprinkler system kicks in, soaking my hair, sweater, and pants.

I step into the fresh air, immediately realizing how badly my eyes are burning, and start coughing. A paramedic rushes over to check on me, but I wave her off and insist I'm fine.

"We should treat you for smoke inhalation. Just to be safe."

Everything else around me fades out and I only hear my own sobbing. Clearly, the only reason I'm having trouble catching my breath is because I'm crying so hard. The paramedic assesses me and deems me in need of oxygen, so she has me sit at the edge of the ambulance, places a mask over my mouth and nose, and wraps me in a foil blanket.

It doesn't help. No oxygen is going to help me when my sweet—maybe not to the general population, but sweet to me—baby is afraid and alone. I feel afraid and alone without him.

I don't think it's possible for the day to get any worse. Until it does.

Burn It Up

I was sitting in my office, trying to get some research done, but my thoughts kept drifting to Dina. My mother is still refusing to see beyond ancestry, and her close-mindedness has broken my heart in two different ways. The obvious one being that Dina is no longer in my life, and that reality hurts more than I thought possible. The second reason being, I can't believe my mother even had formed an opinion someone is superior or inferior because of their skin colour, let alone had enough conviction in that mentality to demand I end my relationship.

My mind is a raging battlefield with no end to the carnage in sight.

Boyd appears at our office door, panting, snapping me out of my inner torment. "The library is on fire."

"Which library?"

"The public library!" He steps into the office and uses his phone to show me the local news crew on the scene.

The cameras pan the area, and what I see renders me paralyzed. Dina is sitting in the open doors of an ambulance, in hysterics, with an oxygen mask on her face.

"That's Dina," Boyd states.

It takes a few seconds, but Boyd's sharp words bring me back to reality.

Now I'm running down the sidewalk along Bathurst Street toward the scene. Thankfully, the rain has let up, so it's no longer falling, but the streets are soaked. Each step is splashing water halfway up my thighs. My pants and shoes are getting heavier as I run farther. My adrenaline is pushing me forward, even though I can barely breathe myself. The motivation I feel after seeing the image of Dina sitting in that ambulance, wrapped in a foil blanket, is stronger than the pain from my burning lungs.

I round the corner and see her. Still seated in the ambulance, still crying. Firefighters try to keep me back, but I shout at them and tell them my girlfriend is in the ambulance. Finally, someone takes pity on me and lets me through. Hopefully, they don't ask her for clarification on that title.

"Dina!" I run the final few metres and crouch in front of her, so I'm level with her eyes. "Are you hurt? What's wrong?"

She blinks several times before shaking her head. "Na-na—" Her breathing becomes erratic, so I try to calm her.

The paramedic at Dina's side informs me if I'm upsetting her, I'll have to leave. I can't leave her. Not until I know what's wrong.

Then I realize her bags are not with her. Dina almost always has her bags.

"Dina, where's Nacho? Did you leave him at home?" Stupid me for asking. She wouldn't be crying so hard if she had.

She shakes her head again and blubbers, "Nacho..."

The paramedic pushes me back and asks me to give Dina space.

From fifteen feet away, I shout, "I'm going to find him. Don't worry, okay? I'm going to find him."

My first course of action is calling Boyd to report in and see if he can come help me and bring one of Phoebe's coats, since it looks like Dina doesn't have one. He's on his way. I try calling Phil and Sam, but neither of them answers. Their weird working hours mean they're probably sleeping. Next, I want to call Angel, but I don't know her number, so I take a minute to track her down on social media and send her a message with my number. I do the same with Hollis, hoping neither of them blocked me in solidarity after what I did to Dina. Worst-case scenario, if we don't find Nacho, she's going to need people around.

Boyd arrives fifteen minutes later, poised to help me find the angry little dog. He questions firefighters while I speak to other library patrons. I find Julie, who is being interviewed by a police officer, so I wait a moment until she's free.

"Julie, have you seen Dina's dog?" I whisper, not wanting others to know Julie was aware a canine was being smuggled inside.

She gasps and claps her hand over her mouth. "No. I didn't even know Dina was here. Have you spoken to her?"

"Not really. She's in the ambulance with an oxygen mask on. I tried to speak to her, but she's too upset."

"Oh, the poor dear. No, I haven't seen a dog anywhere. Does she know if he came outside? I hope he's not inside anywhere." She glances at the library, which isn't engulfed in flames, but heavy smoke is dissipating from a couple of upper windows.

The firemen are slowly filing out of the building. I watch as Boyd intercepts them and flashes a photo of Nacho on his phone. Each of them shakes their head.

"I hope so too."

I make my way over to where I left Dina and find her with a blanket still wrapped around her shoulders, but the oxygen mask has been removed. That's a positive sign. I drape

Phoebe's puffy coat over Dina's shoulders, engulfing her and the metallic sheet.

"Hey." I place a hand on her shoulder, and she collapses against my chest, sobbing. "We're going to find him. I won't stop looking." I kiss the top of her head, even though that's not my right anymore. It gives me too much credit to say I broke her heart, but if I meant a fraction to her that she does to me, I'm certain breaking up with her has taken its toll.

What I can do is find the one male creature she loves more than anything who won't break her heart.

Dina settles after a few moments, and her breathing regulates. She leans back, pulling herself away from me. "I'm sorry. Nacho has never been anywhere but home alone. I-I'm so scared."

Boyd rushes up behind me. "Good news and bad news."

I try to put my arm around Dina to brace her for the bad news, but she leans away.

Boyd continues, "They didn't find Nacho inside and they've done a full sweep. But the good news is, nothing much burned. There's just a lot of smoke damage. So if he is hiding in there somewhere, chances are he's okay."

Our options are limited right now. We can't get inside to search and have to leave that to the professionals. So I devise a plan. Addressing Dina, I say, "You wait here so you can be around while the firefighters do their sweep. Boyd and I will start canvassing the area. He's small, so he could have gotten out when people were rushing outside."

That prompts a fresh wave of tears, though Dina keeps herself composed enough to nod.

"I messaged Angel and Hollis, but neither of them replied. Do you have your phone?"

She reaches into her back pocket and pulls out her phone. "Yeah. I'll call them."

"We're going to find him. There are people everywhere. Someone must have seen him and you know he wouldn't cooperate to go home with anyone else."

Dina chuckles, relieving some of my worry. "That's true."

"Okay, text or call me with any updates."

With a quick nod from Dina, Boyd and I head in opposite directions. Him toward the pet store Dina and Nacho frequent, and me toward the Fort York National Historic Site where Dina walks him every day. I'm not sure how he would have gotten across a busy city street, but anything is possible. He could have darted across while traffic was at a stand-still.

Each person I pass along the way, I show a photo of Nacho on my phone and ask if they've seen him. Chances are they'd remember a tiny demon dog. If I see anyone with shredded pant legs, I'll know I'm on the right track.

I cross at the main intersection, walk past the bus stop, making sure I ask each waiting person, but still have no luck. Then I head into the beautifully manicured space that was once the scene of a dark and dramatic event in the city's history from the War of 1812. On any other day, I'd revel in the historical significance of the site and take in the immensity of what happened on this very land. Today, I revel in the historical significance in my relationship with Dina. We started and ended in this spot.

The site itself is over forty acres, so I won't be able to cover all that ground myself, but I'm hoping with the help of other pedestrians, I'll be able to mend this broken piece of Dina's soul.

As for the other part I'm responsible for, I'm unsure how to ever fix that.

41

DINA

Hopeless

Angel is on her way. Hollis is in the middle of a shift for her internship, but promised she'll get here as soon as she can. She offered to leave, but I can't let her screw up that opportunity for a mission I'm sure is futile. I have very little hope that anyone will find my tiny dog in this area. Between the people, the streetcars, subways, busses, and other vehicles, plus the expansive area, it feels hopeless.

How could I have been so stupid? To leave him alone like I did? I should have just made sure my bibliography was complete the first time I read each book, then none of this would be happening right now. We'd be home, cuddled on my couch. This is all my fault.

"Dina?"

I look up to see Julie approaching me. The paramedic gave me the all clear with some signs to look for if I need to seek further treatment, but she was confident I'd be fine. I'm not confident I will. That has nothing to do with smoke inhalation.

"Is everyone okay? I can't believe this happened."

"Me either. Apparently, it was an electrical fire from faulty wiring connected to the automatic doors. There was a raging fire behind the wall before anyone knew what was happening.

Everyone got out safely, as far as we know." She sits on the bench beside me. "Any word on your dog? Holden said he was missing."

Well, it's happened. I've dehydrated myself enough, I can't produce any more tears. "No, nothing yet. I'm not sure if he's inside hiding, or if he got out unnoticed in the foot traffic."

"Oh, darling. I'm so sorry. I'm sure someone will find him. Have you asked the firefighters to look for him?"

I nod. "Holden's brother spoke with each of them and showed everyone a picture."

"Oh, good. That boy really likes you, you know? I can tell."

That comment nearly has my body turning blood into paste just to produce enough liquid to create new tears. "No, he broke up with me," I choke out. "And I don't even know why."

Julie wraps her right arm around my shoulders, pulling me toward her. "I may be an old spinster, but there's no mistaking the way he looks at you. Today has been a trying day, so maybe not now, but when you feel up to it, have a heart-to-heart with him. He wouldn't have shown up here with his brother if he didn't care." With that, she pats my knee, stands, and walks away to speak to someone else.

Seconds later, I hear my name again and spot my sister running through the crowd toward me. On her days at home, she often spends her days in loungewear. Today is no exception, and she didn't even take the time to change out of it before showing up here.

"Are you okay? You're sure you're not hurt? Where's Nacho?" She pulls me in for a tight, seated hug.

"Nobody has found him yet. Holden and his brother are looking. He's not even wearing his sweater. He's probably so cold." I know I'd be freezing if I didn't have this coat. Wet clothes and near-freezing temperatures are not a good combination.

"He's a dog, Dina. I know he's used to being pampered, but he's resilient. He'll be okay. And you know he's not letting anyone dognap him."

"Holden said the same thing."

We both laugh. Who knew my dog's grouchy demeanour would one day be helpful?

Angel asks several more times if I'm okay before she's convinced, then makes her way to the firefighters packing up their gear to ask if anyone has seen signs of Nacho. Judging by all the shaking heads, I'm assuming not. She also makes calls to the city's bylaw office, then the animal enforcement office and several area shelters to recruit some more help.

My phone buzzes, so I rush to yank it from my pocket to see if Holden is sending me good news.

Hollis: *On my way. Any luck?*

Dina: *Nothing yet. Holden is out looking.*

Hollis: *THE Holden?*

As far as Hollis is concerned, we hate Holden for breaking my heart. And maybe I should, but it's really hard to go from caring so much about someone to hating them, regardless of their actions or how deserving they may be of said hatred.

Dina: *Yes. And his brother. I'll update you when you get here.*

I tuck my phone back into my pocket as Angel returns to inform me no one saw any signs of Nacho, and he hasn't attacked any ankles, so chances are slim that he's inside. As much as I was hoping he wasn't inside because his little lungs wouldn't be able to tolerate much smoke, the thought of him being lost on the city streets is equally terrifying.

Angel and I work on a plan until Hollis arrives, then we divide and conquer. Hollis heads north toward Front Street just to be thorough, but there is so much open space with train tracks and greenery, that's hopeless. Angel travels south east to check the south side of Canoe Landing Park. I walk south along Bathurst toward Lakeshore. Now we have people in every direction. Still, big city, tiny dog.

Hours pass and none of the messages I've gotten from anyone have provided a glimmer of hope. I've talked to more people today than I have in my life, which is a bit ironic considering this day was meant to play out with my nose in some books, snuggling my dog—the two activities I partake in to *avoid* people.

The girls and I meet back up at the library, but Holden hasn't replied to my message that we were reconvening, and I don't have Boyd's number.

"How did Holden end up here?" Hollis asks, which I'm sure she's been dying to all day.

"I don't know. He just showed up here out of breath, like he had run the whole way. There was a news crew here, so he must have seen something and came to check on the library."

Hollis and Angel both stare at me.

"What do you want me to say? I didn't ask him to come, and I wasn't planning on ever seeing him again. It was as much a surprise to me."

"No, it's not that." Hollis looks at Angel again without turning her head away from me. "It sounds like he came for you and I just... I don't know. After everything, that seems a little strange. Mixed signals, I guess."

"Tell me about it." I won't mention how I cried into his chest. Nor how he kissed the top of my head or tried to put his arm around me. His signals have been hacked, crossed, and they're suffering from a power outage.

"Just be careful, okay? I don't want him worming his way back in and breaking your heart the next time his mother has an attitude problem. I appreciate that he's helping find Nacho, but that doesn't mean I forgive him for how he treated you." Hollis pulls me in for a hug.

She's right. As much as I hoped him being here means more than it does, I can't forgive him.

Angel wraps her arms around us both. "You know I'm not opposed to physical violence if the situation calls for it."

Hollis and I both laugh. I've always admired my sister's strength. Without her, I would have been lost years ago, but her presence through this situation with Holden has been invaluable.

We're all getting cold since the air is damp, the sun is setting, and the temperature is dropping. Nacho must be freezing. Suddenly, I'm overcome with sadness again and start sobbing while wrapped in the arms of my sister and best friend.

"Shh. It will be okay. We're going to find him." Angel rubs my back in soothing circles, like only a big sister can. "Everything will be fine. There are a lot of eyes looking for him and I gave them my number. The second I hear something, we'll be right there."

I sniffle as Hollis and Angel release our embrace and the cool air becomes really noticeable without collective body heat. I can only hope Nacho has found a non-rabid raccoon or sewer rat to snuggle up with to keep warm—even if they are three times the size of him.

Just as I'm picturing Nacho trying to infiltrate a city rat's hideout, Boyd rounds the corner, rubbing his hands together and blowing on them. "Any word from Holden?"

I shake my head. "I'm assuming you didn't have any luck either?"

"No, sorry, Dina. I started in the pet store you guys go to and then branched out from there. No sign of him, but I gave everyone my number."

My interaction with Boyd was limited, but I'm pretty confident he doesn't share the same prickly demeanour as his mother. He's been friendly and kind, even if he always seems distracted.

"Thanks for trying. I know you're busy and probably have a hundred other things to be doing."

"Listen, Dina..." Boyd shoves his hands in his coat pockets and exhales a breath that disappears in a mist. "I know things with you and my brother are—"

"Dina, look!" Angel shouts, slapping me on the shoulder.

The sight cures my laboured breathing better than any oxygen tank.

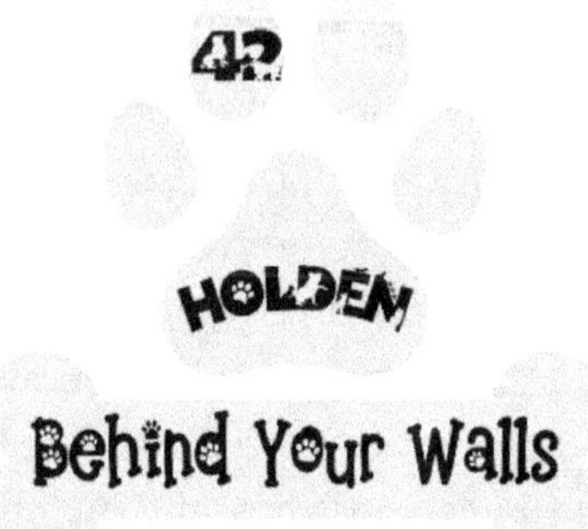

Dina's face when I cross the street with Nacho wrapped in my jacket is worth the miserable cold I'm bound to have for the next few days.

She runs toward me with a wide smile and tears streaming down her cheeks.

"My baby! You found him!" She pulls Nacho from my arms without looking at me. It appears there's only one male who she's excited to see, but I have no right to be upset about that.

"He was over near the Fort York Visitor Centre, hiding behind one of the cannons."

Dina laughs and sniffles loudly, clutching Nacho to her chest. "Of course he was. The little war lord has been itching to figure those things out." She pulls my sister's jacket up to wipe the tears from her eyes, creating two wet patches on the dark pink fabric. "Thank you, Holden. You didn't have to come, but I can't thank you enough."

I glance up to see Hollis and Angel staring at me with a mix of emotions on their faces. No doubt they hate me for hurting Dina—I hate myself for it, too. This sequence of events has made things crystal clear for me. I'm not going to be Napoleon Bonaparte; a great man, ruined by stupid decisions. Fearing I'll never get a chance to say it again, I remind her, "I love you, Minnie."

Dina snuggles her little dog, wrapped in my jacket, not looking at me. "We can't do this, Holden. I appreciate what you did for me today, but you don't love me. I'm not sure you ever really did. Not enough, anyway." She unwraps Nacho, handing me the jacket with one hand and tucking him inside hers. "Maybe I'll see you around."

"Please, just… now isn't the time to explain, but I do love you. Breaking up with you wasn't really my choice. I mean—"

"Let me stop you there." She steps closer to me, her tears long gone and now replaced with a palpable anger. "Last I checked, you were a grown man. So don't claim that your actions were anything *but* your choice. Don't put this on anyone else. You and you alone broke my heart. I don't need to know why. I don't need to hear you skirt responsibility. What I need is to move on and focus on what I should have been focusing on before you crashed into my life, only to leave me in tears. You, of all people, know those who don't learn history are doomed to repeat it. But I am well aware of our history, Dickens. I laid awake at night, replaying it for the last two months. I *will not* repeat it."

Her words, coupled with the conviction with which she's saying them, twists my heart and stomach in opposite directions. Like I'm having the life wrung out of me. I'm not sure I've ever felt such deep emotional pain before. Even when I broke up with her, it hurt, but in my heart it wasn't the end. This… it feels final.

Today has been an emotional day; both Dina and Nacho should get home to dry off and warm up. But the fear gripping me at the thought of letting her go right now is preventing me from saying another word.

"Good luck with everything, Holden. Thanks again for your help."

My brother claps me on the back of the shoulder. "We should let these ladies get home."

I nod, even though silently I'm screaming no.

Dina walks away without looking back. I watch as she climbs in the back of a black Range Rover, Angel hops in the front, and Hollis gets in the back on the driver's side. I feel a swell of pride seeing her climb in the car, even as they drive away.

"Come on. Let's get home. I'll make you a coffee."

"Yeah, thanks." We start walking north, but we're no more than twenty metres from the library before I blurt, "I screwed up bad."

Boyd exaggerates an exhale. "You were given an impossible choice. I don't think there was a way to handle the situation without something being screwed up. But it's Mum that screwed up. Not you."

We might live together, but Boyd and I haven't been close since we share bunk beds. Today was an anomaly. A nice one. Despite the fact we spent far more time apart than together, it felt nice to know my brother had my back.

A few steps later, Boyd asks, "What are you going to do?"

"I don't know."

"Yeah, you do."

I look at my brother as we walk in stride toward King Street. "What do you mean?"

"I mean, you know what you're going to do. You just need to convince yourself you can."

A street car squeals along the tracks in the opposite direction, giving me pause to consider his words. "It's not a straightforward decision. You know how Mum is."

"You know, I'm familiar with the concept that some things can be open to interpretation. That sometimes people do the wrong things for the right reason and they can be forgiven. But in this case, Mum is wrong. Full stop."

"I know that! You don't think I know that? But that doesn't mean Dina deserves to be treated like a second-class citizen. This isn't about me."

Boyd and I finally reach home, where he slides off his shoes and heads straight for the kitchen, continuing his big brother speech. "Mum will get over it. She loves you, and despite her determination to control certain aspects of our lives, she can't. You say this isn't about you, but really, it isn't about Mum."

I shake my head as I sink into the couch. Everyone seems to think this situation is easily resolved. Am I just too much of a coward to try?

"This sad face of yours is going to be the death of me." Phoebe tosses a box of tissues in my lap, distracting me from replaying my last conversation with Dina for the seventy-third time. Or thereabouts.

I set her weapon of choice on the end table, paste on a cheesy fake smile, grit my teeth, and try to speak. "Is this better?"

"No, that's terrifying. You're going to scare my child."

I relax my features, and they automatically return to my perpetual scowl. "She survived your singing; she's equipped to handle anything, now."

"I'm not that—"

"Yes, you are. Please don't try to prove it because I'm already miserable enough."

Phoebe places Grace in her swing, pressing the button to sway the child into La-La Land, now that she tolerates it. "Why don't you call her?"

My chest deflates from the long sigh I release. "Everyone keeps saying that like it's easy. But I saw her. She doesn't want anything to do with me anymore. You didn't see the look on her face."

"Maybe she just—"

"Phoebe, I appreciate what you're trying to do, but she told me she wants to move on. That she won't repeat our history ever again."

My sister drops into the seat beside me and rests her head on my shoulder. The two of us are quite a pair. Her rocking the new mom look with her frizzy hair piled atop her head and a stained oversized T-shirt; me in worn university sweats with a grease stain down the front and overgrown hair that's desperate for a cut.

"I love you, little brother. But you're wrong about this. You need to make your own choice. When Aaron—"

I stand in a rush, leaving Phoebe to topple over onto my now vacated seat. "This is nothing I haven't heard already, but it's easy to say when you're not making the choice yourself. When it's not someone *you love* having to face the consequences. I appreciate that you're trying to help, but it doesn't." Rather than waiting for her to reply, I add, "I'd like everyone to respect that I'm trying to do the right thing for Dina." Then I walk through her front hall and out the door to retreat into my own house that I resent more with each passing day.

Up in my office, I pull up my working copy of my thesis proposal and stare at it. Every ounce of motivation I once had for this project has been zapped out of me. So I search for a little flicker of inspiration in the album of old photos on my phone. Where all I find is the woman I love, her misunderstood chihuahua, and the smile I don't think I'll ever wear again.

43

DINA

It'll Be a Long Time

Today's events are the culmination of almost six years of work. Countless hours of researching, reading, studying, analyzing, writing, and revising. The nausea pooling in my stomach isn't on account of facing the thesis advisory committee. It's not a fear that my second reader won't show up. It's because this marks the end of an era, and I'm not sure I'm ready to face what comes next. To go from master's student Dina to a functioning adult with a job and other responsibilities.

Ready or not, here it comes.

Angel loaned me a blazer and dress pants so I can look the part when I walk in to contend with the serious faces poised to decide my future. I paired the smart suit with a sky blue blouse and sensible shoes for the weather. I'm taking a ride-share by myself for the first time in my life. One thing I've learned from my brief relationship with Holden is that if I want something to change, I need to do it myself. Relying on someone else is cowardly. And I, Dina Blake, am no coward. Not anymore.

I exit my condo building, where I find my ride waiting out front. I climb in the back and notice the driver is a gorgeous brunette woman who is about my age. On one hand, that makes me feel less likely to be kidnapped, but on the other, I wonder how well she drives. That's really judgemental, but she can't have many years of driving experience under her belt.

"Big day?" she says as she pulls her Honda Civic onto Fleet Street to circle back around.

"The biggest." I take a deep breath to ease the mounting anxiety—from both my academic pursuits and riding in a rolling death trap. "The past two years of my life come down to this day. Thesis defence."

She glances in the rear-view mirror and smiles. "Wow! That's amazing, girl. Good for you. Smart and beautiful; a double threat."

"I don't know about that. The only thing I seem to threaten is my sanity."

"Don't we all?" She chuckles, then continues to drive our conversation and the car simultaneously. She does such an excellent job at distracting me, I don't even notice we're pulling onto campus until she rolls to a stop.

"This is it." I close my eyes, preparing myself for this pivotal moment in my future.

My driver spins around to face me. "You've got this, okay?" She scribbles something on a small piece of paper and hands it to me. "I'm not supposed to do this, but if you need a ride home, text me. My name is Aven, by the way. Aven Becker. I'm invested now, so I want to hear how it goes." The smile she gives me seems to regulate my breathing.

I take the paper and inspect it to make sure I can read the numbers. I'm splurging on a car to get here, but I wasn't planning to take a ride home too. Then again, now that my studies are done, there's nothing stopping me from getting a job. I've successfully made it through six years of post-secondary education within my tight budget. If there's ever a day to indulge, it's today.

"Okay. But if you're busy, don't worry. It could be a few hours." Before I exit the car, I face Aven and add, "I'm Dina, by the way. Thank you for this. For the distraction and pumping me up. You have no idea how much I needed both."

"Go embrace your inner warrior, Dina. Nothing can stop you."

I climb out of the little blue sedan and realize I've overcome a lot in my life. Aven may be a stranger, but her words give me a new wave of inspiration.

I've got this.

Defence of my work took sixty-four minutes. I was afraid I'd chosen the wrong thesis to defend, but once I got speaking about it and answering the questions asked, I knew I was prepared. I knew my material inside and out—thanks to our AQ5R method—and more importantly, I was passionate about it.

I was so passionate, that now, standing outside in the cool spring air, I feel as if I've come down from a high and I need something to mimic the excitement I felt twenty minutes ago. Hollis and Angel are busy, so even though I'm sure they'd be happy to hear my news, I don't want to disrupt them.

There's one person I do want to call, but I won't. I don't even want to post anything on social media to share this moment because I know it will sting when Holden doesn't respond. It's not like I have a wide circle of online friends. My largest social media platform is *Goodreads*, and I don't think anyone on there cares that I've achieved this milestone.

So instead of calling the one person I want to talk to, I call a virtual stranger.

"Heya."

"Um... Aven? This is Dina. You dropped me off earlier."

A soft chuckle confirms she remembers me. "How did it go?"

"Good. I think. I think it went well." I take a deep breath to stop myself from blabbering. Standing in front of the group of accomplished academics didn't make me this nervous. I really should practice speaking to real-life people more often. "I'll find out soon if I passed one or both portions."

"I'm sure I'm not the first to say it, but congratulations! Do you need a lift now?"

Her assumption has me lost in a sequence of sad thoughts. The fact this is the biggest day of my life, and the first person to congratulate me is a stranger. The fact I don't have a network of people to call who would sing a song for me at the bar and celebrate with me. What good is a degree when I have no one around me to mark these moments?

"Dina? Do you need a ride?" she repeats.

I shake my head to rid myself of the depressing reality that my life has become. "Oh, I don't mind walking, but I didn't want to leave you in suspense." That's not entirely true. Really, I just wanted to tell someone.

"No, girl. I got you. I'm just dropping someone at the Eaton Centre. Let me clock out and I'll be there in ten minutes. Same place I dropped you off?"

She sounds determined, so I agree. In the few minutes I have before she arrives, I rush to find an ATM to withdraw some money. If she's clocking out, I can't pay her through the app like I did earlier.

Aven pulls up in the exact spot she did less than two hours ago, giving me an enthusiastic wave. I walk to the rear passenger door, stopping myself short. For the first time in my life, I climb into the front seat. It's not the driver's seat, but it still feels a lot more in control. It feels symbolic of what's to come in my future. Like a power move.

Thirty seconds into our drive, I blurt, "You know, until a couple of months ago, I hadn't been in a car since I was thirteen?"

"What? Why?"

Another way I've grown, I'm no longer afraid of my past. "My parents died in a car accident. I've been too terrified ever since."

Aven jerks her head to look at me, which I only notice from the corner of my eye as I pick at my fingernails.

"That's awful. I'm really sorry."

More growth. My reaction isn't to get defensive and tell her I don't want her pity. Instead, I take a breath and say, "Thanks. This is a new era for me."

"Amen to that. The world is your oyster, or however the saying goes. Actually, that doesn't make any sense at all. Why would anyone want to be restricted to an oyster?"

I chuckle as I watch pedestrians pass in a blur along University Avenue. "It's from Shakespeare, but it's been altered from its original meaning. Now it just means that everything is open to you, and you might find something special."

"Okay, I knew you were smart, but how do you know random things like that?" Aven's smile is wide and bright, eliciting a matching one from me.

"I read a lot."

We turn onto Fort York Boulevard as Aven replies, "Whatever you're doing, don't give up. I have a good feeling about you, Dina. You're going places."

As she pulls up in front of my condo, I scramble to take some cash from my bag.

"Same price as the way there?"

She puts the car in park and rests a hand on top of my arm digging through my bag. "Your money is no good to me. I didn't ask you to call so I could make money off of you. You looked like you needed a friend. My treat."

I'm speechless. For all the years I shut people out, I probably missed out on a lot of genuinely good people. Of all the growth I've made in the past few months, this is the most life changing. I'm not going to continue isolating myself because I'm afraid to lose people I love.

44

HOLDEN

A Thousand Days

Dina hasn't posted anything on social media since before the library fire two-and-a-half weeks ago. I didn't realize how much those status updates and silly selfies were keeping me afloat. My entire world has imploded, and the only person who doesn't try to give me advice is Grace. That makes her my favourite, even if she's constantly covering me in drool because she's teething.

My thesis proposal is stalled, my advisor is already threatening to quit, and I can't type more than ten words at a time. Making sense of the endless research I've done is another issue entirely. It's all hopeless.

I did what I thought was the right thing, but my family has still fallen apart as a result. My siblings have been boycotting family dinners in solidarity. My mother hates me for turning them against her, despite their insistence it was her actions driving their decision. We tried to have a conversation as a family, but she refuses to change her stance. I think in her mind, it's become more a matter of winning.

Winning what? That's what I can't figure out. She just doesn't want to concede or admit she's wrong. Her stubborn nature has ruined everything she held so dear our entire lives.

Meanwhile, I'm left mourning the loss of someone who is less than two kilometres away, not able to explain why love isn't enough. That it's hatred steering our course.

"How's it coming?" Boyd pops his head in the office doorway, wearing his work uniform.

I blow out a long breath that says more than an actual answer would. "Stuck on the synopsis."

"Is it the synopsis you're stuck on? Or Dina?"

I spin in my chair to face my big brother. Our relationship has been a lot better over the past few weeks, and I almost feel guilty that we've bonded over something so... awful? Stupid? Disgraceful? All of the above. Along with Sam, Phil, and Phoebe, Boyd has gone above and beyond to cheer me up or encourage me to stay focused. It's a nice change from the distant cohabitation arrangement we had for the past several years.

"I don't know what to do. She..."

Boyd steps into our shared office he rarely enters at the same time as me, plopping himself on the edge of his desk. "What do you want? Mum aside. If it was your choice, what would you do?"

"We've been over this. It's not that simple. I can't just make a decision and pretend it doesn't have anything to do with family. Or that it wouldn't have an effect on Dina."

"I'm not asking real life. I'm asking hypothetical."

"Since when do you ask hypotheticals? I thought everything had to be presented with logic and evidence."

Boyd is nothing if not pragmatic. But he insists, "This time, hypothetical is logical. What would you do if there were no external factors?"

My stomach is in knots because my heart is so confident in my answer, but my mind knows it's not possible. Playing fairytale isn't going to help matters. "I love her. It's as simple as that. And I know it probably sounds crazy because we haven't known each other that long—"

"It's not crazy." His interruption is full of conviction and understanding.

For some reason, my brother's validation is important to me. Even while we're talking about no external influences on my relationship with Dina. The real-life support matters. I know Phoebe supports me, too.

"Have you thought about telling her the truth?" Boyd flashes a sympathetic smile with one side of his mouth.

"Yes. No. I've thought about it, but every time I come to the conclusion it's selfish of me. Just because I want to be with her doesn't mean she should feel obligated to put up with things she doesn't deserve." The mention of this reality still makes me sick to my stomach. No matter how I spin it, there's no scenario in which it makes sense.

"I know we haven't been close over the past few years, and that's on me. I put my life on hold when Dad got sick, but that was my choice. And to be honest, it was an easy excuse to drop out because I was barely passing my classes." He stares down at the floor as I watch in shock. This is a brand new revelation. "Taking that break renewed my focus and now I'm in a better place because of it." He rubs a hand on the back of his neck and scrunches his face. "Point being, I've always wanted what was best for you. If you ever had a different impression, it's because I was mad at myself."

A huge part of me wants to get up and wrap my big brother in a bear hug, but I get the impression he's not done. I nod to encourage him to continue.

"One thing I've learned, though, is that success isn't about academic or career accolades. None of that means anything if you're not happy." He chuckles, making his face relax. "I don't know when I turned into a Hallmark card."

Now I don't care if he's finished speaking or not. I stand and pull him in for a tight, brotherly hug. For the first time in years. I'm man enough to admit I get a little choked up for no real reason. Or maybe a lot of reasons.

Because one relationship that's important to me is healing, while another is still a gaping, oozing wound.

Because my mother has prioritized her bias over my happiness.

Because I feel lost, with no clear direction for a life I had carefully mapped out.

"You've made me so proud—you and Phoebe both, to be honest. You both inspire me to pursue what's important, and if Dina is important, don't let her go. Give her a chance to decide."

My brother is not what I'd ever call an open book. He has a natural way of commanding attention, but he's also the first person to avoid any limelight. He's notoriously reserved and closed off. This sharing session is the first time he's ever confessed actual feelings. So while I'm busy processing that, I'm trying to consider his advice, too. I don't think he'd intentionally steer me wrong, but I don't see a way out of this. Not unless Mum changes her mind, which won't happen.

"Thanks, man. Sorry if I've been a wet blanket the past couple of months."

"Nah, don't sweat it. I get it. More than you know."

That's ominous. I want to continue this deep dive into his feelings, but before I can ask what he's talking about, he brushes his hands down his clothes, mutters a quick "See ya later," and he's gone.

His departure leaves me alone with thoughts I can't make sense of. In all my years of studying, diving deeper into an inquiry helps clarify the facts. When you need an answer, you search for it, and eventually, you find what you're looking for. There are few historical mysteries that have plagued historians for centuries. Was King Arthur a real person? What happened to the Ark of the Covenant? Did Atlantis really exist? Some things we'll never know. And based on the last several weeks of analyzing, questioning, and obsessing over a solution, I'm confident my current plight will go down in history without answers, too.

I drop back into my chair, which makes it roll across the hardwood a few feet. Instead of resisting, I go along for the ride. My computer screen has gone black from inactivity, and since it put itself to sleep, I figure it's time I do the same. The fact it's 11am is irrelevant. So is my impending deadline. I've been letting that blinking cursor taunt me for two hours. The fourteen words I added to the twelve-page document hardly qualify as a contribution to society's understanding of anything.

So I leave my sleeping computer, walk into my bedroom, draw the blinds, and crawl back into bed.

Heartbreak hurts like the dickens.

45

DINA

Rise and fall

Now I understand what Holden was talking about all those months ago. This limbo between finishing your mammoth tasks and waiting for results. If I fail either the written or oral portion of my thesis, I'll have six months to make corrections and try again. If I fail a second time, I'll be "excused" from the university. All of my hard work would be for nothing. That cannot happen. I did not survive on ramen and processed cheese for the past three years just to fail.

The waiting game is torturous, so I've been occupying my time by taking Nacho to observe other dogs at Coronation Dog Park, since the one at Red Canoe Landing has been tainted forever. I can't look at a red canoe without feeling the crushing weight of heartbreak all over again. Based on the assumption I passed and I'll be able to start a job in the near future, I even purchased a few new toys for Nacho to replace his deceased squirrels.

Happy chihuahua, happy life. Right?

Aven and I have become fast friends, but it's been less than two weeks since we met, so I'm still treading lightly. We went out with Hollis, Angel, and a couple of Angel's friends this past weekend for a girls' night, and the break from my own nagging thoughts was nice.

Today, though, I'm lounging on my sofa watching a mini-series on YouTube. Of all the choices, I settled on *War and Peace*. The entire series is a little over six hours, and I'm halfway through, with no plans of pausing between episodes.

I hear a knock at my door, which sends Nacho scurrying across the wood flooring to let the person know their presence is unwelcome. I assume it's some dumb kids who got into the building and think it's a funny April Fool's prank, so I don't pause my show. Except a few seconds later, another softer knock sounds, along with a quiet, "Dina?"

My heart leaps into my throat at the voice. I rush to shut off my laptop—because I've never had the budget for a real TV—then grab Nacho and close him in my bedroom. I smooth my ratty house clothes as I walk to the door. There's no hope of making this outfit presentable, but a girl can try.

I peek through the peephole to confirm I'm not imagining what I heard. Nope, I'm not losing my mind. When I open the door, I see one person I never expected to see at my door.

"Hi." I'm stumped on how to proceed from here. 'How can I help you?' No; too formal. 'How do you know where I live?' No; that's irrelevant right now. Or 'What do you want?' No; that's rude. I settle for a blank stare.

"Can I come in for a minute?" Boyd asks with a shy smile.

"Sure. I… don't have anything to offer except water."

He steps in slowly, scanning the small space. "That's fine. I won't stay long." He doesn't move any farther inside than necessary, tucking his hands in his pockets. "My brother loves you. I know you doubted that after the fire, but I don't doubt it at all."

Of all the awkward conversations Holden and I ever had, talking to his brother about our relationship is a hundred times worse. Once upon a time—a very short time—I didn't doubt

Holden's love either. I had no questions about whether what I felt for him was reciprocated. But that backfired.

"Maybe he thinks he does or thought he did, but he doesn't."

"He does." Boyd runs his hand over his hair that looks like Holden's would if he cut or styled it. "There was more to it than you know, and he'd probably punch me if he knew I was here, but I can't let him live with regrets forever."

It doesn't take a genius to understand that 'more' is their mother. "I respect his decision. He chose his mother over someone he barely knew, and I can't blame him for that."

"You know?" Boyd's hazel eyes widen as he backs up into my living room until his legs hit the edge of the sofa and he drops on a cushion.

"I assumed it had to do with your mom, yes. Our dinner was so awkward, people in Iceland probably felt the tension."

He shakes his head, but not one single hair shifts. "It's not... I get why he didn't want to say anything, but he can't move on. He can't forgive himself. And it's not even his fault."

"I'll tell you the same thing I told him. At the end of the day, it was his choice. But, like I said, I respect his decision. As someone who doesn't have parents, if they were around, I'd take their opinion seriously."

Boyd leans forward, resting his elbows on his knees, and sinks his face into his palms. So many seconds pass, I'm convinced the conversation is over, until he blurts, "Our mum told him to break up with you because of your skin colour."

For some reason, that never occurred to me. I drop in one of my wooden dining chairs and stare at the artwork Angel created hanging above the sofa, wrestling with a slew of emotions. Anger, upset, dejection, resentment, outrage. They all make an appearance.

It's not a new concept for me. Being raised with my aunt, Angel and I were too brown to be white, but too white to be brown. As if being a hybrid of two skin colours makes a person unwelcome in their own family. Before our parents died, my heritage never crossed my mind. I was just Dina. But suddenly, being without parents who loved us unconditionally, Angel and I faced a world where we weren't welcome.

After I process Boyd's confession, I drone on, explaining my previous experience with the same mentality. Turns out, along with their United Kingdom roots, Imogen and my aunt have a lot in common. Not good things.

"I'm sorry, Dina."

"It's fine. It's really not your fault, and it won't be the last time I deal with it, I'm sure. I've been pretty lucky to see a fraction of the discrimination a lot of people do." I choke on my words because even though that's true, it has caused a lot of heartache.

"Holden is a mess. His proposal for his thesis is due in a few days and he can't string a sentence together. I looked over his shoulder yesterday, and under methodology, he wrote, 'I'll read stuff.'"

Romance novels never told me that love comes with so much fear. You're no longer held captive by your own fears, but by worry and concern for those you love. When Nacho was missing, I experienced a fear more intense than I've ever felt. Riding in a car was nothing by comparison. But hearing that Holden is struggling to complete his thesis proposal is another kind of fear. Because I love him and I don't want him to fail.

Still, I try to dismiss the truth because it's done me no favours thus far. "We didn't even know each other that long. He shouldn't be hung up on me."

"Are you hung up on him?"

I freeze. "That's irrelevant."

"No, it's not. Holden isn't hung up on you. He's in love with you, and that has never changed. The only reason he broke up with you is because our mother has some narrow-minded way of thinking, which was made infinitely worse by the division in the Royal Family. I kid you not; the woman is obsessed with royal drama.”

“That’s ridiculous. For one, there are two sides to every story, so whatever drama people have is theirs to deal with. No one outside of that relationship can truly grasp what’s happening. Two, last I checked, Holden wasn’t sixth in line for the throne.”

“Trust me. I know. It’s silly, since whoever is sixth in line will never be at the top of the list, anyway.” He chuckles, and I get the impression that was meant to be a joke, but I can’t laugh.

I sigh, long and intentional. “The best I can do is let him know I forgive him. I know after he found Nacho, emotions were high, and I was harsh with him. I’ll apologize and tell him I don’t hate him.” Despite his initials, I don’t feel that way toward him at all. I still love him, but it hurts too much to hold on to something that can’t happen.

Boyd pushes himself to stand, straightening his apron. “That’s not the outcome I was hoping for, but I understand. I’m sorry you were ever put in this position to begin with.”

“Again, it’s not your fault. But thank you for explaining it to me.”

“I’ve got to get to work, but if you ever want to stop in at *Just Add Coffee* on Queen Street, I’ll make you a flat white that’ll knock your socks off. My treat.”

I smile at Boyd and walk him to the door.

Fear may prevent me from pursuing the relationship I want, but it won’t stop me from making sure Holden is able to pursue his dreams without me holding him back.

My chat with Boyd left me a combination of sad, surprised, and determined. With emotions all over the map, I confide in my sister about how to proceed. She is justifiably angry with Imogen for dredging up wounds we'd both long buried, but she's supportive of my decision.

The least I can do is put the past to rest and move on with my future. Even if I can't do that with one person I wanted there.

45

HOLDEN

All I Want

Despite the efforts of my friends and siblings, nothing is pulling me out of my funk. With no hope of anything changing, I'm going through the motions, but my passion has disappeared. I'd say it's stuck somewhere in a fourth-floor condo on Fort York Boulevard.

It's been three weeks since I saw Dina. For the first time since the day of the fire, I suddenly feel consumed by anger toward my mother. I'm stuck between two hard choices, but the longer time goes on, the more clear my decision gets.

With renewed confidence in my choice, I march to my parents' house and walk in without knocking. The space feels foreign. Unwelcoming. Not like the home I grew up in.

I find her in the kitchen, puttering away at something she's deemed important.

"You know one of the main things I've learned from history?"

She looks at me, no hint of surprise at seeing me here.

"Nothing good has ever come from failing to consider someone else's perspective. Human beings have caused hatred, division, violence, even full-blown wars, and it largely boils down to failing to see that the other parties involved as their own entities, with the right to decide for themselves."

My mother stares at me, her typical stoic glare that says a thousand things behind her hazel eyes. "This is not the same."

"It is Mum. What you're doing *is* the same. I don't know if you can't see or you don't care, but I'm miserable. I've *always* listened to you, and I've always appreciated everything you've done, but this time, I can't. Not anymore. I hope you'll come around and see things from my perspective. Until then, I'm making my own decision."

I don't wait for her to reply. A respectful conversation with my mother will be a priority in the near future, but for now, she can digest everything I've said. I need to see Dina. I pull my phone from my pocket to text her as I walk out the front door of my parents' home. A photo of her and me together the night of Sam's gig back in November serves as a reminder of how that night changed the direction of my life forever. And I don't want to turn it back.

"Hi."

I stop walking, looking to see where that voice came from. My eyes land on my front step. On Dina. On her tentative, but still gorgeous, smile. Her long curly hair and deep brown eyes. Her olive-green jacket and knee-high boots. I take it all in. Every inch of her.

"Hey. How did you—"

"Boyd. He… uh… he came to see me on Saturday."

That sentence causes my eyebrows to collapse together.

"He told me why you broke up with me. So I'm not here to make things harder or to ask you to make a choice. You're lucky to have a family who loves you so much. I guess… well, I'm just here to tell you it's okay. No hard feelings. Toward you or your mother. She obviously wants what's best for you, so I respect that. I needed to tell you that in person." She fiddles with a button on her jacket for a moment. "Oh, and to thank you for helping me find Nacho. I don't know what I would have done without him."

I walk closer to her, and once she's within arms' reach, I place a hand on her forearm, guiding her down the single step. We're inches apart and the proximity immediately makes me whole again.

"Dina, I love you. You deserve so much better, and I refused to let you ever feel uncomfortable. But it was *never* because I didn't want you or didn't love you enough. I thought I was doing the right thing."

Tears are pooling in her eyes, which are like a death grip on my heart.

"But I'm selfish. My family may not be perfect… we're a mess most of the time… but we love each other in our own weird way. And if you'll let me, I'll love you with all that I have. And before you say anything, I'm not choosing you over my family. I'm choosing to give my mother time to see her mistake and discover how incredible you are."

She sniffles as a pair of tears trail down her pink cheeks. "What if she doesn't? I'd give anything to have even one more day with my mom. I'd hate myself for becoming a wedge between you and yours." She wipes her tears with the sleeve I'm not holding and straightens her posture. "I love you, Dickens, which is why I came to see your face one last time. To tell you, I understand why you made the choice you did, and I accept it, as much as it hurts. I want what's best for you too, even if that's not me." With that, she places a palm on my cheek, looks into my eyes for a brief second, then attempts to step past me.

"Wait!"

Dina and I both turn our attention to two doors down, and find my mother in her slippers, walking out her front door. Boyd exits behind her, wearing an uncharacteristic smile directed at me. He seems to have materialized out of thin air.

Mum shuffles down the sidewalk toward us. She stops a few feet away and releases a steadying breath, not looking at either of us. "I'm not okay with this, but I won't stop you."

If she came out here to mend fences, she's a long way off. "Mum, you know I love you, but you either accept Dina, or you continue this nonsense. Because if she'll have me… If she can forgive me—"

The sound of a door closing has the four of us turning our heads again, spotting Phoebe backing out her front door with a stroller. Boyd rushes over to help her traverse the step.

"What are you doing here?" Phoebe greets Dina with a big smile, ignoring the rest of us.

I deserve it though, because I've barely spoken to her since I stormed out of her house two weeks ago.

"I'm not entirely sure." Dina's posture is a case study on awkward body language. Arms crossed. Eyes directed at the ground. Teeth gnawing at her bottom lip.

"Grace and I are walking over to the Little Free Library a few blocks away, since the public library will be closed for a while. Want to walk with us?"

I love my sister, but her attempt to get Dina out of this situation is as obvious as the Cheeto stains on her sweater.

"We were in the middle of something. Can you give us a minute?" I ask.

She glances at Dina, then at the rest of us who have all formed some weird faction of the Ruin Holden's Relationship Club. I don't know if I'm the guest of honour or the president, but it needs to be disbanded.

"Sure. What are we in the middle of?"

I stammer, looking for the words because I don't want to make an awkward situation worse. "Mum was just apologizing… to Dina… and me. Yep, she was telling us how sorry she was for her lapse in judgement."

My mother glares at me and remains silent, telling me she's not falling for my ploy.

"Oh, for goodness' sake, Mum. Get over it, would ya? Holden is a grown man and he can date whoever he wants. Dina is lovely, and if you remember, you hated Aaron at first, too. Now he's the only one to compliment your dry pie crust."

The rest of us are stunned speechless, including Grace.

I'm the first one to break the silence. "She hated Aaron?" I thought Aaron was beyond reproach. Likeable on all accounts. Hardworking, respectful, kind. The epitome of a knight in shining armour. Having him next door even makes *me* feel safe.

"Oh, she thought he was a Gypsy or some nonsense. He had a lapse in his lease agreements when we started dating, so he stayed in a couple hostels or short-term rentals until he got into his next apartment." Phoebe looks at our mother, who actually returns the eye contact. "Point is, Mum, you have to give people a chance. No offence, but if I had listened to you, I would have missed out on the best part of my life, including this beautiful baby girl."

That revelation makes me feel like a total schmuck. That's probably what Phoebe was trying to tell me that day at her place. I didn't know Mum had tried to break up her and Aaron, too. But Phoebe had the guts to fight for the man she loved.

I'm such a coward.

I don't care if everyone is watching and listening. "Dina, I was wrong. I was wrong to let anyone come between us because only we know what we have. I can't blame you if you have doubts about us now, but I don't. You're everything I didn't know I needed. Please, can you forgive me? Can we try again?"

Dina keeps her eyes trained on the sidewalk, not hinting at an answer for several seconds. When she focuses on me, it's another punch to the gut. "You broke my heart. Really shattered it. I'm not sure it's that easy to just pick up where we left off. I didn't come here to mend fences; I came to help us both move on."

My throat is painfully dry as I struggle to redirect the conversation. "Then we start over. I know I screwed up, trust me. I broke my own heart too, and it was the worst decision I've ever made. But tell me what you want me to do, and I'll do it. Wherever you want to start."

The long silence is painful. I can feel the anticipation radiating off of our spectators, like this is the season finale of the year's greatest primetime drama. I'd expect nothing less than a pivotal moment in our relationship being marked by awkwardness.

Everyone collectively takes a deep breath as Dina starts to speak. "I guess we start by putting each other back together."

I can actually feel my face light up as I register her words. "Yeah?"

"Yeah." She nods as more tears spill down her face. Tears that I hope are ones of happiness.

I react instinctively, rushing forward, wrapping my arms around her waist and spinning us both. My lips find hers and without missing a beat, we find our perfect rhythm once again. I missed everything about her. More than the way she tastes or how her skin feels. I missed her mind. Her generous spirit. Her spunky clap backs. I pull away so I can take in her smile, which I may have missed most of all.

"One other thing," she adds.

"Nacho ran out of squirrels?"

She laughs, and I stand corrected. I missed *that* most of all.

"No. Well, he is, but we'll talk about that later." She pauses, her face brightening even more. "I got my master's."

I nearly drop her, but she catches herself by grabbing tighter around my neck.

"What? How did you…? When? This is huge."

"This morning. I mean, nothing official yet, but my advisor called me to say I passed." Her smile falters as I gently set her down. "I wanted to call to tell you, but… it didn't seem right."

"Dina, I'm so sorry. You have no idea how proud I am. How proud your parents would be."

She nods, still battling with tears. I wipe one away with my thumb, then slide my hand into her hair to pull her in for another kiss.

My ridiculous siblings start clapping in the background, but I don't pay them any mind. I get lost in Dina, and if I have it my way, I'll never miss another big moment in her life again.

DIMA
epilogue

We Are One

"I'm so proud of you, Dr. Edwards."

"That sounds really weird. All I can picture is being in a restaurant or on an airplane and someone shouts, 'Is anyone here a doctor?' I raise my hand and realize someone is having a heart attack. 'Oh, sorry. Not that kind of doctor. But if you need any information on historical gender roles, let me know.'" He gives a cheesy wink and two thumbs up.

That scenario makes me laugh—only because it's hypothetical. Someone having a heart attack is no laughing matter. "You know, I think that could make a great book. What would you call it?"

He leads me into our living room, responding, "*Doctor Dickens Doesn't Save the World*."

"Well, I'd read that one. As long as you don't spoil the ending."

"I'm learning to enjoy a surprise ending." Holden smirks as he drops on the sofa, pulling my hand so I follow suit. We only have a few minutes alone before our company will arrive.

It's been eighteen months since Holden and I reconciled, and we haven't looked back. His mother is coming around, but still seems upset that Holden went against her wishes. I'd be lying if I said it didn't bother me, but I hope one day she'll see I'm just a woman who loves her son. Because of the tension, he moved out of the house with his brother a year ago and we bought a small condo closer to the university—and my sister.

"What do you think about us taking a weekend away? Maybe The Couples' Resort in Algonquin or camping in Tobermory? I've heard they're both beautiful, and I've never been."

Excitement bubbles through me at his suggestion. We've talked about our next step—at length—and my one stipulation was that he finish his PhD first. Now that he's done, it makes sense for us to take that leap. That sounds like a perfect romantic getaway to, at the very least, discuss a future wedding. I have no doubts that's what I want.

"That sounds perfect. Just let me know the days you have planned so I can book them off work." My job as an assistant librarian—at the renovated public branch that was destroyed by the fire—has been so rewarding and a great learning experience. Ideally, I'd like to get into a university library someday, but for now, I'm content working under Julie and learning the ropes. If Holden takes on a job as a professor, that may require relocating, so I can re-evaluate when the time comes.

"Which one do you think you'd like better? Hiking or hot tubs?" he asks.

"Probably hiking. That way we can bring Nacho. He might even find some real squirrels, and learn that he's not as tough as he thinks he is."

My handsome graduate laughs. Then, like he's been waiting all day, he pulls me in for a kiss. "Hiking it is, then. I've wanted to visit Tobermory for years."

We're interrupted by a knock at the door. We shut Nacho in the bedroom, because he still has a tendency to snarl at people, though he is getting better. Boyd arrives, looking smart and handsome in equal measure. I've been so happy watching his and Holden's relationship return to one that resembles friends as much as brothers.

Not long after Boyd, Phil and Sam enter. Sam has his guitar, and Phil holds a twelve-pack of beer. Holden welcomes them inside, where they greet me as enthusiastically as they always do.

We congregate in the living room, Sam in the lone chair, Holden and me on the loveseat, Phil and Boyd on the sofa. It's only a few more minutes before Angel, Hollis, Aven, Phoebe, Aaron, and Grace arrive. It's a full house, but that doesn't stop the little toddler heading straight for her favourite uncle, whom she calls "Unk". It's been a point of pride for Holden, who insists I trained Grace to call him "hunk". I told him I considered teaching her his actual nickname, but was afraid it would go terribly wrong. Holden lifts her onto his lap and kisses her head.

Baby fever may not be an actual medical condition, but I swear I suffer from symptoms every time I see these two together.

Thirty minutes later, a knock at the door interrupts the clamoring consuming the living room.

"Pizza's here!" Phil shouts as he jogs toward the door. He swings it open, but the people on the other side aren't holding a pizza.

Alfie and Imogen Edwards step into the front hall. Alfie is holding his wife's hand, looking confident, but Mrs. Edwards is staring at the floor. Panic rises in my chest seeing them here. On one hand, I'm grateful they've shown up, but on the other, I'm afraid they'll come in between us again. It's already difficult to swallow the fact I've unwillingly come between parents and children.

"Dad." Holden reaches out his hand to shake his father's. Then, with a brief hesitation, he hugs his mother. "Mum."

Boyd, Phoebe, Aaron, Sam, Phil and Grace all go through the process to greet the newcomers. Angel and my friends follow suit. I'm last in line. Alfie gives me a weak side hug and a smile, but says nothing. When I step in front of Imogen, I'm begging my hands to stop shaking on account of the nerves coursing through me. In what I'd consider one of the greatest shocks of my life, she wraps her arms around me—my torso and arms, so I'm locked in her hold—and the realization she isn't going to body slam me offers little relief. She's hugging me. And... crying.

Without the ability to pat her back or offer some sort of comfort, I'm stuck and desperate for a rescue. I plead with Holden, and now, after two years, he's finally learned to pick up on my signals.

So what does he do? Wraps his arms around both of us. Maybe he's privy to something I'm not, but I'm wondering if I should fear for my life.

An eternity later, Holden and Imogen release me so I can use my arms again. Though I'm not sure for what. The way the tiny woman is staring at me, I don't think I'll have to fight my way out.

"I'm sorry," she whispers. Literally whispers.

Sorry for what? The awkward extended hug? Pretending I haven't existed for nearly two years? For giving your son the cold shoulder because he stood up for himself? Or for the prejudice against me based on my skin colour? I could ask for clarification. Demand she prove how sorry she is. Let her know what an impact her interference had on our relationship. But I don't do any of those things. Today isn't about me.

"I know. I'm happy you're here for your son."

It's the truth. Holden has worked hard for nine years. He's sacrificed a lot to achieve what he has, and he deserves to know they're proud of him. His accomplishment should be celebrated.

His parents don't stay, though. When the pizza delivery woman appears at the door, Alfie and Imogen make a hasty exit. It doesn't feel like anything was resolved, but it feels like a weight off, knowing there's been an acknowledgement that something needs to change. Something we can work on in the future.

The rest of us sit down in the living room, and Holden drops a stack of paper plates beside the boxes of pizza.

Sam pulls out his guitar and announces, "Before we eat, I have a little song I want to play in honour of the coolest nerd I know." He starts singing the intro before he strums a single note and it doesn't take long to recognize this tune as *Why Don't You Get a Job?* by The Offspring. I laugh; I'm familiar enough with the lyrics to know it's about a guy whose friend has a deadbeat girlfriend.

But Sam has completely rewritten the words. So instead of saying the friend wants to dump his girl, he sings about having a girlfriend he loves. I set my drink down to give Sam my full attention as he belts out, "Man, I wanna make her my wedded wife, in the worst kind of way."

My eyes widen as Sam looks at me and winks, then turns his attention to beside me, all while continuing the re-written song.

When I follow his eyes to my left, Holden is crouched beside me, holding open a box. Not a ring box, like a normal person; a pizza box. Inside the top, is a message: *You have a pizza my heart. Will you marry me?*

My hands fly to my mouth—half in shock and half trying to stop myself from laughing as hard as I did when he pulled this stunt before.

"What do you say? Can you and I make a deluxe combo?" The smile on Holden's face is almost as cheesy as his joke.

I love him so much. Him and his terrible pizza puns. "You are well and truly a weird-dough, Dickens. Nothing could make me happier."

Holden sets the pizza on the coffee table and pulls me to stand along with him. This time, when he kisses me, it's full of promise and anticipation. Whatever our next step will be, we'll make it together. And that's not so scary anymore.

Our perfect moment and electric kiss is interrupted by Phil saying, "Another one bites the crust. Am-I-right?"

Amongst the cheering and clapping, everyone is laughing. It's the perfect soundtrack to the happiest moment of my life.

"We're going to have a good life, Minnie."

I slap him on the chest and reply, "We better, Dickens. I have *Great Expectations*."

THE END

If you enjoyed this book, please consider leaving a review on Amazon or the retailer's website where you purchased the book from. I love hearing from my readers.

If you'd like to hear from me, find all of my links here: linktr.ee/TiffanyAndrea, including some free stories and social media links.

To my readers, I want to say thank you for reading. I sincerely hope you enjoyed Dina and Holden's story. I wanted to take a moment to address the uncomfortable reality that I wrote about in this story. One that, as a white woman, people may think I have no right to write about. So I wanted to clarify a few things.

First being that my intention with addressing any difficult subject in my books is never to discount what anyone has gone through. I'd never intentionally glance over a subject in an attempt to make it seem "not so bad," or even imply that one person's experience is how it is for everyone—especially not a fictional one in a story that's got a guaranteed happily ever after. It's not reality.

Second, I wrote this story from personal experience. My husband and I, as a mixed couple and parents of mixed children, have experienced similar situations to what Dina dealt with. Like "Dina" mentioned, the discrimination she faced was a fraction of what some people go through, but it still hurts. My family has been abandoned by people we once considered "friends," refused service at restaurants, and pulled over by police when doing nothing wrong. We've had to consider if an area we wanted to move to was "too white", and so on. I'm not saying this to garner sympathy or pretend like I fully grasp what many people deal with, but I wanted to validate the reality that it does impact lives on a daily basis. Most often in ways that never make the news.

So, I know the conversation surrounding racism is a supercharged one, and I don't pretend to understand what many people contend with, but I'm not one to shy away from tough topics. The issues I delve into in all of my stories are ones I have firsthand experience with to some extent, so I write them from my perspective as a white woman who wants to see better in the world. As someone who wants to make people question their own perspectives and potential bias. As one who just wants love to prevail. I want to write stories that make people laugh, but also make you think.

I hope this one achieved both for you.

One other note, I did extensive research on the master's and PhD process at Toronto universities and tried to craft a story based on said research. In an effort to keep the story focused on their relationship and not so heavily on their studies, I kept details vague. If you are a former, current, or future master's or PhD student, I commend you for your dedication, but please remember, this book is a work of fiction. It's meant to be an opportunity to suspend reality and just enjoy a fictional world. I'm a writer, not an advance degree student, so my focus was on a feel-good story, and not a how-to guide on pursuing an advance degree.

Again, thank you for reading, and stay tuned for Boyd's story next! (Hollis, Sam, Phil, and Aven will all get their turn too.)

SPECIAL THANKS

First, I have to give a shout out to my beta readers, who went above and beyond to help me polish up this story. Sara, your emoji reactions and critical eye had such a great impact on both this story and my confidence in it. Harriet, your tough love helped me take note of my questionable writing habits and made me a more conscientious writer. Thank you both.

To my husband and daughters, you guys will forever by my endless source of inspiration and encouragement. I'd be nothing without you.

Lastly, with all of my books, I always choose a theme. My chapter titles always have some sort of connection that helps me to craft a story, start to finish. With a lot of my books, I've used music. For this one, you probably noticed The Offspring mentioned a few times. If you're not familiar with their music, all of the chapter titles are their songs. I chose them for inspiration for this book because, as Holden mentioned, the lead singer obtained his PhD, and one of the original members is a gynecological oncologist. That similarity to my characters made them a perfect choice. So, as I always do, here's a master list of the songs used for inspiration.

Please note, I do not have any association with The Offspring and make no claims to their music or lyrics. I'm simply stating where I found inspiration for this story.

Cool to Hate
The Blurb *
Special Delivery
No Reason Why *
Gotta Get Away
Can't Get My Head Around You
Days Go By
So Alone
I'll Be Waiting
Autonomy
Next To You
Disclaimer
One Fine Day
Amazed
Change the World
Get It Right
Feelings
Session
She's Got Issues
Spare Me the Details
Want You Bad
Bad Habit
Denial, Revisited
Time to Relax
Leave it Behind
Fix You
Long Way Home
The Meaning of Life
Something to Believe In
Living in Chaos

Fire & Ice
Come Out Swinging
Have You Ever
Take It Like a Man
Hurting As One
Let's Hear it For Rock Bottom
Intermission
Kick Him When He's Down
Let the Bad Times Roll
Burn it Up
Hopeless
Behind Your Walls
It'll Be a Long Time
A Thousand Days
Rise and Fall
All I Want
We Are One

Special Mention
Pretty Fly For a White Guy
Why Don't You Get a Job?

*Indicates song is not available on Spotify Canada at the time of publishing

<u>**You Are Enough Series:**</u>
We're All a Little Broken: Book 1 (Zara's story)
We're All a Little Overwhelmed: Book 1.5 (Zara's extended epilogue)
We're All a Little Guarded: Book 2 (Chelsea's story)
We're All a Little Tired: Book 2.5 (Chelsea's extended epilogue)
We're All a Little Scared: Book 3 (Isla's story)
We're All a Little Determined: Short Story Collection (Available free on my website)

This women's fiction series focuses on various aspects of mental health and overcoming trauma. It addresses anxiety, depression, panic disorders, miscarriage, adoption, grief and loss, racism, discrimination, and more, but in a light hearted way that will also make you laugh. The entire series is set in Muskoka/Bracebridge, Ontario.

Dear Sister, Never Again: Available free on my website as an eBook, or through Amazon as a paperback. This women's fiction novella explores the concept that DNA is not the only factor to determine family.

Suburban Watchdogs: This silly PG-13 crime comedy features four dads, three idiotic criminals, one slobbery dog, a determined cop, and a nosey nonagenarian neighbour. It's full of vigilante nonsense, terrible dad jokes, and a pursuit for justice.

Set in a small town north of the big city, these dads are not going to let criminals waltz into their neighbourhood without resistance.

A New Leash on Life Series:

This series will consist of twenty interconnected standalone romantic comedies. Some characters from Suburban Watchdogs and the You Are Enough series will have cameos or their own starring role!

Total Bull (Angel and Damian)
Ay Chihuahua (Dina and Holden)
Tell-Tail Sign (Sophie and Boyd)
The Pugly Truth (Hannah and Caleb) *Spring 2023*
Chemistry Lab (Hollis and Myer) *Summer 2023*
Pitty Party (Oscar and Frankie) *Fall 2023*

Con Artist: This standalone romantic comedy follows the story of an FBI agent tasked with investigating an art theft ring. The only thing his number one suspect makes away with, is his heart. *February 2023*.

Trip and Fall: This standalone road trip romance follows two twenty-somethings who each have a different reason for wanting to leave town and explore the countryside. One out of a sense of wonder; the other, a sense of desperation. Will they find more than the adventure they were looking for? *Summer 2023*

Sign up for my newsletter, access my website, or follow me on social media to keep up to date with new releases and sneak peeks.
Linktr.ee/TiffanyAndrea

* 9 7 8 1 9 9 0 7 2 4 2 9 9 *